AMANDA CADABRA

AND THE HIDEY-HOLE TRUTH

HOLLY BELL

Other titles by Holly Bell

Amanda Cadabra and The Cellar of Secrets
(The Amanda Cadabra Cozy Mysteries Book 2)

Amanda Cadabra and The Flawless Plan
(The Amanda Cadabra Cozy Mysteries Book 3)

Amanda Cadabra and The Rise of Sunken Madley
(The Amanda Cadabra Cozy Mysteries Book 4)

Other books published by Heypressto

50 Feel-better Films
50 Feel-better Songs: from Film and TV
25 Feel-better Free Downloads

www.amandacadabra.com

www.heypressto.com

Cover art by Daniel Becerril Ureña
Cover concept by Chartreuse at Heypressto

Chartreuse@heypressto.com
HollyBell@amandacadabra.com
Twitter: @holly_b_author

Sign up an stay in touch

AMANDA CADABRA

AND THE HIDEY-HOLE TRUTH

HOLLY BELL

To Bim and Philippa

The world is full of magic things,

patiently waiting for our senses to grow sharper

W.B. Yeats

CONTENTS

KEY

1. Amanda's House
2. Sunken Madley Manor
3. Sinner's Rue Pub
4. The Library
5. St Ursula's-without-Barnet
6. Medical Centre
7. Priory Ruins
8. Playing Fields
9. The Snout and Trough Pub
10. Post Office/Corner Shop
11. The Orchard
12. School
13. The Grange
14. The Elms
15. The Market
16. Vintage Vehicles
17. Church Hall
18. Vicarage

THE VILLAGE OF SUNKEN MADLEY

Introduction

Please note that to enhance the reader's experience of Amanda's world, this British-set story, by a British author, uses British English spelling, vocabulary, grammar and usage, and includes local and foreign accents, dialects and a magical language that vary from different versions of English as it is written and spoken in other parts of our wonderful, diverse world.

For your reading pleasure, there is a glossary of British English usage and vocabulary at the end of the book, followed by a note about accents and Wicc'hudol

Chapter 1

❧

THE DAY OF THE INCIDENT

'Fresh blood,' observed Mrs Cadabra.

Detective Sergeant Thomas Trelawney looked at her doubtfully. She registered that he was in his late thirties, tall, light-haired, grey-suited and attractive in a manner appropriate to a policeman.

'Do come in.'

He stepped over the threshold and into the clean, bright hall. She closed the door behind him.

Trelawney's boss, Chief Inspector Hogarth, was on the verge of retirement and had sent his junior to acquaint himself with a case that had remained open for 28 years.

Mrs Cadabra led the way into the living room, gestured to the sergeant to sit down, then decisively pulled a photo album from one of the stacked bookshelves flanking the brick fireplace. She laid it open on his knees and pointed to a portrait of a power-dressed couple holding a baby.

'1987. Our darling Amanda, held by my obnoxious daughter,' she uttered in clipped tones. 'That's her husband. I need only say that they were well matched. And if that assessment gives me a motive for murder, Sergeant, then you're welcome to investigate it,' she declared challengingly.

Trelawney suppressed a grin. Hogarth had told him what to expect in the redoubtable old lady sitting beside him on the chintz sofa. He had not exaggerated. Senara Cadabra was every inch the imperious aristocrat to which Hogarth had compared her. She lifted a hand to tuck in a hairgrip, pinning her white victory roll even more tightly into place. One of her piercing violet eyes was slightly larger than the other. This, coupled with her upright posture and cut-glass English accent, created an unnerving effect.

Mrs Cadabra glanced down at the photograph. Mercifully, there was no sign of Amanda's gifts at that time, she commented to herself. Not *then*.

'Lamentably,' she continued, 'Amanda's parents had no time for her — or interest in her — and she was mostly cared for by my husband and myself. However, if you were to assume that little Amanda was traumatised by the sudden change in her situation following the "incident", you'd be wrong,' she stated, keen to stay one step ahead of any conclusions that the sergeant might be drawing.

While the detective jotted in his ubiquitous police notebook, he took a surreptitious look at his surroundings. The Cadabra's circumstances were noticeably comfortable. Their house lay a mere thirteen miles from The Houses of Parliament to the south and just three miles from the Hertfordshire border to the north. The village of Sunken Madley was populated not only by locals, some with lineage reaching back the 1500s when the manor and church were built, but also by a selection of reclusive celebrities. Seeking privacy, and with a taste for gracious living, the VIPs had acquired several of the grander residences. By contrast, the Cadabra's house was a modest three-bedroom cottage at the end of Orchard Row, just where the village gave way to a field of apple trees, now flowering with faintly blushing, bridal blossom. Number 26 had a spacious garden accommodating a small neat lawn, well-kept vegetable beds and, most importantly, a sizeable furniture restorer's workshop.

Trelawney brought his gaze back to the photograph of the infant Amanda and her parents. Mrs Cadabra flicked towards the front of the album, each page taking them further back in time. Gesturing dismissively, she indicated her three other unsmiling children, Amanda's aunts and uncles, and their smirking, blank-eyed or scowling offspring. Mrs Cadabra turned a few more pages back to her own generation, remarking on her siblings and their brood with equal distaste.

'As for my own children, I could never bear any of them once they became teenagers.' She barked out a laugh. 'I bore them once; I feel that was quite enough.' Trelawney allowed himself a smile for the first time. It did not go unnoticed by Mrs Cadabra, who awarded it eight of ten for charm.

'Thank you for your frankness, Mrs Cadabra. And now, could you please tell me what you remember of the events leading up to the incident?'

Mrs Cadabra repositioned herself, straightening her back more than ever. 'My husband and I had each received a note and —'

'Was there anything that stood out about it?' interjected Trelawney. 'Was it typed or written? The kind of paper, the envelope —?'

'It was handwritten in purple-black ink and —'

'Did you recognise the —?' he began.

'— the writing?' she forestalled Trelawney, 'No, I did not.'

'Normal paper?'

'Interesting that you should ask. It was quite peculiar, thick but oddly transparent.'

'What did it say?' he asked, making notes.

'It said that transport would arrive on 9th September at 9 o'clock in the morning. We would be taken to a location, and there, apparently, we would learn something to our advantage. It went on to say,' said Mrs Cadabra, leaning towards him for emphasis, 'and I remember this precisely: "It is essential, however, that all members of your family be present."'

'Curious,' commented Trelawney.

'Exactly. And it was signed "A well-wisher". Hm! Well-wisher indeed!' said Mrs Cadabra indignantly, twitching the cushion behind her more firmly into place.

'I see,' said Trelawney, 'And what did you and Mr Cadabra make of all this?'

'Why, that it was fishy, of course!' she exclaimed, stating the obvious.

'But you decided to go?'

'Yes,' said Mrs Cadabra, 'but *reluctantly*. And not to serve our own interests, of course. Hardly. No, it was so that if we should derive some benefit from the exercise, we could have left it to Amanda. That is the only reason that it would have been worth enduring the company of our odious family for any length of a journey.'

'Did anyone in the family encourage you to go?' Trelawney enquired.

'Oh yes.' Mrs Cadabra's face registered her distaste. 'We received quite a flurry of unwelcome messages from them, but we'd already made up our minds to attend. They were all desperately keen, needless to say. A more mercenary bunch you'd be hard pushed to find.' She snapped the album shut and put it down on the inlaid coffee table.

Trelawney sat back. 'So what happened on the day of the incident?' he asked.

'Poor little Amanda had been awake all night with a frightful cough. She was only three, and she'd never been a very strong child. And since she'd developed asthma, we'd had to be especially careful. Well, by that morning, Amanda's condition had worsened, and she was clearly not fit for the journey,' recalled Senara Cadabra with an emphatic shake of her head. 'And considering our unease about the whole affair, we decided that neither we, nor our Amanda, should have any part of it. So when the transport arrived, we didn't get on board. It sat there and waited for fifteen minutes and then finally left.' She folded her hands. 'And that was that.'

'You didn't go out to tell the driver that you weren't going?' pressed Trelawney.

'No,' replied Mrs Cadabra. 'We simply didn't want anything to do with it.'

'Did you notice the vehicle?'

'I did. It obscured the view of our Princess Margaret roses,' said Mrs Cadabra indignantly.

'And what did it —?'

'Horse manure.'

'I beg your pardon?' asked Trelawney, startled.

'Oh, I mean no disrespect to the dear Princess herself,' Mrs Cadabra assured him. 'No, indeed. Just that it's the best thing for roses. But only after three years of composting. *Not* when fresh. I'm sure Her Royal Highness would echo my every word.' Having successfully diverted the subject to horticulture, she placed one still delicate hand over the other, signifying that she considered the discussion of the transport to be closed.

Trelawney, however, returned to the matter at hand. 'But the *vehicle*, what was it like? Can you recall?'

'It was a grey minibus of some description,' she answered.

'Good condition?' continued Trelawney.

'Yes, I think so,' she answered, with a careless shrug of her shoulders. 'I am not a motor car engineer, but it certainly didn't seem to be in an advanced state of disrepair, if that's what you're asking.'

'You didn't notice anything special about it?' Mrs Cadabra shook her head. 'The registration?' Trelawney looked at her hopefully.

'No idea. I heard it start up. By the time I went to look out of the window, it had gone.'

'And these notes that you received. What became of them?'

'They disappeared,' she declared.

'Disappeared?'

'Vanished. Without a trace.'

'Really?' Trelawney remarked. He wrote in his book. 'Mr Cadabra's note as well?'

The back door to the kitchen closed audibly followed by a hollow clatter as discarded work boots hit the mat. There came the sound of a tap running.

'You can ask him yourself,' Mrs Cadabra said.

A tall, grey-haired man, in dark work trousers and jumper over shirt and tie, opened the living room door, and entered the room. He was of that generation of craftsmen who took so great a pride in their occupation and appearance that they wore a shirt and tie even to work. The persistent briskness of the British climate had prompted him to cover up with a sweater. He smiled a kind welcome at the case officer.

'Ah, very generous of you to come all this way, Mr Trelawney, is it?' Mr Cadabra held out a clean but French-polish-stained hand.

'Detective Sergeant Trelawney, sir,' said the policeman, accepting the handshake.

'Please call me Perran. Although my wife likes strangers to call me Mr Cadabra.' He gave her an affectionate twinkle, which she returned. 'Has Senara been making you feel at home?' The trace of a West Country burr in the man's gentle voice appealed to the Cornwall-born-and-bred Trelawney.

'Pleasure to meet you. Perran? A good Cornish name, if I may say so. Yes, Mrs Cadabra has been most helpfully relating the events of the day when …' Trelawney paused, tactfully avoiding an explicit reference to the sensitive details of the incident.

'Yes … a tragic business,' said Mr Cadabra, helpfully filling the gap. 'I *will* say, it's good of the police to keep taking an interest after all these years. We've given up any hope of a resolution. But at any rate, is there anything I can tell you that my good lady hasn't already shared with you?'

'If you have time,' said Trelawney politely.

'Of course.' Mr Cadabra carefully sat down on the edge of a Queen Anne armchair, aware that he was in his work clothes.

'Your wife told me about a note. I understand that you received one of your own,' Trelawney prompted.

'Yes, that's right.'

'And there were some distinctive things about it?'

'Oh, yes, purplish ink and odd paper,' replied Mr Cadabra confirming what his wife had said.

'Do you still have it?' asked Trelawney, checking Senara's statement.

'No. No, it disappeared,' Mr Cadabra said in a regretful voice. 'I could have sworn I'd put it in my overalls pocket, but when I went to look for it, it was gone. I remember I turned out *all* of my pockets, thinking it might have got lost amongst the bits and pieces. But no.'

'Thank you.' Trelawney left a brief silence while his pencil scribbled away.

'Now, could you both tell me what happened later that day?' asked Trelawney looking from one to the other.

After a brief exchange of glances between the couple, it was Mrs Cadabra who answered, 'About six hours after the car left, the telephone rang. We were in here. Perran was having his afternoon tea-break with me. I remember it as clearly as if it happened yesterday. It rang, and he put his hand on my arm and said the oddest thing.' She looked at her husband. Perran nodded supportively. Trelawney's pencil hovered about his open notebook, waiting.

Finally, Mrs Cadabra spoke.

'"Senara," he said, "Whatever you do, *don't* answer that."'

Chapter 2

୶

DEATH AND MAGIC

'And why did you say that, Perran?' Trelawney asked quietly.

Mr Cadabra shrugged. 'I just had a *feeling*. Usually my Senara here is the intuitive one, but I just had this strong feeling that whatever was on the other end of that line wasn't … *wholesome*.' He rubbed his hands together as though washing away something unpleasant.

Trelawney turned to Senara. 'So *why* did you pick up the phone, Mrs Cadabra?'

'It was odd,' said Senara, 'but, I felt I *had* to answer it. I don't really know why.'

'Tell me about the call, if you could,' Trelawney requested. 'Who was the caller?'

'I can't be certain, but I think that it was a woman. A woman with rather a deep voice. Claimed she was from the police; called herself Detective Carlyon.'

'I see. A typical Cornish name,' said Trelawney, writing it down. 'And what did she say?'

'First, she asked me if I was Mrs Senara Cadabra. Then she

wanted to know if my husband was with me, because she had some bad news. I said "yes" to both. Then she told me that she was very sorry to inform me that there'd been an accident and had I heard? I said, "Heard what?", not having the least idea what she was talking about. And then she told me.' Mrs Cadabra became indignant. 'It wasn't the news that upset me; it was *her*. She went on to ask me some thoroughly impertinent questions. I didn't care for her *or* her manner at all!' Senara shook her head in disgust. 'Highly unprofessional! And then, furthermore,' she waved towards the front door, 'a few hours later the police arrived and told me face to face. I explained that I'd already had a telephone call, but they insisted that no one from their office had rung me; apparently such things are best done in person, and,' continued Senara, folding her arms and tilting her head significantly, 'then they told me that there was no such person as Detective Carlyon on their force!'

'How interesting,' responded Trelawney making rapid notes. 'But that aside, you weren't distressed by the news?' he asked in surprise.

'That the whole boiling of my revolting family had driven over a cliff in Cornwall? Hardly! I've never made any bones about my feelings toward them, Mr Trelawney, and, no doubt, to some people that would make me appear suspicious. Nevertheless, if I'm your chief suspect after thirty years then I'm far from impressed with your department's efforts to solve this mystery, young man,' she announced truculently.

'No, Mrs Cadabra, you are not my chief suspect.' the detective replied meekly. 'I assure you I am not here to make an arrest!' he added with a touch of playfulness belying his solemn expression.

'Hm,' responded Senara with a responsive glint of amusement in her larger eye. 'I thought the police had no sense of humour.'

Trelawney's face was inscrutable. 'Not … *officially*.'

'Ha!' laughed Senara appreciatively. Trelawney was relieved

at having, finally, established some sort of rapport with Mrs Cadabra. He knew from experience that it was essential to achieve a measure of concord with a witness, especially when interviewing them regarding a possible murder investigation.

'There is one question I should like to ask, given that your family perishing does not seem to be quite the sensitive subject that it might have been —'

'Do go on,' Senara prompted.

'Just on the off-chance that something may, now, in retrospect, spring to mind,' he said tentatively.

'Get to the point, young man,' she uttered.

'Can you think of anyone who would could have wanted to bring about the untimely deaths of your family?'

Senara replied without hesitation, 'Anyone who had met them, I would have thought!'

Trelawney turned to Perran, who responded, 'If their habitual disregard for their baby daughter is anything to go by, Sergeant, I shouldn't think they endeared themselves to many people.'

Trelawney gauged that this was the best he could do with that line of enquiry.

'If the perpetrator's aim was to wipe out your entire family … have you had any threats to your own lives?'

'Oh, dear me, no,' chuckled Senara.

Trelawney decided that the person who would attempt to get the better of Mrs Cadabra would be exceptionally brave, desperate or foolhardy.

'Well … thank you both for you, er … frankness and for allowing me to run over what is probably well-trodden ground.'

Mrs Cadabra nodded graciously.

'I am here, as you know,' he recapped, 'at the request of Chief Inspector Michael Hogarth, who is retiring. He has continued to take an interest in the case. He always considered it unfinished business, you see, and now that he is only two weeks away from his last day at the office, he is passing it on to me to see if I can make any further progress.'

'Good,' Senara returned approvingly, 'because as *you* will know, the coroner declared that the family did not perish as a result of the accident, and the cause of the deaths was inconclusive, and,' she continued, punctuating with a waggle of her index finger, 'without death certificates, there is no probate, and without that, young Amanda cannot inherit what is rightfully hers. I hope you see, Mr Trelawney,' she added with a hint of pathos, 'that this is gross injustice against a poor orphaned girl.'

At that moment, 'the poor orphaned girl' in question, was in the workshop, singing along under her dust mask to *Don't Worry, Be Happy.* Using the rhythm to help her as she worked, Amanda Cadabra moved her arm back and forth, gently sanding the rough edges off a sliver of oak veneer. It was destined to replace a missing piece from a 19th-century bookstand, sitting on the other end of her workbench. This was delicate work, a process that she needed to attend to carefully by herself. Meanwhile, there were certain other tasks that Amanda could delegate. Twisting around, she looked at the brush resting in the gluepot, warming on the single ring electric hob on the opposite side of the workshop.

'*Mecsge ynentel*,' she bade it. Instantly, by itself, the brush moved from leaning to vertical, so that it stood upright in its lake of adhesive. Then, as if guided by an invisible hand, gently it began to stir the Scotch glue.

Satisfied that the task was under control, next Amanda turned her attention to a hammer she'd left beside the loose backboard laid in place upon a cupboard. She had already tapped the panel pins lightly into place. At her word, '*frapka*', the hammer picked itself up and commenced banging the thin nails into place, to the pulse of the bass of the song that was playing.

'Don't worry,' sang Amanda. 'Be happy.'

In the vice attached to her grandfather's workbench, a particularly dense block of Brazilian walnut was clamped. A saw sat still in the shallow cut Amanda had managed to make earlier. Rather than attempting to apply herself physically to the task, she said over her shoulder, '*Ahiwske*'.

Energised, the saw began to move to and fro to the beat of the music.

Amanda relied on this magical assistance. Overexertion could trigger her asthma but while she was by no means an athlete she was not a weakling either. Nor was she entirely lacking in stature. At 5 feet 4 inches, Amanda was almost of average height, and liked to think that she was nearly as tall as Emma Watson — except a dress size or two would have stood between her and Burberry-model-stardom.

The intercom from the house buzzed and flashed. Amanda turned off the iPod player, pressed the speakerphone button with a blue vinyl-gloved knuckle, and stripped off her dust mask.

'Amanda, dear!' her grandmother's voice boomed out. Senara believed that all communication devices required considerable volume for the speaker to be heard, rendering her audible throughout the building. But, on this occasion, Senara wanted to be doubly sure that her granddaughter would hear her loud and clear: 'The *detective* is here!'

Chapter 3

∾

TEA AND EVASION

'Are you fit to be seen?' Senara's voice asked through the intercom from the house.

Amanda looked back at the workshop. This last sentence was the arranged signal to cease all magical activity, no matter how small, with immediate effect. It had been rehearsed frequently, a system by which they could avoid a visitor walking uninvited into the workshop and seeing things that would confuse and alarm them.

'I will be! And then I'll be right there, Granny.' Amanda turned back to the tools that were busily working away as commanded. '*Eol wicc'hudol sessablin*!' Instantly they stopped their tasks. The stripping brush subsided onto its handle, and the glue brush leaned itself neatly against the inner rim of the pot with a 'thup' and lay motionless. The saw came to a halt, and the hammer lay down on the backboard. Amanda looked at the bookstand as she waved a hand. '*Aereval lytaz.*' As instructed, it rose sedately until it hovered a few inches above the bench. She gestured palm up across her body. '*Cledstre.*' At this word the bookstand moved to the left until it was over the floor, suspended in midair. '*Sedaasig*', she said, and it gracefully lowered itself to the ground and was still.

Amanda checked herself in an antique mirror leaning against an armoire. Her light brown hair was still pinned up in its messy plait, her lip salve had mostly been eaten off, and her face had a fine powdering of sawdust that defined where her mask had been, and also coated her boiler suit.

She looked carefully at the reflection of her eyes behind her close-work lenses aware that they were a giveaway. Amanda's irises were an unusual mixture of blue and brown; chestnut continents, floating in a sea of pale indigo, that were sometimes growing, sometimes shrinking. It was a small but unfortunately revealing side-effect of her magical nature; brown predominated when she used her mystical abilities.

Just in case this colour change was the sort of thing a detective might notice from one visit to the next, Amanda put on some clear glass spectacles to help disguise the effect, the reflection of the lenses being more visible than the eyes.

Amanda also thought that they made her look plainer and more intelligent. Dearly as she loved her Granny, she was weary of Senara's efforts to find her a husband. Her grandmother homed in on any potentially eligible man under sixty years of age that showed the least sign of sufficient intellect and understanding to accept her gifts, and regardless of how unsuitable her granddaughter might find them. But Amanda remained good-humoured and generally compliant, long nights in the local hospital during her childhood battling for her life with asthma had taught her not to sweat the small stuff. All the same, the relentless matchmaking brought out a hereditary rebellious streak.

Amanda Cadabra came out of the workshop and shut the door behind her, startling a blackbird hunting for earthworms in the garden. It gave an irritated warble and shot away across the fences. She made her way down the path between the vegetable beds where her grandfather had been mulching and putting in poles for the runner beans. As Amanda walked, unwittingly she collected a few stray petals of breeze-blown blossom, floating into her hair from his favourite fruit trees. She paused as she reached the back door, breathing in the scents of rosemary and tarragon from the pots on either side of it, then pushed down the handle.

'Boots!' came her grandmother's unnecessary reminder. Amanda grinned and bent to loosen the laces. Straightening, she was greeted by the sight of Trelawney, who had been dispatched to the kitchen to 'help Amanda with the tea'.

'Hello, Miss Cadabra,' he said, smiling. 'Detective Sergeant Thomas Trelawney, Devon and Cornwall Police.'

'Amanda,' she introduced herself confidently. 'Don't tell me: my grandmother's sent you to help with the tea.'

It was Senara's customary device for getting Amanda 'alone with the young man', whoever that happened to be.

She looked entertained but sympathetic as they shook hands. Trelawney noticed that her right index finger was covered in polish, like the stains on Mr Cadabra's hands.

'Although I'm sure that you're more than competent,' he replied, affably,

'Well, I can manage to make *tea*,' Amanda agreed, moving to the sink. Trelawney leaned against the kitchen counter where he would be out of her way. She certainly exuded a quiet efficiency, he observed, and was hardly the frail waif he'd somehow expected. Nevertheless, she did have an air of fragility, something hard to define. Trelawney thought he understood why Hogarth had asked him to keep an eye on her.

While the kettle boiled and Amanda spooned Earl Grey into the teapot, she glanced up with a serious expression and met Trelawney's eye. The mood changed. 'Is there any … news?'

Trelawney shook his head regretfully. 'I'm afraid not. I'm just here to meet your family and hear their evidence for myself, just in case.'

'Just in case …?' Amanda prompted.

'A teapot?' Trelawney leaned over to inspect the large

brown-and-beige-ringed vessel. 'You don't see many of those used nowadays.'

'Granny likes things done properly,' Amanda confided. She began assembling the tea tray.

'How is your asthma these days?' he asked casually.

The abrupt change of subject caught Amanda by surprise.

'My asthma?' she asked defensively.

'I'm sorry, I didn't mean to ask an insensitive question. It's simply that your grandmother mentioned that you developed it as a child.'

Amanda responded cheerfully, keen to appear strong enough to deal with both the question and the condition in equal measure. 'Oh, I have ways to work around it.'

'Can I carry the tray for you?' he offered gallantly.

'Thank you,' she said, pleasantly. Picking up a large round tin on their way out of the kitchen, she followed him into the living room.

'And how are you two getting on?' Senara looked from Amanda to Trelawney in search of evidence of a spark. Amanda shot a look of amused but strained patience at her grandmother.

'I was just enquiring after Amanda's health,' responded Trelawney, setting the tray down on the coffee table. 'Asthma and furniture restoration.' It was an anomaly, and it was niggling him. 'That's an unusual combination.'

'Victoria Sandwich,' said Senara resoundingly.

Trelawney was thrown by this unexpected reply.

'Won't you have some, Sergeant?' she invited him. 'I baked it myself, and I pride myself on my cakes,' she uttered challengingly. 'Ammy sweetheart, do serve our guest.'

'Thank you,' Trelawney accepted politely, sitting down on the sofa.

Amanda gave him a glance of rueful sympathy due to a man under test by Granny. She sat down beside Trelawney, pulled the lid off the vintage tin, cut a slice and passed it to him on a delicate rose-patterned plate, with a white linen napkin underneath it.

Senara eyed him keenly while he sampled the cream, jam and sponge confection.

'This is excellent,' he remarked with genuine appreciation, relieved that he would not have to dissemble.

'Organic free-range eggs,' she declared. 'From Henpecke Farm. *Local*,' Senara added, to put the outsider in his place.

Trelawney was unabashed. He laid his cake fork on the plate, applying the napkin to his lips to ensure they were crumb-free before continuing. 'I expect it's especially important for your granddaughter to eat healthily.' His glance returned to Amanda. 'In view of your ... condition.' He added pointedly, 'Especially considering the work that you do.'

'It's important for a girl to have meaningful work, Sergeant. I'm sure you agree,' Senara stated, receiving her cup and saucer from Amanda. 'Thank you, dear.' She took a sip and redirected her piercing gaze at Trelawney. 'I *myself* drove an ambulance during the War.'

Yes, for three weeks before it ended, said Amanda wryly to herself, handing her grandfather his tea.

'Just like Mrs Uberhausfest in Rattling Bridge Row,' Senara announced. 'We all did our bit. Of course, she did it for Other Side, but that's all in the past and I'm the first to say that I'm glad we've buried the hatchet!'

'I agree, Mrs Cadabra, that it's important for everyone to have work that is meaningful.' Trelawney was not to be diverted. 'But it does seem an odd choice for someone whose condition is surely aggravated by a workshop where carpentry takes place.'

Mr Cadabra supplied the response. 'I trained little Amanda from when she first took an interest.' He stirred his tea and continued mildly, 'She used to toddle up the path and bang on the door, demanding for me to let her in. Not to be denied, were you, Amanda? I had to adapt a mask for you. All the same, Sergeant, I got used to keeping the workshop *very* clean just to be certain. And after all's said and done, you can't dampen enthusiasm, can you? So I started her off with bit of painting when she was just three years old, didn't I, Ammy?' he said to her, then looked back to the sergeant. 'And it just went on from there,' he ended vaguely.

Trelawney said nothing. His mind was grappling with the picture of the family that was building up, as he was merging the old facts he'd read in Hogarth's report with the real-life impressions he was receiving. Like a splinter on half-sanded wood, something about it all was snagging. His mind went back to his training.

Hogarth had been Trelawney's mentor from day one.

'What is the first rule of interviewing?' he asked the young Detective Constable.

'How to tell if someone is lying, sir?' Trelawney answered smartly.

'No,' Hogarth corrected him. 'How to tell if someone is leaving something *out.*'

Trelawney had never forgotten those words, but now they rang out in his head. And drinking Earl Grey tea and eating home-made cake from bone china on this pleasant March morning years later, Trelawney had the overwhelming instinct that a page was missing from the Cadabras' story; not just a page either; more like several entire volumes.

However, whether that had anything to do with the incident of the minibus going over the cliff, was another question.

Chapter 4

༧

SUNKEN MADLEY

Rewind 2,000 years. In the South of England, and to the north of the great River Thames, a tribe is settling and spreading. They are the tribe called the Catuvellauni. The Ancient Forest that once covered the country is long gone, and they tend their flocks on the ground cleared for crops and pasture. Yet still there are deep woods, and here, within their shade, on a raised plateau, subterranean water is forced into the light of day at a spring. Beside it, a woman stands, a staff in her hand. With her is a young couple, waiting anxiously. For this is a place of magic, of healing, of insight.

The woman points her rod at the freshet and speaks the words of a spell. She passes her hands near the body of the girl. Together the three cast herbs and flowers into the tiny stream. The girl and her husband embrace the woman and with smiles depart. In the spring, a child will be born.

Fifty years pass and here are the Romans building Verulam to the north of what will one day be Amanda Cadabra's village. To the south, on a river that is to be called the Thames, they construct Londinium, just a dot now but in the future, it will spread and rise to become the city called London.

A thousand years pass. The Romans have long gone. The Saxons, from what, in the future, will be Germany, have invaded, and the south of Britain begins to be called Angla Lond. England.

Now to the north of London, from ground still shrouded by a green canopy, still sheltering the sacred spring, and so high it dominates the surrounding landscape and draws level with the Ural Mountains thousands of miles to the East, smoke rises. An open space is being made by cutting down the trees and setting fire to the wood, and from this, the place gets its name: 'Bærnet' meaning 'a clearing made by burning'. A Roman road still runs through it, and off this road, amongst coppices and thickets, villages of cottages and churches are forming. A priory appears. The Benedictine monks in their black habits are tending the gardens.

It is 500 hundred years later; the brothers are leaving the priory. Now the land is rent by the Civil War. A battle rages through and around our village. Lives are given and taken, until a hard-won peace returns. The dead are commemorated. A new church rises on the site of the devastated old one, and more farmhouses appear. The abandoned priory falls into ruin. The fields of rye give way to barley, and the barley to wheat and vegetables, sharing space with flocks and herds. The sacred spring serves only as a water source for the land, the people and animals. Its mystical past is forgotten by all but the very few.

In our village, a stately dwelling is built of timber from the forest. Gardens are planted next to it, and the land around is fenced in. Cottages and a village inn spring up nearby around a triangle formed by the fork in the road. It is a patch of pasture that is called 'the green' and has a pond where horses, cattle and sheep can drink on the way to market. One day, humans — fearful fools who have forgotten the legacy of magic of this place — gather around it, shouting and waving their arms. They commit a heinous deed. And after that day the village becomes known as Sunken Madley.

The stately house is none other than Sunken Madley Manor, built by Lord Dunkley, the first Baron of that name. A man and woman leave one afternoon in a horse-drawn carriage and, disappearing into the trees, do not return. Over the following decades, sometimes at night, figures are seen creeping anxiously into the house or leaving in secret.

Passed down from generation to generation, the Manor is extended, new wings are added, sometimes with remarkable flamboyance, and then dismantled by a successive son on grounds of either health and safety or good taste. The male line of barons is broken and the lords become misters. Nearby the once feared Church grows kindly over the decades. Shops spring up. Periodically the Dunkleys sell some of their land, on which more houses appear. A school is built overlooking the village green, and the wide space of grass behind becomes the playing fields. Still, the forest shelters the village in its emerald arms. On one side, an orchard laps at the edge of its south-eastern border where there stands a lone cottage. It is often visited by the folk of Sunken Madley. Now a line of houses is being built linking the single dwelling to the centre of the village along on a lane called Orchard Row.

Here comes a young couple, moving into that last house in Orchard Row. Their children are seen playing in the garden, growing up and leaving for the last time. Now there is another baby playing on the lawn. She too grows up, and the couple grows older. There is a car pulling up outside the house, and a man gets out. He wears a well-fitting grey suit and discreet matching tie that he straightens. After a few paces up the garden path and a short wait, he goes inside.

Time is slowing down, and it is a full hour before he leaves. The door closes behind him. He stands at his car and thoughtfully looks up at the house. He gets in and he, none other than Detective Sergeant Thomas Trelawney, drives north to the M25, the orbital road that circles London. Sometimes he switches on the radio and listens to the traffic news. He wanders between his favourite talk and music stations, occasionally singing along. But mostly he thinks about the conversations he has had at the house in Orchard Row. He heads for the M3, the motorway that will take him to the far South East, beyond the River Tamar. This is the old border behind which lies the one-time Kingdom of the Cornovii tribe; ancient Britons forced into the corners of the mainland by the Anglo Saxons. Their descendants, the 21st century Cornish, are a different breed from their English countrymen. They are a Brythonic-speaking people. With a long history of magic.

Chapter 5

༄

GUT FEELING

Trelawney drove over the Tamar as the sun was westering. He turned toward the sea, and his journey ended in a car park next to a police station. He went inside to see his boss.

'Thomas.' Hogarth was pleased, as usual, to see Trelawney. He'd helped the criminal psychology graduate, with the light of enthusiasm in his hazel eyes and fire in his soul to change the world, to mould himself into a steady, professional detective. Now touching 40, Thomas was a credit to his mentor. The intense focus and intelligence had been leavened with patience, and Hogarth liked Thomas's courteous way with interviewees and his flashes of humour. Hogarth had both nurtured and increasingly respected Thomas's intuition, and that was what he needed from him now.

Hogarth beckoned him with a welcoming wave of the hand.

'Come in, close the door and sit down. Got your coffee? Good.' He let his junior take off his suit jacket and settle himself in a chair at the side of Hogarth's tidy-ish desk. He waited patiently, contemplating the yellow catkins on the evergreen oak beside the car park, while Thomas took a few sips of his reviving beverage.

'Well now,' began Hogarth for openers. 'What did you make of the Cadabras?'

Trelawney, digging his left hand into his trouser pocket, turned down the corners of his mouth. He wasn't too sure how close his boss was to Senara and Perran. He fielded the question.

'They seem like nice people.'

'I agree,' said Hogarth. He put the question another way. 'But from a detective's point of view … first, let's take Mr and Mrs Cadabra. Impressions?'

Fortified by caffeine, and feeling more confident, Trelawney recommenced.

'Well, if you put it like that; Senara Cadabra is a terrifying grande dame, and Perran is an unassuming gentleman with a comforting presence. Both as shrewd as they can hold together, in their different ways. Senara is apparently a cards-on-the-table sort; very forthright about her dislike of her family and her joy at their collective demise. Perran seemed relaxed about my visit, and content with his family and life in general. In short, I didn't learn much from them that isn't in your file. Oh, except, horse manure needs to be cured for three years before being fed to the roses,' he added wryly. Hogarth smiled. Thomas summarised, 'I felt they gave me exactly what they wanted to and no more.'

'How about the granddaughter?' asked Hogarth, leaning back in his chair.

'Hm. Bright … polite … friendly … but there was one thing about her. They knew I was coming; after all, you had made an appointment for me, but …' Thomas frowned at the memory, 'well … the old lady was precise to a pin, well dressed and not a hair out of place. Her husband was fresh from the workshop but presentable. However, the granddaughter, Amanda … boiler suit and glasses, covered in dust, hair in a mess. It was like she'd deliberately made no effort. A sort of teenage rebellion. Odd for someone who's about 30.' He sighed and shook his head as though to clear it. 'Oh, it's nothing, I've got it all wrong —

she's a working woman.' He stopped speaking, feeling irked by a detail that probably was meaningless. Hogarth waited for him to continue. Trelawney resumed.

'And here's the thing that doesn't make any sense at all. Amanda Cadabra has asthma, it's been potentially lethal to her in the past, but she works in the worst possible conditions for it. A furniture restorer in a workshop with sawdust and fumes from toxic liquids! And none of them really *explained* that. I felt the old lady especially was batting away questions about it. In fact, any questions that led in *any* direction she didn't want to go.'

Trelawney remembered something else. 'I noticed that Perran Cadabra still has a faint Cornish accent after all these years, but not Senara. I expect her family thought she was marrying beneath her.'

'Perhaps when you get to know them better you can ask them about that,' suggested his boss.

'I will.' Thomas paused, looking into his coffee cup as though for enlightenment there.

'Gut feeling?' Hogarth invited. Thomas looked up and spoke with certainty.

'That they know, or at least suspect, some underlying cause that led to the minibus accident. But,' he added regretfully, 'I don't think I made any progress beyond what you've already made, sir. I'm sorry.'

'Not at all, Thomas,' Hogarth reassured him. 'You've done well. You've picked up what I hoped you'd pick up.'

'Thank you, sir.'

'Remember what I told you when I gave you the file for this case. You're in this for the long game. It's already lasted two and a half decades, and maybe goes back far further than that. You've only a fraction of the jigsaw pieces in that document folder, and probably you'll find a fish-farm-full of red herrings. So starting with your instincts is the only way, and you've made a good beginning. Now ... what else is bothering you?'

Trelawney sat with pursed lips and creased forehead. At

last, he spoke. 'It felt so … '

There was a diffident knock at the door, and a shapely figure could be seen through the frosted glass.

'"Speak friend and enter,"' Hogarth called out, quoting from his favourite book, *The Lord of the Rings*.

A youthful policewoman came in, carrying a plate of biscuits.

'Sorry to interrupt, sir, but I got these on the way back to the station and thought you might like them.' She placed the dish on Hogarth's desk and retreated, flashing a quick, shy smile at Trelawney.

'Thank you, Constable, very considerate of you,' Hogarth said, as she closed the door. He inspected the offering. 'Hm. Now, what do we deduce from this, Thomas? An apparently innocent plate of biscuits. *Allegedly* acquired especially for *my* delectation. Except! What do we find? Aha. These are not *my* favourites. I, as is well known throughout the station, am a Hobnobs man. These, however, are …,' pronounced Hogarth, leaning in and pretending to inspect the biscuits with a magnifying glass, '… shortcake. The chosen confection of … who can it be?'

Thomas was grinning, torn between amusement at his senior's playful narrative and his own embarrassment.

'All right, yes, I *do* like shortcake.'

'Can we deduce from this that our fledgeling constable has a crush on you, Thomas?'

'I have done nothing to encourage that, sir,' protested Trelawney.

'I don't doubt it.' Hogarth gestured towards the biscuits. 'Go on, help yourself. And go on with what you were saying. I asked what else was bothering you and you said that it felt so …?'

'Yes,' said Thomas, much more at ease after the humorous interlude. 'It felt so *staged*.'

'Then,' replied Hogarth, 'I suggest next time you go back unheralded. Just drop in, when you're on one of your trips to London. How is your mother by the way? Still living in Crouch End?'

Thomas's mood lightened. 'She's well, thank you. Yes, still there.'

'And your aunt?'

'Just the same: still loathes my father, as all the London lot do.'

'But they're very fond of *you*. And it does you good to go up there as often as you can. You always come back a new man,' observed Hogarth. 'You know … I could call in a few favours and get you posted to Hertfordshire. I know you don't get on with your father's bunch in these parts.'

Thomas shook his head. 'I appreciate the offer, sir. But you're retiring in a couple of weeks, and this is unfinished business, isn't it? My place is here until this case is, not just closed but, solved,' he said with determination.

'Hmm, the sentiment does you credit, Thomas. We'll see. Bide your time. Let them smooth their feathers for a few months, think you've forgotten all about them. I tell you what: let me tip you off when the time is right.'

'Even after you've retired, sir?'

'You know I'll keep in touch. My cottage is just up the road. Not going anywhere for the time being. And I meant what I said, come and see me whenever you want.'

'Thank you, sir. It'll be pretty often then.' Thomas drained his cup.

'Good,' approved Hogarth.

Chapter 6

ᴄ๛

THE FIRST SIGN

It is the day after the 'accident'. A 12-year-old boy is buying a newspaper at London's Paddington Station, where his mother, newly divorced, has just dropped him off. The headline has caught his eye: 'Mysterious Death of Cornish Family'. Bound for his father's home in Cornwall, he takes the Great Western Railway to Plymouth. Before the train passes over the Wessex Downs, he knows what his future career will be.

* * * * *

Shortly after Amanda was orphaned, Senara and Perran had formally applied to become first her guardians and then to adopt her. They had received visits from two sets of social workers to assess their suitability for the role of permanent legal carers. The second pair, a woman in a tight blue suit and a man with odd socks, came only once. They observed Amanda carefully, looked at her eyes and asked about her development.

'Anything unusual?' Blue-suit had asked earnestly, holding her hands a few inches either side of Amanda's body, as though trying to detect any aura emanating from the child.

'Unusual? In *my* granddaughter?' Senara had responded with outrage. But the pair had seemed convinced that Amanda was a tediously normal infant, and soon left.

Eventually, the adoption papers were signed. Amanda became Amanda Cadabra, both the legal child and the natural grandchild of Senara and Perran. Amanda, whom Perran, from the time of her birth, had called his *bian*, Cornish for baby, truly became his.

Amanda's asthma continued to trouble her. She tried attending nursery school, but was disorientated, distressed and off sick so often that Senara and Perran decided to educate her themselves at home. Granny had had a university education, and Grandpa was well versed in any number of practical skills, so they were more than qualified. Amanda was relieved, and happy with the arrangement. She felt shy and awkward around her peers, lacking the physical stamina for their games. Being of above average intelligence and used to interacting with her grandparents, she found children of her own age strange, confusing and exhausting.

Each day, Amanda got up, had breakfast with her grandparents, then moved between the workshop with Grandpa, when it was clean enough, and the dining room with Granny where they would sit and pursue whatever subject was firing her interest. The grandparents regarded themselves as facilitators rather than teachers. They threw themselves into designing games and finding books and places to take little Amanda where she could sponge up whatever data she was currently craving.

Over the next three years, Amanda's asthma worsened, and life was dominated by prescriptions, nebulisers, inhalers, emergency visits to Barnet General Hospital and appointments with specialists at the Royal Brompton allergy clinic. There were tests for dust, feathers, mites, milk, dander, chalk and cheese. Amanda's workshop time was strictly limited, and the space had to be thoroughly vacuumed first. Even her two plush teddy bears, Honey and Marmalade, had to take it in frequent turns to go for a spin in the washing machine and spend some time drying on the radiator.

And so life continued, with asthma and education, until, what they came to call, 'The Day of the Mustard Spoon.'

It happened at the polished oak dining table. Amanda was 6 years old and liked English mustard with her bacon in the mornings. Granny served the thick, savoury, yellow paste in a little green-glazed earthenware container that had its own tiny beechwood spoon. That day, Granny had laid the clean mini ladle on the table beyond the mustard pot where it happened to be just out of Amanda's reach. Perran watched Amanda stretch out her little hand. Senara was just about to tell her not to reach across the table … when they saw it. All else was still. No one had shaken the solid piece of furniture they were eating on. But two inches from Amanda's fingers, the spoon … rocked. The couple froze with shock. It was the first sign.

With every appearance of being at ease, Senara picked up the wooden implement and handed it to Amanda, as if she had noticed nothing unusual.

Later, when their granddaughter was tucked up asleep in her bedroom under the eves, Perran and Senara were free to talk.

'I couldn't believe my eyes, Perran,' Senara said, bringing the pudding dishes into the kitchen.

'She has it, all right. After *all*.' Perran had made a start on the washing up from dinner.

'Very unusual for it to take six years to show itself,' remarked Senara.

'Very *lucky*, I'd say,' said her husband.

'True,' she agreed with feeling, picking up a dishcloth

and disappearing into the dining room to wipe the table.

'The main thing is,' said Perran on her return,' that it didn't upset her. The *bian's* perfectly natural with it. She didn't think anything of it. And now it's started it's not going to go away anytime soon.' He took the dishcloth from his wife and passed her a towel. 'I think we should start her training tomorrow.'

Granny was less relaxed than her husband. 'You know where this could lead.' She wiped her hands anxiously. 'And do we *tell* her? Surely not. Then what do we *say* to her?'

'Now, there's no need to be agitated, Senara. There might not be any threat at all. At least, not immediately. We tell her just enough,' replied Perran 'Begin by explaining to her what she is and see how she takes it.'

'She'll have a lot of questions,' Senara warned him, taking up a tea towel and drying the cutlery.

'That's all right. But I'll bet she'll love it, and she'll lap it up.'

'That's just what worries me.'

'Then teach her control right from the start,' suggested Perran. 'Like I taught her with the tools in the workshop. Health and Safety for Witchcraft,' he joked.

Senara gave a half-smile. She considered for a few moments, as she slotted the knives carefully into the block, then said confidently, 'All right. Let's be positive. She's as sharp as a tack. Give Amanda a rule and she'll remember it, and she'll *keep* it.' She paused and said, hope rising, 'Yes, dear, we just have to tell her to keep it secret. *Very* secret.'

'No need to worry her with why, love,' added Perran, 'It may be that the danger has long passed.'

The following morning, with the autumn sun slanting into the living room, the grandparents sat Amanda down on the sofa, her feet leaning against a needlepoint covered stool, and Granny beside her.

'Amanda,' said Senara, tucking a stray strand of the little

girl's hair gently into place.

'Yes, Granny?' She looked up, with her happy, alert blue-brown eyes fixed on Senara's face.

'I want you to listen carefully to what I am going to tell you. I have good news for you,' her grandmother began reassuringly.

'Yes, Granny?' Amanda's face was alive with expectation.

'You,' said Senara with a congratulatory air, 'are …'

'Yes?' Amanda nodded encouragingly.

Granny paused so long that Amanda filled it with guesses, 'Going to the seaside?'

'Er, not today. No, you —'

'— are having roast beef for dinner? On a weekday? Oh wow, it's my fav —'

'No, dear, no. Something even better.'

'Better than —'

'You are a … witch.'

'A witch,' repeated Amanda. She took a moment to absorb this. 'Really, Granny?' Her small face registered her concentration as she rapidly considered this information. Images of Samantha from *Bewitched* twitching her nose, the Fairy Godmother from *Cinderella*, benevolent Glynda from the *Wizard of Oz*, Miss Price from *Bedknobs and Broomsticks* passed before her mind's eye. But what about the sorceress from *Snow White*, she thought, and the —'

'A *good* witch,' emphasised Granny, correctly reading the consternation in Amanda's expression.

'Ah. A *good* witch.' The child smiled with relief.

'Yes, dear, and that's why you could make the mustard spoon move when you reached towards it.' Granny explained, in the most everyday tone she could manage.

Amanda paused for thought. What else might I be able to do? she wondered in the privacy of her head. Is this an all-good thing? Or like double cream that's yummy and then makes it hard to breathe when it brings on my asthma? Where has this thing come from? All of which was distilled into a single word:

'Why?'

'Why what, Ammy?' asked Grandpa.

'Am I a witch?'

They'd prepared for this question. 'Most likely because *I* am a witch and so is your grandfather,' Senara replied, patiently.

'Why don't you do spells then?' asked Amanda curiously, getting straight to the point.

Perran and Senara had discussed how they'd deal with this one too. 'Because,' said Grandpa, 'we thought you were a Normal, and we wanted you to have the chance of a normal life.'

'We shall explain more about this as you get older,' Granny added reassuringly, hoping to end the conversation for now.

Amanda wasn't sure about how to take Granny's news. Although of a naturally cheerful disposition, her health had given her a practical view of life at an early age. Right now, it seemed that being a witch was just one more thing that made her a weird kid. On the other hand:

'If I learn to do spells and things, maybe I can make myself well? Will I be able to run and climb like the other children?'

'Possibly,' conceded Grandpa, noncommittally.

'Will it make me strong?' Amanda was hopeful.

Senara put an arm around her granddaughter and drew her close, then answered, 'Yes, in a way, my dear'. Senara didn't want the child to think that she would necessarily be able to cure herself and live an ordinary life. In fact, her life was going to be anything *but* ordinary. However, Amanda had already decided:

'I'm glad. I *want* to be a witch, and I want to learn *witchcraft*.' She turned her eager blue-brown gaze on each of them, 'Please, Granny and Grandpa, *teach* me.'

It took some time for sleep to overcome Amanda's excitement that night. Her grandparents were awake until the early hours discussing the questions of how. 'How do we answer her if she asks …?' and 'How powerful might she become?' and most importantly of all, 'How do we protect her?'

Trelawney got up and headed for the door. He turned. 'So you'll tell me when to visit them again?'

'Yes. But you may have caused some ripples. So, for now, let the waters calm.'

Chapter 7

᙮

CAREERS ADVICE

The next morning, Perran went to the workshop and left Senara and Amanda to it. In the dining room where they usually studied, Amanda was sitting up straight in her chair, as Granny had taught her, on a stack of three red velvet cushions to bring her elbows up to table height. She had set out a notebook and pencil before her like a place setting. Her diminutive hands were clasped in her lap as she waited impatiently for Granny to sit down and begin her first lesson in Magic. Finally, Granny finished clattering around in the kitchen, gathering her thoughts, and came in. Amanda patted Senara's chair, encouraging her to hurry. Granny lowered herself gracefully onto the brocade-upholstered seat. Amanda fixed an intense stare on her grandmother's business-like face.

Senara took a breath and began. 'This is the first lesson and the most important of all.' Amanda nodded earnestly, her mouse-brown ponytail bouncing on her neck.

'Making others feel uncomfortable is a social solecism. Do you know what that is, Amanda, dear?'

'Bad form. Being ill-mannered,' Amanda, who liked

dipping into the *Oxford English Dictionary*, answered confidently.

'Correct,' Senara said approvingly. 'Witchcraft makes non-witches uncomfortable, and therefore we keep it private. We do not perform it or speak of it either *before* them or *to* them. To do so would be impolite, and we are never rude.'

Amanda thought Granny was frequently rude, but Granny called it 'speaking one's mind'.

'Therefore,' Senara continued, 'the use of magic must be strictly controlled. Now you, my dear, are a natural witch and to control something that is natural takes discipline and practice.' Amanda nodded, indicating she understood. 'Are you, Amanda Cadabra, prepared for the rigorous training that this will involve?' Senara asked her seriously.

Amanda took a resolute breath in that ended in a wheeze and a cough. 'Yes, Granny,' she said through her handkerchief.

'Very well,' said Senara with acceptance. 'Then, after every lesson on using Magic, there will also be one on how to appear Normal.'

Amanda's eyes grew large, as she took in the unexpected gravity of her new, exciting situation.

* * * * *

At that moment, a 15-year-old boy, starting his half-term holiday, was settling into a seat on the Plymouth to London train. He took out a worn, lime green paperback and began reading. The title and the boy's involvement with the story were presently noted by a man in his late thirties. He wore a dark suit and was leafing through a copy of *The Western Morning News,* Devon and Cornwall's daily newspaper, until the boy looked up from his book. The man smiled and nodded.

'Which case have you just finished?'

The teenager grinned.

'"The Speckled Band". My favourite. *So* clever.'

'Glad you didn't say "The Hound of the Baskervilles",' the man responded. 'Not that that isn't good too.'

'It's just the most famous *Sherlock Holmes* story,' observed the boy, 'thanks to the films. But I don't think it's the best.'

'What is it that you like about the cases of the world's most famous detective?'

The boy shrugged. 'I guess it's the puzzles. Only they're not abstract … like crosswords … they're in real life. Real-life detectives solve real-life mysteries … problems … crimes. They make the world a better place. Or, at least, they make sense of things.'

'Hm. It sounds like you want to be one of them.'

'A detective? Yes!' the teenager replied fervently.

'I see. So what are you studying at school?'

'The sciences, history, psychology.'

'Good. But as for reading, Conan Doyle's *Sherlock* will only get you so far.'

'Should I read other detective novels?' asked the boy.

'Not necessarily just novels. I could suggest a reading list if you like,' the man offered.

'Are you a careers advisor?' asked the boy curiously.

'No.'

Another, more exciting possibility occurred to the boy. 'You're not a *detective*, are you?'

'Well …,' the man replied slowly, 'in my own small way, I do have an interest.'

'Then yes, please, a reading list would be great!'

'Ok, I'll write one out for you now.' The man got out a notebook and pencil and began to scribble away

'Thanks!' said the boy.

The man didn't give his name, and the boy didn't think it polite to ask. Later, the boy got off the train with the list clutched in his hand, and they were soon separated in the crowd. Inside the station, he looked around for his benefactor … but the man had gone.

* * * * *

The next morning, Amanda began her Magic lessons. Over the following weeks she practised making the mustard spoon rock again; then rolling a ping pong ball, a marble, and an egg, all without touching them. They got out Amanda's train set, and, using only the power of her intention, she repeated moving the engine on the tracks, forwards and backwards, then added carriages and freight. Senara encouraged Amanda to tumble tennis and cricket balls in different directions at different speeds. In the workshop, Perran made little obstacle courses with tools on a bench so she could practice her emerging mystical skills sliding chunks of wood around them.

Amanda couldn't do everything at the first attempt.

'What am I doing wrong?' she asked, trying to analyse her method.

'It's not about concentrating so much,' explained Grandpa. 'It's more about feeling the thing moving, and then focusing that feeling. And then watching it happen.'

In spite of Amanda's urging, Perran and Senara refused to use magic themselves, and they had her practice behaving like an ordinary child.

'So, Amanda, you are moving your train set with magic, and you hear or see a Normal nearby —'

'Yes, yes, I stop using my magic and push it with my hands, Granny,' she repeated a shade wearily.

'And why do you —'

'Because it is unforgivably rude to use magic around Normals. I *know*.'

'Good,' approved Senara.

* * * * *

On one momentous day, sitting on the end of her Grandpa's bench in the only-just-spring-cleaned workshop, Amanda smiled idly at a blonde curl of pine wood shaving, gleaming in the sunshine, wanting to stroke it. She stretched out her little boiler-suited arm, and the curl rose a few inches into the air. Suddenly, realising what she had done, Amanda clapped her hands with delight, and the wood peel fell back down onto the bench.

'Look Grandpa! Look!' she cried. Her blue-brown eyes had turned chestnut with enchantment.

'I saw!' said Perran, picking her up and whirling her around. 'Who's a clever little witch, then?'

'Let's tell Granny!' she chirped, excitedly,

As Amanda's power and control increased, the asthma eased off. The day she raised the tea strainer, so much heavier than the wood shaving, two inches off its dish, Perran began to teach her Workshop Witchcraft, and Senara made a decision.

Chapter 8

⟶

WICC'HULDOL AND AMANDA'S FIRST TEST

One afternoon, while Amanda was in the workshop with her grandfather learning how to make French polish from shellac flakes and methylated spirits, Senara went up into the attic. She found a spot opposite a particular roof beam and knelt on the floor. Senara put her hand on an ordinary-looking floorboard and pronounced, '*Agertyn forrag Senara, atdha mina vocleav.*'

At the sound of her voice, two lines appeared about eighteen inches apart across three boards that invisibly formed a hatch on a hinge. The little trapdoor popped open. Senara reached inside the cavity and withdrew a hefty tome. It bore the legend *Wicc'huldol Galdorwrd Nha Koomwrtdreno Aon.*

'*Bespredna,*' she instructed the floor; and the hatch shut gently. The floorboards assumed their customary aspect.

Downstairs, Senara gave the volume a good vacuuming and wipe, wrapped it in a tea towel, and stowed it under the sink behind the washing up bowl.

After Amanda was in bed, while Senara and Perran were clearing up after a dinner of rabbit stew and jam roly-poly, Senara said, 'Let's go up to the workshop when we're done. I need to show you something.'

Ten minutes later, Perran was looking down in consternation at the book on his workshop bench.

'Are you really going to give her that ... *thing*?' he asked his wife incredulously. 'She's *seven* years old.'

'It does say "1",' Senara offered.

'It says "*Witchcraft: Spells and Potions: 1*" and it's stuffed full of notes and addenda by Jowanet Cardiubarn! And heaven only knows who she inherited this — this homicidal book from,' Perran protested with unusual vehemence.

Senara lifted her hands in surrender. 'Very well. We can go through it together, and you personally can put sealing spells on the parts that you think are unsuitable.'

'We'll be here all night then,' said Perran, opening at the first spell. 'Fortunately most of it's in Wicc'yeth rather than English.'

'It'll give her the opportunity to learn that too,' replied Senara with an optimistic air.

'Hm,' commented Perran unenthusiastically. He turned over the first five pages and found an age-yellowed piece of notepaper inscribed with a schoolgirl's hand-writing. 'Look at this, will you? "How to Put Upon a Rat the Legs of a Lizard",' he translated with distaste.

'Yes, yes, great-great-grandmother Jowanet was a revolting child but ...,' Senara waved her hand over the paper. The writing faded and was gone. 'We can remove things like that.'

Perran shook his head distrustfully.

'Oh, come now,' cajoled his wife. 'It's a primer. There are a great many useful, simple spells in here for the beginner ...'

As a precaution, since she was about to introduce her little granddaughter to a tome with a rather dark history, Senara waited until the next morning when the sun was shining brightly before she heaved *Wicc'huldol* onto the dining room table. Amanda knelt up in her chair, leaning curiously towards the ancient lexicon.

Granny slid it towards her granddaughter.

'Put your hands on the book, dear, and close your eyes. If you can find the thing that is hidden, you are ready for it, and you can have it. It's a kind of game, my sweet.'

Granny was smiling and nodding. Amanda shut her eyes tightly and ran her hands over the cover of the book. It was lumpy with embossing. She opened it and touched the pages. Then she stopped guessing, stopped thinking and felt … and there it was: a pull. A pull toward the centre of the pages. Amanda could feel the stitching, but it was *under* the stitching. She gasped and shut the book. Her thumb pressed against the three-inch-wide spine and detected a ridge. She followed it down, then back up. Her face lit with delight.

'*I* know!' she exclaimed. Amanda pushed two small fingers down inside the spine and drew out a wand. She opened her eyes as Granny applauded.

'Well done, Ammy, clever girl!'

As Amanda learned to use the wand and spells to focus her energy, she developed, for her age, formidable powers of levitation. Soon she could make the Hoover vacuum the workshop, and lift a small chest of drawers onto a workbench. Amanda could make a hammer bang in a nail without touching it, and make a saw cut into a piece of pine. Not yet a straight cut, though.

'It's coming on, *bian*. Looks a bit less like the River Nile today,' her grandfather teased her affectionately, pushing back into place the scarf that protected her silky hair from dust. 'I wish there was a spell to keep *that* where it should be!'

At 9 years of age, she faced her first real test.

'Remember the most important lesson, Ammy?' asked Perran.

'To appear normal. To resist any temptation to use magic in the presence of the Normals,' Amanda recited.

'Very good, love. So your Granny's invited an old friend of ours to tea on Sunday. Ms Amelia Reading from Muswell Hill. We think it's safe now that you're doing so well with your studies.'

Ms Reading arrived in a swathe of long sweeping purple skirt and cashmere jumper. This ensemble was revealed when she removed her black furry coat that matched her dark hair and eyes and reached all the way down to the ankles. Amelia Reading wore both a shawl and a scarf, dropping first one, then the other and apologising. She had a large, black velvet bag that she kept close to her. Although Amanda thought Amelia sweet and comical, she was also on her guard.

Tea was set out in the dining room. Amelia sat next to Amanda and asked her how she liked being her grandfather's assistant. As Amanda was answering, Amelia accidentally pushed her crumpet off her plate. Amanda deftly caught it.

'Oops!' said Amelia. 'Thank you, sweetie.'

A few minutes later, Amelia somehow managed to wedge the butter knife under the pot of damson jam, and sent it flying towards Amanda, who dodged then retrieved it from under the sideboard.

'Oh dear, I do seem to be accident-prone today,' Amelia said remorsefully, waving one end of her shawl in a flustered manner. 'What a helpful girl you are.'

Shortly after, Amelia's elbow nudged her Royal Doulton teacup and sent it tumbling towards the carpet. Amanda did nothing to save it, avoided the splashes and went to the kitchen to get a cloth. She wondered what was the matter with this strange exotic lady.

Once Amanda was back in her seat, Amelia smiled at her and said, 'Well done, my dear, very well done indeed. You have passed. Flying colours.'

'Ms Reading is one of us, Amanda,' said her grandmother, beaming with pleasure.

'You have been well taught in the art of suppressing your magical gifts in the presence of Normals,' Amelia complemented her. 'I am here to supplement your grandparents' splendid instruction with some tuition in my specialist areas,' announced Amelia.

Amanda's eyes shone.

After tea, Amanda was introduced to The Crystal Ball, which had been concealed in Amelia's bag. Lessons in the basics of divination followed every Tuesday with Ms Reading. She was now 'Aunt Amelia,' had unaccountably stopped dropping her woollen drapery on the floor, and her clumsiness had vanished.

'We are not fortune-tellers, Ammy,' explained Amelia. 'No one knows the future. We see only possibilities, openings, opportunities. Do you see? We make our *own* destiny, and we can change it in a moment.' She continued kindly, 'Remember that the ball, the cards, the tea leaves, the crystals, and the candles are just ways to help us concentrate. The power to see is in each of us. The hardest thing is to read for oneself. We are too dominated by what we wish to see. Just like healing. The hardest thing is to heal *oneself*.'

'Is that why I haven't found a healing spell that works?' asked Amanda, a little troubled.

'You haven't found it *yet*. That's all I can say, my pet,' said Amelia, patting her hand encouragingly.

Chapter 9

༄

ROMEO AND JULIET, BECOMING AMANDA, AND THE VOICE IN THE NIGHT

Amanda did not distinguish herself at divination. The tea leaves always looked like a cup and saucer. Her candles went out when she stared at them. Her crystal ball invariably turned orange and appeared to fill with goldfish.

Amelia had once been a glass-blower, renowned in artistic circles. Over the years, she had created a dazzlingly beautiful collection of crystal balls. Amanda tried an array of them but the only alternative she could achieve to the fish tank, was a snow globe of an especially plastic version of Paris. Amanda's failures increased her respect for Aunt Amelia's talents. Additionally, she had become Amanda's confidante and source of information. Senara and Perran had given Amelia carte blanche to provide Amanda with little titbits about them, as and when Amelia thought necessary. Today was one of those days.

'Can this thing tell you about the past?' asked Amanda, staring into the eyes of a curious goldfish that had, as usual, appeared in the crystal ball.

'Yes, sweetie.'

'Hm, pity I can't make it work.'

'What is it that you want to know?' Amelia asked, helpfully.

'Granny and Grandpa are Cornish, right?' Amanda checked.

'Yes,' answered Amelia, guessing at what was coming.

'And I'm Cornish too?'

'You are,' Amelia replied levelly.

'So ... why don't we live in Cornwall?'

Amelia collected her thoughts and then said, 'Would you like to hear a story?'

'Oo yes, please, Aunt Amelia,' Amanda replied, eagerly.

'All right ... so,' — she cleared her throat —, 'once upon a time there were two young people. Let's call them Romeo and Juliet —'

'— that's Shakespeare, Aunt Amelia. I already know that story.'

'Well, this was *another* Romeo and Juliet,' Amelia responded, patiently.

'OK.'

'Just like in the play, their families were ...?' Amelia paused for Amanda to finish the sentence.

'... enemies.'

'Yes, Amanda. So ... what do you think our Romeo and Juliet did?'

'Killed themselves?' she answered, brightly.

'No, they did something much more practical. They knew they could never have a life in their home country, so they eloped!

'Wow!'

'They ran away one night and crossed the border into another country, and they got married. But where in that country were they going to live?'

'I don't know,' answered Amanda.

'Well, there had been a war and, during that time, Juliet had made a friend. Let's call her Viola. Viola lived in Romeo and Juliet's new country in a beautiful village, and she wrote and told

Juliet all about it, and said that she and Romeo could have a peaceful life there.'

'So that's where they went to live?'

'Yes.'

'And they lived happily ever after?' asked Amanda hopefully.

'Yes,' smiled Amelia.

Amanda considered the narrative.

'Romeo and Juliet are Grandpa and Granny, aren't they, Aunt Amelia?'

'They could be.'

'And the village is Sunken Madley?'

'Perhaps,' replied Amelia.

'Who is Julia's war friend? And Romeo and Juliet had children, yes? And one of those had a baby? But they didn't want it, did they? And that's why Romeo and Juliet looked after it,' said Amanda, consternation rising in her voice.

'Sweetie,' interrupted Amelia. Amanda stopped and looked at her with wide, empty eyes until Amelia said, 'This tale is a happy tale, remember?' Amanda calmed and managed a half-smile.

'But,' Amelia continued lightly, 'it does not reveal everything.'

Amanda nodded.

'All you need to know right now is that you are in Sunken Madley because your grandparents, who are your legal parents, are here. And they love you very much and wanted you with all their hearts. All right?'

Amanda nodded again, this time cheerfully.

'Now … how would you like to learn a little crystal magic?'

'Yes, I'd like that,' replied Amanda, successfully distracted. 'At least I couldn't be worse at it than I am at divination!'

* * * * *

Just as Amanda's esteem for Amelia had grown, so her admiration for Granny was now considerable. In fact, she made Senara her role model. Granny had always worn black cotton dresses for housework. She had a bolt of the cloth in the airing cupboard upstairs.

'It's hard-wearing, serviceable and doesn't show stains,' Granny said. Now that Amanda's magical training had moved on to being increasingly practical, Granny often put on one of her dark outfits. Her granddaughter's misfired spells could get messy, especially in the kitchen.

One rainy September afternoon, 9-year-old Amanda looked up from memorising some of her spellbook vocabulary.

'Granny.'

'Yes, dear,' Senara responded, continued looking down at the blanket she was hemming.

'Please, would you make me a dress like yours?'

'Black cotton?' asked Granny.

'Yes, please.'

'Just for at home, now. Nothing says "witch" like going about all in black like the Adam's Family,' Senara pointed out.

'Yes, Granny, I know. Outside I'll keep wearing my favourite orange and yellow.'

'Right, then.'

A few days later, after getting the sewing machine humming and having several fittings, Amanda got her first black dress. It was slightly high-waisted, gathered at the back of the shoulders, and had detachable white collar and cuffs. Hems were extra long and turned up to allow for growth. Amanda looked at herself in the mirror and, for the first time, was extremely pleased with what she saw.

Amanda had long noticed that Granny took down her victory roll at night and arranged her white hair in a long plait that hung down her back. Except sometimes at night or early in the morning, it would be loose, and Granny would have a sort of glow about her, that it took Amanda a few more years to identify.

Inspired by Granny's coiffure but old enough to want her own version, Amanda came down to breakfast one day with her hair tied in two plaits and asked Granny for black ribbon. When Perran saw her, he applauded.

'You look complete to a shade, Miss Cadabra!' He studied her and then said, 'Well … almost'. He gave Granny a speaking look. 'What do you say, love?'

'Not yet,' was Senara's judgement.

'What "not yet"?' asked Amanda excitedly, her plaits rebounding on her shoulders as she jumped up and down.

'Never you mind,' said Senara.

* * * *

That evening, 400 miles to the south-west, an 18-year-old was in his bedroom packing and preparing for his first term at university.

His father came to the open door.

'Got all your course books?'

'Yes, thanks,' smiled his son. He'd asked the same question all through school, checking the boy had whatever he needed.

'Notepad, pencils, stationary?'

'Yup.'

'Set your alarm for the morning?'

The young man laughed affectionately.

'Yes, Dad.'

His father looked at the rare poster of Sir Arthur Conan Doyle on his son's wall.

'You sure about this? Taking Criminal Studies with Psychology? You used to be so keen on being an archaeologist.'

'When I was *11*.'

The man gestured towards Sir Arthur.

'You really think you can be the next Sherlock Holmes and make a good living at that?'

'Sherlock Holmes was a *fictional* character, Dad. Out of Conan Doyle's head. I'm going to be the *real thing*.'

'Well, if you're set on it,' his father sighed. 'You'll be careful though, won't you? It won't be like school, you know.'

'Dad, I'll be fine. It's just Plymouth. I'll be home every evening just like before, at least for the first year. And I really appreciate the car, by the way.'

'Oh, it's just an old banger. Get you there and back. I'd rather you were driving than going on the train with all sorts. Mind yourself on the fast roads, though.'

'I will.' He closed his bag and set it by the door. 'Dad?'

'Son?'

'There's just one thing. Well, I'm 18 now. Legally, I'm an adult. So ... I was wondering if ... you'd feel you could tell me ... now. You know? Man to man?'

'What?'

'Why you and Mum broke up.'

He couldn't remember a time when his parents had been ecstatically happy. They'd never argued in front of him, but sometimes, late at night, when he awakened from a dream, he had thought he'd heard his parents talking in the kitchen downstairs. Their conversations sounded urgent, anxious, pleading but hushed. They never raised their voices, and that's why it stood out in his memory. And because it was the evening of his 10th birthday. His mother's voice tearing the night with a single accusing, fearful cry: 'Sorcery!' Soon after that, his parents had told him that they were getting a divorce, and his life was never the same again.

'Can't you tell me *now*, Dad?'

But his father responded as he always did.

'Cultural differences, son.'

Chapter 10

༄

PERRAN CADABRA, AND MAGIC FEVER

Tuition in the workshop with Grandpa was very different from studies in the house with Granny. Perran was adamant that, in his domain, Amanda should learn to do things the Normal way. First, he taught her to use hand-tools. She had to become proficient in the use of saws, planes and chisels, as well as sharpening and cleaning them. Only then was Amanda allowed to use power tools, and always under his supervision.

'Why can't I use *magic*?' nagged Amanda. 'It's so much easier and quicker!'

'Because this is a trade that you're taking out into the world, where you can't use magic, not in front of Normals,' her grandfather repeated for the fifth time that morning.

'But there aren't any Normals here *now*,' Amanda argued. 'And I'm not going to go out on any jobs yet. I'm only 11.'

'This is the time of your apprenticeship where you develop your skills, learn to appreciate what crafters before you accomplished *without* resorting to spells, and to fix the things that they made when they get damaged. Besides, you are learning the magic *too*, especially with your Granny.'

Still, Amanda's frustration was apparent, and Perran saw that he needed to change his teaching tactics. Cleaning up the workshop at the end of the day, he looked up towards the house and Amanda's bedroom window. What he detected through the glass, gave him an idea. Half an hour later he tapped on her door.

'It's Grandpa,' he called.

'Erm … yeah … just a minute … ok, come in,' he heard her flustered reply. Perran smiled, knowing why his granddaughter had stalled for time. There were origami aeroplanes, haphazardly arranged on every surface in the room. He looked at her teasingly as he came in.

'It's alright. I'm not the Magic Police.'

'Phew! You won't say anything will you, Grandpa?'

'No, but don't worry. In spite of Granny's embargo on magic in the house for recreation, she knows you fly your paper planes around your room, and, as long as its *only* in your room, she's prepared to turn a blind eye.'

'Thank goodness,' breathed Amanda, making room for him next to her, and her bears, Honey and Marmalade, on the bed.

'But,' he said sitting down, 'how would you like to fly something *better* than bits of origami?'

'What d'you mean?'

'How about if we make it a workshop project to make all of the Spitfires, that you're so fond of, between Mark 1 and 24 and …' But he was interrupted by a crushing hug.

'Oh, Grandpa!'

'And any other plane you want, a Messerschmitt and a Japanese Zero —'

'— and a P-51? And a P-47? And a —'

'Yes,' Grandpa laughed, 'anything you like. But you'll have to stop strangling me if want me to be able to help you!'

'Grandpa, thank you!' she said releasing her affectionate grip. 'That's a brilliant idea. You're a genius! I can't wait.'

'Now,' he said steadyingly, '… my little witch … making

these will need precision. A precision that's within the scope of your manual dexterity to develop. But this work is far too delicate for anything you could do with levitation; you do understand that?'

'Yes, Grandpa. I know. I don't mind. Can we start tomorrow?'

Amanda rose to the challenge, and her old enthusiasm returned. However, a year later, on one of her Tuesday sessions with Aunt Amelia, Amanda couldn't help remarking on the contrast between her grandparents. Her crystal ball was as unco-operative as ever, so, as a diversion, Amelia asked how Amanda was getting on with carpentry.

'I do love Grandpa and what I'm doing in the workshop. It's just that with Granny I learn so much more magic and it's hard not to think about it when I'm with Grandpa because it's what I really want to be *doing*!' insisted Amanda. 'Sometimes I can't sleep because I'm imagining spells.'

Amelia was quiet. She pushed the crystal ball aside, took out her Tarot cards and put them in front of Amanda.

'Shuffle these, Ammy.' Amanda was surprised, but picked up the cards and rhythmically mixed them until it felt right to stop.

'Let's find out what's going on with you, shall we?' suggested Aunt Amelia.

'OK.'

Amelia laid them out.

'Do the cards tell you anything?' she asked Amanda.

'No,' her student replied forlornly.

'Alright,' Amelia said soothingly. She pointed to one card after another as she spoke. 'You are 12 years old and a young witch. This can be a … trying age. You see this card? This means the fever is upon you — the fever for magic. You must overcome it, or it will overcome you.'

'You mean, I could become … Darkside?' asked Amanda, round-eyed with concern.

'There is that danger,' Amelia warned her. 'You think Granny is exciting and Grandpa is boring.'

'No, not that,' objected Amanda. 'Not that bad.'

'But,' continued Amelia, 'you are learning something essential from Perran, something vitally important.'

'What?'

'What it means to be a Lightside witch.'

Amanda frowned at the cards. 'What do you mean?'

'Perran is a good witch,' stated Amelia. 'He comes from a line of good witches and to be a good witch is far harder than to be a bad one. Why do you think that is?'

Amanda applied her mind to the question and then suggested, 'Because you can't do just anything you want. You have to keep the rules?'

'Exactly. And that is what Perran is teaching you. And make no mistake — see this card here? It represents your Grandpa. Perran Cadabra is a powerful witch in his own right; it's from his side that you get your power of levitation. You would do well to remember and to respect that, Amanda.'

Her little apprentice felt abashed and blushed. Amelia smiled.

'I'm not reproving you, sweetie. I tell you what. Let's call in your Granny and get her to tell you about Perran's family and the legendary magical feat they performed in the Year of the Great Storm.'

Chapter 11

༉

HEIRLOOMS

Amelia's words about Perran provided Amanda with food for thought. She began to see training in *not* using magic as important as learning and perfecting spells. She began to understand why Granny made her alternate doing each of her household tasks one week with spells and the next without. Her newfound awareness was noted by her grandparents, and so, after a few months, she was rewarded.

'It's time now, don't you agree, Senara?'

'Yes, dear.'

The workshop got its annual spring clean. On the first warm day, every scrap of furniture, each fixture and fitting was carried out into the garden. The walls, ceiling, floor, shelves and racks were vacuumed and scrubbed. When everything was put back, Perran sent Amanda to get showered and changed into one of her black dresses.

'Put your hair in plaits with your favourite ribbons and then wait for us while we get cleaned up too,' said her grandfather.

Amanda was soon washed, dressed and pacing her room,

looking downstairs and round doorways to see if they were ready. After what seemed an agonisingly long wait, she was called to the workshop.

She went in and saw Perran standing in the middle of the floor. He seemed to fill the space, as though he'd grown taller. Granny sat to one side looking at him. He seemed to have a faint pale gold outline. Amanda felt as though she were seeing him for the first time.

Then suddenly he was Grandpa again, smiling and drawing something out from behind his back. A big black disc. He tilted it, till she saw it had a peak in the middle.

'A hat!' cried Amanda in awe, 'A witch's hat!' She was deeply impressed. 'Wow, Grandpa, it's yours, yes?'

'It is mine. It is a hereditary hat, come through many generations, had the brim re-done, the crown repaired, the fabric replaced but it is still the same entity.'

She remembered what Amelia had said.

'I suppose you have to be a real, important witch to have one of those.'

'It's not just a badge of office, Ammy,' said Grandpa. 'A witch's hat is an amplifier.' Amanda looked mystified. He explained, 'When you wear the hat, it sharpens your awareness of magical activity around you and to a greater distance. Like a radar dish.'

'Oh, I see,' said Amanda, comprehending.

'And when you do a spell, it intensifies it. So you only wear the hat when it really matters. When you have heavy magical work to do.'

She nodded solemnly.

'This hat,' continued Grandpa,' will one day be yours and we think you're ready to begin training in how to use it.'

Amanda's eyes brightened with wonder, and her radiant smile lit the room.

'Really? Can I? You think I'm ready?'

'Stand still,' he said. Perran ceremonially raised the hat and lowered it onto Amanda's head, speaking the words of investiture:

'*Undreceva thoan ricallow haetowr.*' He took a step back. 'Now, let me see you.'

There stood Amanda in her black dress, with white collar and cuffs, her two light brown plaits bound with black and silver ribbon. Her blue-brown eyes glowed with pride and delight from under the brim of the dark purple-black hat.

From that time on, Perran equalled, if not surpassed, Senara in Amanda's esteem. She asked if he would teach her Cornish. Perran and Senara discussed it in private.

'I'm not sure it's a good idea,' said Senara.

'It *is* her birthright,' admitted Perran.

'It'll make her ask to *go* there. What will we say?'

'I'm not sure. It'll surely just frighten her if we tell her that, now she's a witch, if she crosses the Tamar and there are any of *them* left, … they'll sense her.'

'And not just *them*,' added Senara, troubled.

'Let's say to Amanda,' said Perran thoughtfully, 'that people weren't very nice to us there, and that's why we left. She'll want to stay away out of loyalty to us.'

'Yes. That will do it,' agreed Senara.

'So I'll say Cornish is just so she can practice it with me. And with you,' confirmed Perran.

'Yes. Very well.'

That Tuesday, Amanda looked up from trying to get the attention of Flounder. She saw the goldfish in the crystal ball so often she'd decided to give them names.

'Aunt Amelia.'

'Yes, Amanda?'

'Is someone looking for me?' Amelia sat quietly, seeming to peer into the distance. Her eyes narrowed and moved slowly from left to right, as though scanning the horizon. Finally, she said, 'No, sweetie.'

'So … I'm not in danger?' asked Amanda less anxiously.

'No. Why do you ask?'

'Granny and Grandpa are always on about being careful to keep my magic secret, and then when I asked Grandpa if he'd teach me Cornish, he said yes, if I made a promise. And it was *weird.*'

'How?'

'I had to put one hand on Grandpa's spell book and the other on Granny's, and make a solemn oath never to cross the River Tamar — you know the river that divides Devon from Cornwall?'

'And Cornwall from England, some would say but yes, never to cross it ...?

'Never to cross it without them.'

'You know your grandparents have a past there?' Amelia asked.

'Yes,' Amanda confirmed.

'Well ...' Amelia paused as she looked for an example. 'It's like this: would you walk into a dark alley at night in a strange place?'

'No way,' replied Amanda, emphatically.

'Why not?

'I might get mugged by a Normal and not be able to use my magic to defend myself.'

'Yes, or you might come out of the other end unscathed,' replied Amelia 'But it's best not to go looking for trouble, and then trouble won't go looking for you. Right now you are not flagging up on anyone's radar. If you continue to be discreet and stay out of the alley, then there is no reason why you should not remain perfectly safe.'

'Ah, I see,' said Amanda, 'Right now, the other side of the Tamar is like our family's dark alley. OK.' Amanda was content with that. For the time being.

At 13, Amanda was introduced by Grandpa to his even more surprising possession than her prized witch's hat. Again the family spring-cleaned the workshop and themselves, and again Amanda was formally called to attend it.

Grandpa beckoned her to his workbench. There was only one item on it. An old tan leather covered book. The edges of the pages were ragged and yellowed.

'*Forrag Seothe Macungreanz A Aclowundre*,' Amanda read the title, and attempted a translation. '*For the Making of … Wonderful Things*? ' She looked up at him with a puzzled expression. Perran Cadabra seemed to grow in stature as he replied.

'Just as your Granny has a book of spells handed down in her family, so do I. The Cadabras have been carpenters for over 200 years. And before that by another family name. But anyway, these are to speed up the processes in the workshop. You must only use them at great need and out of sight of Normals.' He turned the pages and pointed. 'This is a glue spell. This is a glue removal spell. This one is a clamping spell; the ones in this section are tool-operating spells. And there are lots more that you will learn.'

'When?' asked Amanda eagerly, looking at the book.

'Tomorrow, we can start, if you like. The important thing to know now is that you'll have to control pressure and direction, but they'll do the elbow work for you. The next thing is: be very sure no one is watching,' Perran cautioned her. 'Keep the back gate and the front door locked if you're ever here by yourself using spells.'

Amanda nodded. Magic was clearly a serious business.

Chapter 12

ᘒ

THE STUDENT'S CHOICE, AND THE FAMILIAR

As Amanda was receiving Perran's spell book, a 22-year-old student was giving some unwelcome news to his mother.

'You're *what*?' she said, leaning forward to put her green tea on the fair-trade coffee table in front of them. 'More importantly, *why*, for heaven's sake?' She shook head in disbelief. 'I thought you were going to stay on at uni and take your Masters degree, and go into research or … or set up in business for yourself.'

'It isn't right for me,' insisted her son, 'investigating sordid affaires for suspicious spouses or grubby financial transgressions. And I've never wanted to go into research. I've always said I wanted to be a detective, and I know that this is where I could do work that *means* something.'

'But joining the *poliiiice*, darling!' She raked a hand through her thick, short, well-cut blonde hair and stood up. 'Two years on the beat. After a getting a first-class university degree, you're going to walk the streets of some dreary Cornish town? My son, a local bobby! One of the police; what, in my youth, we used to call the pi—'

'Mum. Please. It isn't all patrol; I'll be doing lots of training. I'll learn how to use my eyes and ears on the job and then, after the two years are up, I can apply to start on the detective ladder.'

His mother paced about the room, straightening the tasteful, abstract, museum prints on the wall, her lean frame taught with agitation.

'Where has this come from? At least tell me that. It's your fath—'

'No,' he chuckled. 'You can't blame Dad for this.'

'Well, *who* then!'

'Partly the uni careers' counsellor and partly talking to Michelle's Dad.'

'I *never* thought she was right for you.'

'She's just a friend, Mum. Anyway, her dad's a detective in Yorkshire. He didn't try and persuade me or anything. We just talked and ... I started thinking and ... I know this is *right* for me.'

'Oh, darling,' replied his mother, sorrowfully. She held out her hand to him. He got his long legs out from under the table and went to her. He had inherited his mother's colouring and so now two pairs of hazel eyes met, one resigned, one hopeful. She hugged him. 'If you're *sure* ... then I suppose we must support you ... foolish boy. Very well. I hope you won't be sorry. By the way, how did your father react?'

He laughed. 'Just like you!'

* * * * *

Amanda enjoyed developing her skills, mystical and otherwise. She was equipped with two spell books, a wand and a hat, all precious heirlooms. Nevertheless, by the age of 15, Amanda had grown restless. She had formed no friendships with any of the teenagers in the village but had enough acquaintances among them to know they were off on school trips, hiking, abseiling, skiing, practising for sports tournaments and generally expanding their tangible world. Amanda felt trapped by her asthma. The physical limitations it imposed irked her increasingly.

Her grandparents, observing this, stepped up the number of trips to the seaside, days out to museums, antique fairs and stone circles. Amanda was appreciative, but still longed to be out striding the moors, exploring forests and climbing mountains, ideally by herself.

Alone in the living room one afternoon, Perran and Senara considered the problem and came to a conclusion.

'It's time for the familiar,' Perran said seriously to Senara.

'I think you're right, dear,' agreed his wife, resignedly.

That night, Senara and Perran were in the workshop till late. In the morning it smelled hot and musty, of burnt hessian, ammonia and Marmite. The product of their sorcery was nowhere to be seen. Perran, bending backwards with his hands on his waist, stretching his back, looked up at the clear blue summer sky. 'Don't worry,' he said humorously to his anxious wife, who was scanning the garden and peering into the shrubbery. 'Lovely day: that'll bring it in, and no mistake.'

By the afternoon tea break, there was still no sign of 'it', but Perran was unperturbed. Senara had already set out the tea tray in the living room, and Perran and Amanda were making themselves comfortable. He had told his granddaughter to, 'leave the back door open to let in the sunshine.'

That was when it slunk in, as though to avoid the fine weather. It was a selection of greys, short-haired and with eyes of a baleful yellow, like a walking collection of storm clouds around two livid lemon fog lamps.

It silently pushed open the living room door, made its sullenly regal progress into the room, spat and promptly coughed up a hairball onto the carpet. Holding the stage, it cast an all-embracing glare at the three Cadabras. Amanda put her hands over her nose and mouth.

'No need, dear,' said Senara, 'This Animal has been hypo allergenised especially for you. This is your familiar. His name is Tempest. By name and by nature. He is an heirloom. Your grandfather and I reincarnated him last night on the larger workbench. I wouldn't work there today if I were you.'

Amanda cautiously lowered her hands.

'Be careful. It scratches,' warned her grandmother.

Tempest looked at Senara and hissed, then crossed to Amanda and sat on her foot. His purr rattled like a thunderstorm and vibrated her leg. Warmth spread up it and into her whole body. She had never touched a cat before. She reached down and let out a sigh of delight, at a softness she had never before imagined.

'Ahhh. He's beautiful!' she said, adoringly.

Tempest stood up. Their foreheads met, and the edges of Amanda's vision crackled black. Disorientated, she leaned back and closed her eyes. At that moment, she saw herself, the armchair she was sitting in, and the bookcase behind her, all from about a foot off the ground. The view was drained of reds, and was a wash of greens and blues. Her peripheral range had widened, but the image was blurred as though she'd become long-sighted. She gasped in surprise and opened her eyes. The vision was gone.

'Wha…?'

Both grandparents nodded in approval.

'Now you know how your cat sees the world,' said Senara.

'It's done,' confirmed Perran. 'One day maybe you'll be able to see through Tempest's eyes at will, though it'll take a lot of practice. But he's bonded with you, and that's the important thing.'

'And no small mercy. He's a vile-tempered old whatnot,' Senara added, looking at the cat with dislike.

'Oh? *Why* is he bad tempered?' asked Amanda.

'Not for me to say. His Worshipfulness will let you know when he's good and ready.'

'So *you* know why?' Amanda queried.

'Oh, indeed I do,' replied her grandmother, testily. 'Hm!'

Amanda was fascinated by her new companion. She soon learned that stroking was only ever at the cat's behest, that one, slow blink meant 'yes', and to recognise the look that meant 'Feed me now.' By the second day, Tempest thought her training was coming on rather well.

* * * *

Meanwhile, in a Cornish police station, a uniformed 24-year-old was waiting outside an office. He was about to meet the one who would train him to become a detective. The young man deliberately calmed his breathing and tried to slow his heart rate. He wanted to appear confident, though, of course, not arrogant. It was essential to him to make the best possible impression on his future mentor. He'd worked towards this day for two years — no, since he was 12-years old, in fact.

'Come in,' called a voice from within. It sounded friendly enough. He opened the door, looked at the man behind the desk and froze on the threshold.

'Sir?' was all he managed to say.

His new senior smiled knowingly.

'Welcome to Baker Street, young Sherlock.'

* * * *

The next evening, Granny advised Amanda to go and have a bath and meditate. By candlelight, Amanda relaxed into hot water under lavender-scented bubbles. She exhaled happily and lowered her lids. Slowly, she began to see through her cat's eyes.

It was not yet fully dark, but Tempest's vision was sharpening by the minute. He was up on the back fence looking into the sky at the almost full moon. Tempest scanned his surroundings then reached a decision. He jumped a horrifyingly long way to the ground and made for the woods.

Tempest picked a path between the silver birches for several yards, until his head twitched and he halted. He waited. Then pounced. Amanda got an unwelcome close-up of the back wings of a hapless moth, before it turned into a snack. Her familiar trotted on, brushing through the undergrowth. Tempest stopped abruptly, looked up to watch a barn owl flitting along the edge of the trees, and then moved on. Now he was cutting a purposeful route through the rest of the wood. It grew darker as a bank of cloud passed over the canopy. The cat paused at the edge of the pasture beyond the trees. Amanda clearly saw the sky through his eyes as he searched it; perhaps for that owl he'd seen.

Still in the shadow of the birches, Tempest's gaze panned from left to right across the open land. There was the sense of arriving for an appointment. The moon was revealed and its light picked out a shape with long ears appearing at the opposite side of the pasture. Tempest went forward slowly, then gathered speed. Long-ears bounded towards the cat. Amanda waited for the almighty clash and bash of claws and teeth. But unexpectedly, Tempest and the hare bounded around one another, sniffing and nuzzling until the cat rolled on his back. A twitching nose zoomed into view and moved down, tickling Tempest's chest while Amanda's fierce new familiar nibbled the bunny's ears playfully.

Amanda had a sudden sense of snooping on something intimate and opened her eyes. She floated in the warm bath, reflecting in wonder at what she had seen. It was stranger and more mystical than any view from the top of a mountain, where other teenagers might be on holiday at this moment. Amanda understood the value of the gift her grandparents had given her.

I can go places and see things in a way no one else can. I'll never feel sorry for myself again, she vowed.

Not entirely accurately but it was a start.

Chapter 13

৩

DR BERGSTROM'S INVENTION AND THE POWER OF PETITE

Amanda was 16 when Perran told her that they were going on a trip to London to meet an exceptional, magical person. Over the years, her witch outfit had modified to suit her changing tastes but was primarily black. That day she wore a skater dress over leggings and medium heeled ankle boots. She packed her hat out of sight in a large velvet holdall, inspired by Aunt Amelia's bag. Amanda knew that this was a momentous occasion because Grandpa had arranged an executive taxi cab, an indulgence reserved for birthday outings to the theatre or the opera. Amanda's mouth was dry with excitement and nervousness at the thought of meeting a mystical VIP. Dressed in her best clothes and riding in the luxurious car, she felt like royalty.

The cab drove them south into London, through Marble Arch and Hyde Park Corner, past Buckingham Palace Gardens and down onto Vauxhall Bridge Road. From there they branched west into Pimlico until the car stopped in a side street outside a well-preserved Georgian hotel.

Perran murmured something to the driver and Senara led the way in. A smartly uniformed attendant ushered them through the elegant marble-floored and columned foyer. They were expected. The attendant escorted the trio into a wrought-iron lift that travelled up to the second floor and from there to a polished mahogany door. He knocked on it discreetly with a white-gloved hand. Hearing a response from within, he opened it, gestured with a bow for them to enter and silently walked away.

Senara went in first. Amanda followed into what looked like a living room. At the same time, through the only other door, an old man entered. He had neatly side-parted, light grey hair, a moustache and beard. He was shorter than Perran, but every bit as upright. The man wore a white shirt, black suit and bow tie. He had an absent-minded air, but his round-framed bespectacled eyes were periwinkle blue and sparkled with intelligence.

'Bertil, *det är kul att se dig*,' Perran greeted him warmly in Swedish.

'*Det har varit för länge!*' said the man, as they hugged hello. 'Senara, you look well.'

Perran turned to include his granddaughter. 'Amanda, this is Dr Bertil Bergstrom, a creative genius.' At which Bertil laughed and put up a deprecating hand. 'Bertil Bergstrom, may I present my granddaughter, Amanda Cadabra.'

Amanda shook the man's hand and wondered if she should curtsey. Mr Bergstrom bowed ceremoniously, then looked keenly but kindly into her eyes.

'Ah, se little vitch,' he said.

'I'm *16*,' Amanda pointed out, uncomfortable with being called 'little'.

'But inside you are still 9 years ohld, yah?' Amanda stared at him.

'Well...' Her natural honesty overcame her reticence. 'That's just how I feel, yes. How did you know?'

'I can see. Your grandparents tell me ahlvays about you as you are growing up. Ahnd I can see this one is 9. Ahlvays 9.'

Amanda looked dismayed

'But sis is good sing, yah?' Bertil said, joyfully. 'To be ahlvays young inside. Sis is a great gift. As great as your magic!' A smile grew on Amanda's lips and spread to her whole face. 'Yah! Kom sit, sit, everyvon, we have coffee here. And cinnamon buns.' Amanda, having thus been put at her ease by the doctor, ate, drank and joined in with the catchup conversation as much as she could.

'How is Kerstin?' asked Senara. Turning to Amanda she added as an aside, 'Dr Bergstrom's wife is a famous magical inventor in her own right, you know.'

'Good, good, yah. She is all excited wis her new proyect in se laboratory. So she does not com sis time herself but sends her love. London is too varm for her, she says!' The three enjoyed the joke and talked about the weather.

Finally, Perran got down to the reason for their meeting. 'Amanda,' he said, 'I will tell you why you are here. Dr Bergstrom … is none other … than the famous Swedish inventor … of the Pocket-wand!'

Amanda looked at Bergstrom doubtfully. Grandpa had one. She'd never seen it because he rarely used magic, and she didn't even know if it worked.

'And today,' continued Perran, 'you are going to have the rare privilege of receiving one of your very own from Dr Bergstrom's hands.'

'Oh, no need for all sis build up, Perran,' interrupted Bertil. He put his fingers into the breast pocket of his jacket, and drew out a light brown object about three inches long. He offered it to Amanda.

'Thank you,' she said politely as she took it. Amanda looked at it. She paused. 'But … but this is …. It … it's an Ikea pencil,' she said in dismay. That caused the three adults amused satisfaction.

'Loook more closely, my dear,' said the inventor.

'Erm … it's got my initials on it …'

'Yes, good. Somesing more sough.'

Amanda detected a hairline crack about a quarter of an inch from the end. 'Is this a sort of lid …? Oh, it's hinged somehow.' Having opened the top of the pencil, she could see a slim rod protruding. The end was studded with a yellow stone. She pulled out a tiny wand. Amanda examined it closely. 'Is this cherry wood?'

'Of a kind,' Birtil answered.

She smiled, 'It's so tiny, so cute.'

'Try it,' he invited her.

'What shall I do?'

'Somesing small …. Let's see. Levitation is your skill, yah?'

'Yes,' she answered confidently.

'Well, so, open sat sideboard door over sere.'

'Er, ok.' Amanda judged by the wand's size that she'd have to use considerable power to make it work. She looked across the room at the piece of furniture, and focused. She flicked the wand hard, and enunciated loudly, '*Agertyn*! '

All at once, both doors in the room, the two sideboard cabinets, the drawers, the ladies' bags, the coffee pot lid, the inventor's umbrella flew open, and suddenly their clothes felt lose as all of the fastenings slipped undone.

'Oh!' cried Granny.

'Ah!' exclaimed Perran.

'Oooh,' gasped Amanda.

She looked around in dismay.

'Come, Amanda. If you'll allow us to use the bathroom, Bertil …' Senara hurried her granddaughter off to get some privacy in which to do up zips and hooks and buttons.

'Sorry!' whispered Amanda as she made herself tidy.

'That's quite all right, dear.'

'Granny! Grandpa can speak Swedish?'

'Yes and French too,' replied Granny.

'Wow.'

'You don't know *every*thing about your grandfather. Come

on, let's go back in.'

By the time the ladies re-entered, the gentlemen had restored their clothes and closed everything in the living room back up. Bertil was speaking, '*Hon kommer att hänga på de.*'

'*Hon är en snabb lärare,*' agreed Perran.

'I am soooo sorry,' said Amanda remorsefully, returning to her seat. 'Dr Bergstrom … I …'

He chuckled. 'You sought a tiny vahnd could do only a tiny bit of magic and you had to give it a big help.'

'Yes,' she said ruefully, 'I won't make that mistake again.'

'Your grandfaser and I were yust saying you will get se hang of it because you are a quvick lerner, yah? All right. So try once more.'

This time, Amanda simply pointed the wand and mouthed the word '*Agertyn*'.

Gently, the cupboard door came ajar. He clapped. 'Very good. So. Now. Sis is yours. You practice wis it, yah? And your big vahnd you keep at home and sis one you cahrry alvays vis you.'

'Yes, Dr Bergstrom,' she nodded and looked down at the wandlet in her hand. 'Wow, this is really something. Thank you so much,' she said with real gratitude.

That day, Amanda gained her most powerful tool, and learned a valuable lesson. She never forgot it. In her mind, she called it The Power of Petite.

Chapter 14

೨

PREPARING

That same year Granny got bronchitis. She was rushed to hospital, then prescribed bed rest for three weeks. Granny took a practical view.

'Perran,' she said, settling herself on the sofa with a hot water bottle and a copy of The Guardian, as he tucked a tartan blanket around her legs, 'after her GCSE exams, Amanda needs to begin to get used to being on her own more.' He nodded.

Starting with the summer holidays, Perran and Senara began taking romantic weekend breaks. They went to the Scottish highlands for fresh air, to Brighton for the Pier, and The White Cliffs of Dover for the Battle of Britain Memorial. Amanda was happy for them and enjoyed the independence and responsibility of having sole charge of the house and workshop. Sometimes they took Amanda with them on other jaunts, so she didn't feel deprived.

Amanda encouraged them to go away for a week at a time, then for two or more, first in the UK and then abroad. Meanwhile, her studies continued with long afternoons of learning spells by heart but for now more advanced magic. She learned delicate motion-manipulation spells, voice print spells, binding and unbinding, raising cones of power, pyramids, time spells, temperature control spells, protection spells, self-defence spells, dimension gate spells, time-delay spells and trigger spells. All the while Amanda was improving her pronunciation and intonation of Wicc'yeth, the language of incantation. However, for the most part, it was only theory. And it was on that basis that Perran consented to open some of the spells he had sealed in Senara's Great-great-grandmother Jowanet Cardiubarn's primer.

'Just in case she needs them,' he said. 'I hope I'm not going to regret this. And no nasty spells involving toads or lizards!'

Alongside her witch training with the grandparents and Aunt Amelia, Amanda studied history and art, maths and science, English, French, Cornish and even a smattering of Swedish. Perran and Senara encouraged Amanda to study out in the fresh air and away from the house. This was intended to give her some variety of scene and also opportunities for social interaction, in which she was never very interested. So when the weather was sunny, Amanda took her books to the village green or the playing fields behind the school. Often Amanda's research took her to the local library, where she studied in the reference section or just outside under the old cedar there.

If Amanda wanted to stay near the house, she sat and leaned against a tree in the orchard in the adjoining field, eating an apple when the fruit was ripe. She liked the staccato piping call of the nuthatches and the purring chirp of the bluetits there. And she didn't meet anyone except occasionally the farmer, who was always happy to see the Cadabras. The three of them were on friendly terms with the orchard's owner and often helped bring in the Hormead Pearmain harvest.

However, Amanda's favourite spot, and usually shared with Tempest, was the most remote. To the north of the village lay the ruins of Madley Priory, a once stout structure that had been unable to survive the ravages of Henry VIII's forceful takeover and the Battle of Barnet. At the highest point, at the top of what may have been the old night stairs, was a small grassy platform that Amanda shored up, using her workshop skills and a little covert magical assistance. From here, she could look towards the village and over at the grand houses along the lane from the hamlet of Upper Muttring and the road from the neighbouring village of Romping-in-the-Heye: most notably, The Grange, The Elms, Sunken Madley Manor, ancestral home of the Dunkleys, and Madley Towers, a vast, somewhat idiosyncratic mansion or a Victorian monstrosity, depending on the viewer's architectural sensibilities.

The church towered above them all, and the chimes of its clock kept Amanda informed of the time at hourly intervals. In the winter, when there were no leaves to bar the view, she could, on a clear day, see down the 10-mile-long slope into London. Not that she often looked up. Amanda would pause her studies though to stroke Tempest when he demanded a behind-the-ears or under-the-chin massage.

If she brought a picnic, Amanda would be guaranteed the company of her familiar. But regardless of whether he was in plain sight or not, Tempest kept a proprietary eye on Amanda, turning up unexpectedly in shops, and places where she was studying.

The villagers learned, soon after his arrival on the scene, the futility of shooing him away or trying to keep him out off their property. The sensible ones kept a tin of tuna handy and hoped for the best. That Dratted Cat was always exactly where he wanted to be, when he wanted to be there and for ever how long.

Although Tempest manifestly had his own means of getting around, he preferred to be driven in the Vauxhall Astra by 'his witch,' as he thought of Amanda, once she had past her driving test. She thought this was amusing. Tempest thought it was appropriate and overlooked her disrespectful mirth whenever he got into the car. Tempest regarded Amanda as his particular charge and, while he would never have admitted to fondness for a mere human, his feelings for her were certainly a stark contrast to the open contempt in which he held the rest of her species.

Amanda passed her A-levels and began her university degree in Arts and Humanities by distance learning. Amanda could converse with her grandmother and Aunt Amelia, almost on equal terms now, about various historical periods, fine art and literature. She could discuss interior and carpentry design with Grandpa who helped her gain accreditations in furniture restoration. Amanda learned the methods and tricks of his profession, and had a light but sure touch.

'Amanda's a better French polisher than I am,' Perran complimented her to a customer, to Amanda's delight.

Perran had paid Amanda a proportion of each client's job that she worked on since she had begun to produce work of a professional standard. Customers started to bring in tasks specifically for Amanda. Perran and Senara could not have been prouder of their granddaughter.

Amanda loved the restoration work. She revelled in the history of each antique piece, and clapped her hands in glee when she correctly identified the different kinds of wood, from birch and beech, oak and teak, willow and pine, mahogany and walnut to the the more obscure ones like lignum vitae and zabrano. She delighted in the organic glow of the various veneers and the patina of the aged golds, silvers and brasses used for trimming and binding.

Not only did she appreciate the artistry that had gone into creating the furniture and fittings that passed through their hands, but also her connection with the apprentices, assistants and master artisans who'd gone before her. Often, when she was alone and the workshop was quiet, Amanda sensed them, felt them, even at times saw them.

Some items played a psychic recording. Amanda enjoyed these the most. Something like a desk or a watch could have a memory attached to it that was like a video projection or an audio track. The right sort of person, and that was Amanda, one of her grandparents or even Tempest, could activate the recording when they were nearby. It would then play out a scene that had happened around the item of furniture or jewellery. Initially, it came as a shock to Amanda. A hooded leather chair kept showing her a Victorian man in evening dress sitting with a maid on his knee who got up with a guilty start whenever Amanda came into the workshop.

Amanda enjoyed the daylight hours and the variety of her chosen profession. Her evenings were spent with her grandparents watching Ealing comedies then hot baths and sharing Tempest's travels through his eyes.

The orchard adjoining the Cadabra's land flowered then fruited. The harvest was gathered and the leaves fell. The branches bared themselves to the winter cold until the buds formed and the blooms opened and once more cast their petals upon the breeze.

And so the days passed.

Until Claire.

Chapter 15

❧

CLAIRE AND A BRAVE NEW WORLD

Claire Ruggieri bought number 24 Orchard Row, the house next door to the Cadabras. Their neighbour old Mr Jackson could no longer manage by himself and was going to live with his son in Eastbourne. The Cadabras thought the move must be a wrench; he put them straight.

'A wrench? Not to me. I've always wanted to live by the sea.' He added irascibly, 'And to get away from this blasted village where everyone has their nose in everyone else's business!'

If Mr Jackson was getting his wish, Amanda was also getting hers. Claire was the fulfilment of Amanda's dream: a best friend closer to her own age. Claire was vivacious, fit, three inches taller than Amanda, with dark chocolate brown hair and deep blue eyes. She worked in media and seemed to know everyone who was anyone. Claire had her share of admirers and fashionable acquaintances in the metropolis but sought the peace of Sunken Madley as a haven from the London throng. As good-natured as she was bright, and in spite of being several years older, Claire bonded with Amanda on sight. Within minutes each had discovered a fellow enthusiast of vintage British cinema, art and history. Claire especially admired Amanda's carpentry skills.

'I'm hopeless with my hands. Unless I'm inflicting bodily harm, that is,' Claire added merrily. 'I'm a karate black belt so if you're alone and need rescuing, just shout for me, daahling!'

Claire had never met anyone quite like Amanda, with an incisive mind yet a strange naïveté about some aspects of life. She saw the warmth and closeness of Amanda's relationship with her grandparents. They had nurtured her, helped her towards achieving independence and Amanda had complete freedom yet she didn't seem to know how to use it. Claire decided she wanted to help.

It was December and Claire declared herself Amanda's Father Christmas. 'Actually,' Claire corrected herself, as they unpacked her box of carefully wrapped wine glasses into a kitchen wall cabinet, 'I am your Fairy Godmother. From now on, you shall go to lots and lots of balls!'

Claire's work was demanding, however. It often took her away for weekends, or for days at a time and kept her late into the evening. That weekend, however, and from then on, when she was free, Claire began to take Amanda out into a world her young friend had never dared to explore alone: bars, live bands, cabarets, and anywhere there was dancing.

Claire was careful not to bring any other friends, knowing that that would probably overwhelm Amanda, and made sure the places they went to were not too hot or crowded. But, arriving early and leaving early, they went by degrees, first north to Hertford, then further and further south into London: to Crouch End, Islington, Camden and, finally, the West End.

Claire delighted in Amanda's enquiring mind and fascination with every new object and situation she encountered. Everywhere they visited, Amanda examined the furniture, asked how the colourful strobe lighting worked, tried cocktails, applauded the performers enthusiastically and carefully watched the dancing.

'You really love all this, don't you?' remarked Claire with amusement, glancing around the bar where they were sitting.

'It's a brave new world,' explained Amanda.' I wouldn't want to live in it all the time, but it's an exciting change from home. And the great thing is that I don't have to talk to anyone!' she added mischievously.

'Well, just me, and some people would say that's more than enough,' quipped Claire. 'But haven't your grandparents ever taken you out?'

'Yes, to the theatre, the opera, to restaurants, museums and trade fairs. But not to anywhere like the places I go with you. I really appreciate it, Claire, all the places you take me to, everything that you're doing for me.'

'Not *for* you; *with* you. I get a great deal of vicarious pleasure seeing you lit by it all.'

She noticed Amanda swaying to the music.

'You like this track?' Claire asked.

'Yes, what is it? Is it reggae?'

'Yes, it's Red Dress.'

'Oh, it's great. What's the band called?' Amanda enquired, leaning closer to hear the answer.

'Magic!'

'What?' asked Amanda, quick to hide her amazement at the co-incidentally apt word. 'Really?'

'Yeah. Want to dance?'

'Oh, don't know how,' Amanda responded shyly.

'Just follow me,' said Claire.

* * * * *

Two weeks later, when she was next available, Claire took Amanda to a reggae bar. They sat with their drinks at a round wooden table that Amanda identified as chipboard and veneer. Suddenly

Amanda jumped to her feet.

'I love this song!' She moved a few feet away and began to dance. Claire laughed with astonishment as she joined her.

'Hey, girlfriend! You've got moves. What happened to Miss I-don't-know-how-to-dance?'

'I've been practising with YouTube videos,' Amanda called over the music.

Claire chuckled. She was getting to know Amanda's practical approach to life. 'Of course, you have, darling! Just one dance at a time though and rest in between, OK? Let's not get you too breathless.'

Once Amanda began experiencing the delights of the dancefloor, she was soon far too hot in her dress and leggings, and Claire, noticing this, said it was time they went clothes shopping. At the following weekend, Claire first took her to the food hall at Fortnum and Mason and bought them hand-dipped cherry liqueurs. After that Amanda got her first little black dress and, in Selfridges New Year sale, a frivolous pair of ridiculously high-heeled red shoes, which she had to practice walking in.

Bit by bit, Claire helped Amanda find her own style that she could wear even under her overalls, and got her to experiment with colours other than black, orange and yellow. With Amanda's confidence running high, Claire tactfully broached the subject of Men.

'Seriously,' asked Amanda. 'Have you seen the single ones in the village?'

'Well, I grant you,' replied Claire, 'the ones that are available in the local pubs, cafés and corner shop may not be among Britain's finest, but they are not the only men in the world. I have a solution!'

'Oh?' Amanda's interest was fairly caught.

'Yes, the time has come. You and I … are going speed-dating.'

It took a couple of weeks to arrange but Claire had the satisfaction of seeing, for the first time, Amanda enjoying the attention of the opposite sex. Although it was Claire who drew the eye, Amanda had an otherworldly charm of her own that intrigued and beguiled.

They were always home long before dawn, not that Senara and Perran stayed up, for they observed how Amanda blossomed and saw their trust in Claire's promise to keep their granddaughter safe rewarded. They often told Claire how good she was for Amanda. Even Tempest showed no active hostility towards her, which passed for approval.

The grandparents thought getting out into the wider world would present Amanda with the possibility of careers other than furniture restoration that she might prefer. But Amanda laughed at the idea and said, 'No, it's "ingrained" in me! Truly, I love what I do.'

Inevitably, Amanda, while still guarding her secret, formed fleeting relationships with what the grandparents referred to as 'unsuitable men'. Amanda's suitors felt an urge to rescue the mysterious and apparently fragile maiden who turned out to be far less fragile and far smarter than they were at home with, and it invariably ended badly. Amanda couldn't imagine telling any of them about her magical side, but she did get some interpersonal experience under her belt, and a clearer idea of the sort of man who might be her match; a kindred spirit.

And Tempest would get a new catnip toy after each breakup as an acknowledgement of his foresight. Every time she brought a man home to meet the family, her protective and disapproving familiar would baptise his shoe and rake his leg with well-sharpened claws.

'Oh, Tempest,' Amanda would say to him later, tickling him behind his ears, 'Oo knew all along, didn't oo?' Tempest had few expressions, but he knew how to look smug.

Chapter 16

✍

A SURPRISE VISIT, AND THE SMELL

By the time Thomas Trelawney crossed the Cadabra threshold for the first time, Perran was semi-retired, and the regular customers trusted Amanda to do their restoration. Although she retained a child-like quality, Amanda was far more confident outside her workshop and house environment than she had ever been before. She travelled to clients, and into London to meet Claire or even went out by herself. So when Amanda insisted that Perran and Senara take their first ever cruise, they complied. At her encouragement, this became a series. 'Come on; you loved it,' said Amanda, 'you know you did. And you've got savings; start enjoying them!'

It was on one Monday morning in October, while Perran and Senara were away on their third voyage, that Detective Sergeant Thomas Trelawney returned.

He had responded as soon as possible to Hogarth's tip-off that the senior Cadabras were to set sail. It was only Thomas's second visit, but the first without an appointment. He wondered how Amanda would react.

Standing on the coir mat with an image of a black cat painted on it, Thomas straightened his sober blue tie, got his hand round the wisteria branches to reach the brass bell and rang it. Amanda answered through the intercom. He announced himself and she asked him, somewhat curtly, to wait. It was a few minutes before she came to the door and Thomas thought her a little flustered but polite.

Amanda invited him into the living room. It was chilly, but she neither lit the fire nor immediately offered him tea. As Thomas sat down, he saw a large, thick-furred cat in a range of stormcloud greys with acid-yellow eyes enter the room. It planted itself opposite Thomas and inspected him from head to toe, making it clear that it was deeply unimpressed with what it saw. Thomas was unnerved. He'd been on the other end of the malevolent stare of hardened criminals, but he had never before been looked at like this by a cat.

'Oh, don't mind Tempest,' said Amanda, 'He's just being protective.'

'Er ... right,' replied Thomas. He cleared his throat, and watched the creature who, having reduced his subject to a suitably submissive state of mind, was stalking out of the room, waving his tail disdainfully.

Thomas then attempted to engage Amanda in casual conversation. However, her responses were short. Yes, she was fine, the grandparents were fine, yes, on a tour of the Greek islands, no, she'd never been. Didn't he have any news about the case?

After having established some sort of connection with the family last time he was there, Thomas felt oddly rebuffed. In an attempt to restore more cordial relations, he tried getting Amanda to talk about something that might warm her up.

'So, what are your current projects in the workshop? Anything of special interest?'

'Actually, I'm working on a Louis XV bergère chair. The owner wants it stained and waxed.' Her face softened as she saw the piece in the mind's eye. 'It's rather lovely in its way, but carved surfaces always makes these things tricky.'

'Er, what does a Louis XV er —?'

'— bergère chair look like?' To Thomas's relief, it seemed that Amanda was beginning to thaw, now on a safe subject that was obviously close to her heart.

'Yes. If you wouldn't mind explaining,' Thomas requested diffidently.

'Well, the arms are continuous with the back —'

'Like a bucket chair?' he guessed.

'Not exactly,' answered Amanda, 'Seat and seat cushion are separate.'

'Like a bucket chair with a cushion on it?'

'Well, sort of …'

'Actually … may I trespass upon your good nature and valuable time, and request a brief glimpse?' he entreated. 'It's not often such things come my way. My job is all paperwork and science; it would be a treat to see something beautiful and artistic before I go back to my prosaic Cornish desk.'

Amanda smiled acquiescently, but he sensed that inside she was bubbling with irritation. Yet, with apparent good grace, Amanda led the way up the back garden path, treading down and whisking up leaves fallen from the fruit trees. She opened the workshop door that swung outwards and went in first. Amanda beckoned Thomas in, then moved over to the centre of the floor where the bergère chair stood, mid-treatment.

As Thomas followed, it hit him. The smell was unmistakable. Under the polish, glue, paint and sawdust there it was: tin and sandalwood … more the taste of tin and scent of sandalwood, but the unmistakable smell … of Magic.

Thomas had paused for only a moment, yet found her eyes fixed on his face. Amanda smiled. 'I work on a few things at the same time. Here's a chandelier I'm repairing. You can see where the hook or link has come apart here, so I've been joining it back up.' She gestured towards a soldering iron and tube of solder, a mixture of copper and tin, lying on a workmate.

'But this,' said Amanda, moving to her workbench, 'is my pride and joy at the moment. It's is an 18th-century clock case. The mechanism is being repaired by someone else. The clock had sustained considerable damage. We're not sure how ....' While she explained at length, Thomas glanced around. The workshop was immaculate. He complimented her on it when she finished her exposition.

'Yes, I know, it's cleaner than the house, but, then you understand why. I open the back door too every now and then to change the air. But that's not so practical on a chillier day. Hence the sandalwood incense. I hope you don't mind it. Helps clean the atmosphere.' She nodded towards an incense burner on the windowsill. Incense in a workshop?

'Very new age,' he commented.

'We try to keep abreast of the times,' Amanda replied, cheerily.

Tin and sandalwood. The smell had been explained very neatly. Too neatly. Thomas had a feeling of being outflanked and, seeing that he would gain no ground today, decided to withdraw in good order.

'Well, thank you for the tea and the tour. I must get back. I've been away for a few days and promised to take my girlfriend out to dinner to make up for my neglect.'

He had no idea why he'd told her that.

'Of course. Enjoy celebrating being reunited,' Amanda replied pleasantly and led him back through the garden and the house to the front door.

'Thank you for your time. Please give my best to your grandparents. Good-bye, Miss Cadabra.'

'Good-bye,' she replied politely.

As Thomas walked up the path, he heard her close the door behind him. He got into his car and looked back at the house with an audible, 'Phew!'

As Amanda shut the door, she shakily dragged her inhaler

from her boiler suit pocket, and gave herself a dose. She made it to the dining room, poured herself a small Gordon's gin, topped it up with Indian tonic and sat down. She'd had a whole array of things working away on enchanted automatic: the Hoover dusting, the spray paint tin shaking, the furniture rearranging, and the sanding block working on a console table. The air must have been thick with magic. Thanks to Grandpa she'd been covered. She'd had moments to stop the spells, to switch on the gas soldering iron, apply the solder, and light the incense. At least Tempest hadn't turned up and wet the man's shoe.

How had Trelawney made her feel that she would be rude if she didn't invite him to see the workshop? She resented how he'd had wangled his way into her private space; leaving her hoping that nothing compromising was on display. How much did he notice? What did he suspect? 'I'll tell Granny and Grandpa as soon as they return,' she told Tempest as he reappeared from under her bench. Suddenly Amanda was missing their comforting presence.

Thomas meanwhile drove on autopilot around the London-orbital M25 and down the M3 motorway to Cornwall, going over and over what he thought he'd seen and heard: Amanda's initial curt greeting, then the formal politeness melting into a wary friendliness, and the apparent ease with which she'd presented her and Perran's workspace as a perfectly ordinary set up.

Yet, ... the smell. Thomas kept coming back to it.

And Amanda's demeanour had been markedly different from that May day, when her grandparents had been there, and they all had had tea and Senara's cake. Of course, Senara had fenced with him and they were all keeping something back, but it had been pleasant, nonetheless. By comparison with his reception today, there had been a warmth, a welcome even. The faintest wave of nostalgia for that lost sense of connection was rising, and Thomas swiftly quelled it. He was not going to let this family get under his skin.

Later, on his return, Perran reassured Amanda, his arm around her shoulders. 'Keep the incense and the solder handy at all times. Keep the doors locked. He may suspect, but he can't prove, and remember witchcraft has been legal in this country since 1951.'

'I don't like it.' Amanda insisted.

'Maybe he likes you,' he suggested.

'No, he doesn't. He's got a girlfriend,' said Amanda firmly, wondering why Trelawney had given her so personal a piece of information.

'How do you know?' Grandpa asked.

'He told me.'

'Did he now?' he said teasingly. 'That's very interesting, that is.'

'Is it? Why?' Amanda demanded.

Grandpa laughed tenderly but enigmatically.

Chapter 17

ॐ

THE ST PIRAN

Hogarth had been expecting Thomas.

'Come in, my lad,' he said, shaking his protégé by the hand and clapping him on the shoulder. He gestured to the living room. 'Make yourself at home.'

Thomas settled onto a comfortable, burgundy Chesterfield sofa to the left of the hearth. He looked around at the off-white walls and ceiling, and the oak beams. There were two Chesterfield chairs, the flatter cushions on the one opposite him identified his host's favourite seat. The coffee table was of warm, aged beech. Around the room hung watercolours of sunny days and calm seas, and, on the floor, lay a thick pile rug of ruby, orange and yellow hues. The sky had become overcast, and the small wood fire was welcomingly warm and cheerful.

Trelawney heard the kettle whistling, water pouring into the hollow of a teapot, and soft chinks of crockery. Hogarth returned and set the tray on the table between them. Thomas noticed he was in a white open neck shirt, olive cashmere sweater and dark green corduroy trousers, so different from his sharp-suited days. Of course, he'd glimpsed his boss in casuals before, but still, it took getting used to.

Hogarth planted himself squarely in his chair by the fire opposite his guest.

'How was the journey? Less than the usual four hours on a Sunday, I hope.'

'Straight through, thank you, sir.'

'Hm. My being sirred days are over, Thomas. You can call me Mike, as a friend should, and I have long regarded you as a friend. I hope you know that.'

'Yes, I think I do. Mike. Feels strange calling you that.'

'You'll get used to it,' said Mike with amusement. 'Help yourself to shortcake; I know it's your favourite.'

'Thank you,' Thomas laughed.

They watched the fire, dunked their biscuits and drank their tea in companionable silence. Finally, Thomas felt grounded, like he was no longer travelling or on duty, but at rest. He took a short breath in and released it slowly.

'So what happened?' his senior invited.

'Well, sir — Mike — I turned up unannounced as we agreed, and thank you for the tip-off about the grandparents going off on a cruise ... er, how did you ...?'

'I may be retired, but I still have my methods and my contacts,' Hogarth returned lightly. The cloud cover had thickened, dimming the early afternoon light, and an ethereal Cornish mist of light drops was sprinkling the window.

'Of course,' Thomas acknowledged. 'Well, Amanda was definitely startled to the point of being curt on the intercom. Then polite when she opened the door. She wasn't especially helpful with the small talk. Oh, and that cat of hers!'

'Aha, you met Tempest the Terrible, did you?' asked Hogarth, sympathetically.

'I'd swear it was staring into my soul and assessed me down to my shoe size.'

Hogarth chuckled. 'And found you as wanting as it found

me, no doubt.'

'Quite ... However, after it went away, I was eventually able to make some progress. You were right; I was able to use her innate good manners to get myself invited into the sanctum.' He paused to finish his tea. Hogarth took his cup and refilled it.

'What did you make of the workshop?'

Thomas began in reporting mode, 'Very clean. Orderly. Miss Cadabra is clearly in control of her workflow. Efficient, professional as far as I, as a layperson, can judge. She seemed to warm up once we were in there, gave me a tour of her projects. She seems to care a great deal about what she does. .... Yes.' Thomas came to a halt, but Hogarth sensed his tale was unfinished.

'But,' he prompted.

'Sir?' Thomas responded out of habit.

'And ...?'

Thomas hesitated.

'What was the main event?' tried Mike.

'The workshop visit,' Thomas replied evasively.

'Thomas, you've told me what you would have put in a report to me at the station. We're off the record, in my sitting room, two friends. This is a safe house.'

'All right, Mike.' Thomas put his cup on the table and leaned his elbows on his knees, rubbing his hands over his face. 'Police work is a science; it's about evidence, facts, forensics, tangible things. This other stuff that I sensed — picked up — oh, I don't know, it just feels like nonsense!' he said in frustration.

Hogarth nodded and remained silent. Then he got up and went to the bookshelf on the wall opposite the window, took out two books side by side and returned to his seat. He found the page he wanted in the smaller one and handed it to Thomas, saying, 'This is about a dive in a Cornish cave about 30 years ago.' He pointed to the last paragraph on the page. 'Read that, lad. Aloud.'

'"Next the divers discovered a cave adorned with a carving of a human figure standing beneath an oak. The figure wears the head of a stag and holds a staff in his left hand, and a wand in his right. It was believed to date from 1500 BC."'

Thomas looked up, frowning.

'Why have I never heard of this before? A mask of a stag, a tree that was regarded as sacred, a staff and a wand, for heaven's sake. This is evidence that magic was practised in Cornwall three and half thousand years ago! Here is a ground-breaking discovery. Why wasn't it at least splashed across the pages of The Western Morning News, or one of the other newspapers?' Thomas closed the book so he could see the title on the cover. 'The Magic Maze: Ancient Cornish stones and carvings by William Barrows. I've never heard of him either.'

'All of his books were withdrawn from publication, and Barrows disappeared in 1987,' Mike answered. 'I couldn't even trace the divers. Very few copies of The Magic Maze made it into circulation.'

'But you have one,' observed Thomas wryly.

'I do indeed. Friends in obscure places, Thomas.'

'But why didn't it make the news?' he asked curiously. 'This is the stuff of headlines.'

'It's evidence of witchcraft far older than anything in the UK. Someone doesn't want that publicised,' Hogarth replied succinctly.

He handed over the second book, indicating a marked passage. 'Read that.' Thomas obliged. '"Cornwall has been a sacred place from pre-historic times. Monuments were built here over millennia. It was known as a magical place, a country of giants, gods, spells and mystical wisdom." Yes, I've heard all that before,' he said sceptically.

'The point is, Thomas, that this is an old land with old bones, old ways, old families.'

Mike let that sink in then asked, 'More tea?'

Thomas was preoccupied and replied vaguely, 'Thanks,'

Hogarth took his friend's cup, refilled it, and put another shortcake biscuit on the saucer. He handed it back to Thomas asking casually, 'Do you know the story of the St Piran?'

'The Cornish flag?'

'That's right.'

'Erm yes …,' Trelawney searched his memory. 'Let me see, a white cross on a field of black … it symbolises the story of when a holy man built a fire on Perran beach, and white liquid seeped out of a black stone, and that's how tin was discovered. The black background of the flag is the stone, and the white cross is the tin, Cornwall's most significant export.'

'Very good, Thomas, but it also stands for something far more important than the mineral wealth of our land.' He paused.

Thomas shrugged and shook his head. 'What?'

'It represents the fight between good and evil. The light rising over and through the darkness.'

Thomas was taken aback. 'I've never heard you talk like this before.'

'Do you want me to go on?'

'Yes. Yes, I do,' Thomas affirmed.

'All right, then.' Mike continued. 'It's only over the last five hundred years that the work of pellars — good witches, you might call them — has become documented and studied. They were healers, advisers and herbalists, among other things. They provided important services to the community. But one of the reasons why people came to them was for the removal of evil spells.'

'Wasn't that all just psychological?' Thomas asked, insistently. 'Or ignorant attempts to understand unfortunate things that actually had a scientific explanation?'

'Could be. But I think you know that's your English side talking. Good and bad, good witches and bad witches, good witch clans and bad witch clans, good magic and —'

'Sorcery,' murmured Thomas.

'Yes. These are entwined in our land's history.'

If anyone else had said these things, Thomas would have dismissed them. But there was no man Thomas respected more than Mike Hogarth. And more convincing even than that, was the memory of his mother's fearful, accusing cry in the night. Not 'magic', not fairies and golden sparkles. But the very word that had just come to unbidden to his lips: 'sorcery'. He nodded imperceptibly. The rain had thickened and was battering the glass now, challenging the crackling of the fire.

'Now,' Mike said gently, 'why don't you tell me what really bothered you about Amanda Cadabra's workshop.'

Chapter 18

∽

MANAGING THOMAS, AND GRANNY TRANSFORMS HERSELF

Several weeks later, Perran and Senara left for a cruise around the Norwegian fjords en route to Sweden to stay with Bertil and Kerstin Bergstrom. The following day, Trelawney rang the bell of 26 Orchard Row.

This time Amanda was prepared. She appeared at the front door, after a short interval, composed and welcoming. Amanda took him into the kitchen, where Tempest came to check on the chance of a snack and put the visitor in his place. Amanda invited Trelawney to get the milk out of the fridge, which he did, giving Tempest a respectfully wide berth, while she switched on the kettle and dropped teabags into mugs. Amanda pointed at them mischievously. 'Granny's not here, so no pot and tea leaves today. This is the mice playing in a very small way.'

'As befits mice,' Thomas agreed amiably. 'Not that any would dare to cross the threshold in the presence of er …' he nodded at Tempest.

'Well, they do occasionally here at home but not willingly!'

Amanda responded. She bent to ruffle Tempest's dusky head, 'Do they, Mr Fluffy-Wuffy?' Her cat preened himself then gave Trelawney a look designed to convey that any such familiarity on the detective's part would be met with swift and severe retribution. Amanda followed Tempest's glare and looking up at Trelawney said, 'No, I wouldn't try and stroke him, if I were you.'

'Indeed,' agreed Trelawney with feeling, 'I've met friendlier serial killers.'

'Oh dear,' said Amanda remorsefully, 'Thinking of the mice and birds he's brought in as trophies, I expect that's what he is! But he's just doing what comes naturally.' She looked back down at the unrepentant Tempest, saying, 'Aren't oo?'

Trelawney wasn't at all convinced.

They talked about the hailstorm last week, while she made them cheddar and Branston pickle sandwiches — a rare treat for her because she usually had to avoid dairy. This time, Amanda herself suggested a visit to the workshop. She seated Trelawney on a 19th-century library chair that was waiting to be collected by the upholsterer for re-covering.

'Try not to touch the wooden frame at the ends of the arms, please; the wax is still hardening,' requested Amanda and went on to explain what she was doing.

There it is, thought Thomas. Deeper and more subtle than last time, but there nevertheless. That smell: Magic. But again, the soldering iron was cooling at the end of the bench and the sandalwood smouldering in the incense burner. Thomas felt like the single member of an audience at a sideshow. Was Amanda Cadabra managing him? He finished his sandwich, thanked her and left.

Restless as the wind-tossed reeds fringing the Sunken Madley village pond, and feeling foiled, Trelawney drove to London.

Amanda treated herself to a small gin and tonic, before stamping up the garden path, catching her sleeve on the gooseberry bush and wrenching it free with unnecessary vehemence. Tempest appeared in the workshop, from under the chair Trelawney had been sitting in.

'Wretched man!' she exclaimed, slamming the door. 'I've been doing nearly everything by hand in case he came here and I'm nearing exhaustion. Thank goodness he's come and gone. I'll ask Grandpa if I can install a camera at the front door and next time he calls I sha'n't answer!' Tempest rrrowled in agreement.

* * * * *

Back in his mother's comfortable house, and in the privacy of his old bedroom, Trelawney phoned Hogarth.

'Hello, Mike?'

'What news, young Thomas?'

'She was ready for me. I learned nothing.'

'That's all right. Change your tactics. Stop trying to catch her out. Concentrate on winning her trust. I think that, deep down, it's what you want to do anyway, isn't it? So from now on, go gently about it.'

* * * * *

Amanda was sad but not surprised. Her grandparents were in their early nineties. They were slowing down, and even having to resort to magic to help them get things done in the house, garden and workshop.

It was January and Granny had bronchitis again, this time with complications. Amanda sat beside Granny who was in bed propped up by pillows, wearing a white, lace-trimmed nightdress under a blue woollen dressing-gown.

'It will be just the same in many ways,' she assured Amanda, holding her hand. 'I'll be right here; you just have to call me.

Remember, the dead cannot harm the living and they cannot help the living unless they are asked. So see that you do ask.'

'Of course, darling Granny,' said Amanda, throwing her arms around her. Senara hugged her then told her not to be sentimental.

'You've been well prepared to be independent, and we're very proud of you.' Senara fell silent and played with the embroidering on the quilt. This awkwardness on Granny's part was quite uncharacteristic, and Amanda was alarmed.

Senara resolutely nodded her head, looked squarely at her granddaughter and began.

'I have a past. I wasn't always as I am now. I did … certain … magically related things that I felt were necessary at the time. Things that may not reflect well on you, I am sorry to say. However, as long as you are discreet and, in time, find an understanding young man who appreciates and respects you and your gifts, and even shares them, this need not trouble you in the least.'

Amanda had spent enough time in the workshop to know gloss when she saw it. 'A past? Do you mean a shady past, Granny? And 'things'? What things are we talking about exactly? I know you eloped with Grandpa, but surely that isn't so terrible?'

Perran came in from the bathroom, drying his hands on a towel. 'She turned over a new leaf when we met, and she's never gone back,' he assured Amanda. 'That's all you need to know for now. For always, I hope. But if the time should come when you do need to know more, you can ask then.'

Amanda very much wanted to know now, but Grandpa had signalled that the subject was closed and she knew better than to pursue it.

Senara was as business-like about death as she was about life. She prepared her last will and testament with her family and had Amelia to dinner. The four of them ate off trays on their laps in the bedroom. Afterwards, the two older women held a brief private conference.

On the day appointed, Senara asked Perran and Amanda to

help her to dress in comfortable, practical clothing. 'Just in case I don't know how to change them at first,' explained Granny as she lay back exhausted on her pillows. She turned her head towards Amanda. 'You've got the list by the phone, haven't you?'

'Yes, Granny.'

'But on the whole, if anyone comes to you on what they'll call "private business" —'

'Yes, I know: send them to Aunt Amelia.'

'And if anyone asks you —'

'Yes, Granny, if they ask me if I have the Knowledge, I send them to Aunt Amelia; we've been over and over this.'

'All right then.' Out of breath from the exertion of dressing and talking, Senara patted her chest. 'Ahhh, what a palaver. Now I don't want any fuss. I've seen this done, so I have a fair idea of how it works. Oh, my goodness, I'm looking forward to getting my energy back ... so ... give me some room .... Now. I'm off out of this old bod,' she declared, closed her eyes, and breathed her last.

Unlike Senara, Amanda had never seen this done before. One moment there was Granny stretched out on the bed and the next there appeared to be another, transparent Granny, sitting up in the same place where the first Granny was still lying.

'Oo!' exclaimed Granny, looking at her see-through hands and flapping her arms experimentally. 'There. That's done. Much better. No aches and pains but a bit — woaah!' she exclaimed as she rose a couple of feet towards the ceiling, '— flighty! Goodness gracious me!' Senara looked down at Amanda. 'Now, don't you think you should get that rice pudding in the oven for after dinner? Finally, I don't have to cook anymore!'

'Granny, I thought you liked cooking?' responded Amanda, feeling disorientated.

'No one likes to cook dear; baking, jam-making, those are fun. But cooking. No. Best left to the professionals, whenever one can afford them! Go along now. You know how your grandfather likes his rice pudding.' Granny waved Amanda towards the bedroom door with a transparent hand. 'Yes, dear, off you go. Leave me to practice floating, and I'll be down as soon as I get the trick of it.'

Granny suddenly spotted Tempest nosily poking his head round the door. 'And get That Cat out of here!' Amanda obediently took herself, and Tempest, off to the kitchen finding it impossible not to smile. It seemed that dying had just made Granny more Granny than ever.

Trelawney turned up for the funeral wearing a deferentially dark suit and coat. The fifteenth-century church of St Ursula-without-Barnet was famous for its stained-glass windows. It was the pride of the parishioners, who rarely entered the hallowed precincts, and the only reason a very few tourists ever visited the village, unless they were lost. Today, however, the nave was full to overflowing. Senara Cadabra may not have been loved, but she had been respected, and had discreetly helped many villagers, and non-residents too, at one time or another.

Mr Jackson, their former next-door neighbour, had come up all the way from Eastbourne with his son. Sunken Madley's oldest and most distinguished patrons graced the event: Miss De Havillande and Miss Armstrong-Witworth from The Grange turned up in their antiquated but still serviceable Range Rover; Mr Hanley-Page arrived in state in his Rolls Royce Phantom II, the star of his collection at Vintage Vehicles. The headmaster had closed Sunken Madley School for the day and all of the staff, children and their parents were in subdued attendance.

After the service, Amanda left Amelia and Claire chatting while she went to thank the Detective Sergeant for making the journey.

'Quite a turnout,' he remarked, looking around the crowded churchyard. Amanda herself was surprised. She had memories stretching back to childhood of Granny's anxious visitors who disappeared into the living room with Senara for long talks then left looking calm and hopeful. Often, after little Amanda was in bed, she would hear the bell, quiet voices in the hall and then a door closing as she drifted off to sleep. But she had had no idea just how many people her Granny had supported in some way.

'Yes,' was all Amanda could think of saying.

Granny ordered Amanda to try and produce a few tears for Trelawney's benefit. The best she could do was to attempt to look bereft. Thomas assured himself that Amanda was bearing up, and then departed.

Amanda had arranged for refreshments for the guests to be served in the village hall. Tempest considered it worth turning up for this. He had considered the funeral a sham; to him, Granny was as real and objectionable as ever. If most of the humans couldn't see this, it was just another mark of their inferiority. This didn't stop him from accepting a sausage roll from Jane the rector, the contents of a Cornish pasty from Amelia, a slice of ham from Miss de Havillande and a piece of smoked salmon from Claire.

While Tempest took it in his stride, for the humans, Granny's transition took a bit of getting accustomed to. Senara had to master floating at floor level, which she seemed to have a great deal of fun doing. Amanda had to learn not to jump at the suddenness of her grandmother's appearance whenever Amanda thought about her. Granny seemed to enjoy that too. Amanda had never known her to be so carefree. As Senara improved at appearing to be solid, it became apparent that she had grown younger both in appearance as well as in manner.

No sooner had Amanda become accustomed to the change, however, another one appeared on the near horizon.

Chapter 19

৵

WHAT THOMAS HEARD

'Ammy, love,' Perran said to her one evening in the living room. The three of them had been watching the original version of *The Ladykillers*, Tempest asleep on Amanda's lap, and Perran in a somewhat distracted mood. Amanda turned down the volume as the closing credits rolled, and asked,

'What's on your mind, Grandpa?'

'Your granny and I,' he replied hesitantly, glancing at his fairly solid wife sitting beside him, 'have been wanting to ask you something.'

Amanda knew what was coming. She'd been expecting it since Granny's transition.

'You want to be in the same dimension as Granny? That's it, isn't it?'

He put an arm around her. 'Thank you for understanding. Would you mind, very much? I'll still be around, just like Granny.'

'Of course,' she said, with kindly resignation. Amanda smiled and added insistently, 'Except you'll refrain from startling me by appearing suddenly like Granny does, right?'

'I will indeed, pet.'

'When will you er …?'

'You say when. I've done the Will. It all goes to you. You've got the money from your Granny to pay the inheritance tax. And I'll be able to help you a lot more in the workshop if you need me. Lately, I've been so tired I've spent most of my time in front of the telly. Never thought I'd get tired of the *Carry On* films but I have to admit … I want my freedom of movement, and I want to be with ….' Perran ended, wistfully.

'I understand,' said Amanda, 'I'll just miss hugging you.'

'Well, you've got Claire for that, and Tempest for that matter, fond of you as he is, in his way, and one day, you'll have the right man to give you all the affection you'd ever want,' her grandfather answered, practically.

'Oh, that,' Amanda said, cynically. She put her head on one side and looked at her grandparents thoughtfully. 'Have you two seen the right man for me?'

Perran and Senara looked at one another conspiratorially.

'Perhaps we have, Ammy,' answered Grandpa, 'perhaps we have.'

Amanda sat and thought. It occurred to her that her grandparents were going to be harder to pin down once they were both operating from another dimension.

'What is it, love?' asked Perran.

'There's something I want you to tell me first.'

'All right,' Perran replied, cautiously.

'Why didn't my parents want me?'

Perran was unprepared for the abruptness of the question. He turned to Senara who held up her hands, indicating that she was leaving it up to him to answer this one.

'Well, now …,' he began, 'I'm afraid your mother and er … her siblings didn't turn out quite as we'd hoped.'

'That's an understatement,' Granny chimed in.

'They moved to Cornwall as soon as they were grown up, to be with your Granny's family, but, when you were going to be born, they decided that they might need some help with looking after you — babysitting. They were both very ... occupied.'

'So you went to stay there?'

'Yes, sort of.'

'And when I was born ...?'

'Your grandmother's side of the family has certain ... certain ... traits.'

'Oh yes?'

'And so when you were born, they looked for those traits in you.'

'We're talking about magical traits, aren't we? But I didn't have them then, right?'

'That's right. They waited to see if they'd develop, but they didn't appear.'

'So they ... let you look after me.'

'Yes,' said Grandpa tentatively, looking for evidence of pain in her expression. But it failed to materialise.

'It's OK. I gather that their rejection of me is a compliment of no mean order.'

Grandpa sighed audibly with relief. 'I'm glad that you can see that.'

Amanda was silent.

'Is there anything else you want to know about it?'

'Nope,' Amanda replied succinctly, thinking that she was lucky to have got this much out of her grandparents. 'Mostly I'd just wondered why my earliest memories are of you two and not my birth parents. Now I know ...,' she said, smiling, 'and I'm glad!' Grandpa took her hand. 'Oh well,' she summed up, 'if the hugging and the Will and the help at the workshop are all taken care of, any time from tomorrow that you want to er ... is fine,' Amanda agreed resolutely.

She could hardly refuse, and soon she had two fond ghosts, one standing beside her and one still bopping inexpertly, as she attended a second funeral. Amelia, who could see them as clearly as Amanda could, stood politely out of the way of Perran and

Senara. Claire, who could not, kept wandering into them and suddenly feeling chilly. Tempest, although he could see them both perfectly well, ignored Amanda's grandparents. There was no chance of any snacks there. Instead, he directed a demanding stare at Claire until she gave him the kitty treat he knew was in her pocket.

Once again, people from the village and further afield thronged the church and graveyard. Among them, Amanda spotted a tall, slim, immaculately dressed woman in the most elegant hat Amanda had ever seen. She seemed to be a tourist, interested only in the stained-glass windows, but nodded respectfully as she passed the funeral party. Bertil and Kerstin flew over from Sweden and had a discreet conversation with Senara and Perran back at Orchard Row after the funeral was over.

Trelawney stood respectfully at the back. Amanda spotted him after the service.

'Thank you for coming, Detective Sergeant Trelawney,' she said, shaking hands. Out of the corner of her eye, she saw Granny appear at her side.

'Detective Inspector, now, actually,' he corrected her modestly.

'Oh, congratulations,' she said with genuine pleasure.

'Thank you, and no need for your thanks for coming. I liked your grandparents. I didn't know them very well, but I liked them. Well ... you seem to be taking it all remarkably bravely.' Thomas mentally kicked himself, remembering Hogarth's words: 'Stop trying to catch her out.'

It had sounded like a question.

'I don't think the shock has hit me yet,' was the reply Amanda hastily came up with.

'Good come back, dear,' said Granny, walking beside them out of the musty nave into the fresh air of the churchyard.

'I'm sorry I couldn't er ... come back ... to the house after the service last time,' Thomas apologised, changing the subject.

'That's quite all right. I'm sure you had things to do,'

Amanda said understandingly.

'It was respectful of him to come at all,' said Perran, hovering next to Granny.

'I wanted to … pay my respects,' Thomas explained. 'Erm … look ….' He took a card from his wallet and gave it to Amanda. 'If you ever need anything at all, this is me. Just call or text or email or …. smoke signal. And if any new evidence, even a hint, surfaces, I'll let you know straight away. I don't want you to feel alone. Hogarth was very insistent that I keep an eye on you. I think he had a soft spot for all three of you.'

'Didn't see that one coming,' said Perran.

'Just in case. Things can happen. When you least … see them coming. So it's good to have a useful contact.' Thomas was aware that he was talking too much.

Amanda was bemused but touched. 'Thank you. I appreciate it,' she responded sincerely.

As Trelawney walked back to his car, Perran and Senara were in a fever of consternation.

'What was going on there?' exclaimed Senara.

'He kept repeating words we used. Do you think he could hear us?' asked Perran, suspiciously.

'Maybe he was picking up a faint echo of you,' suggested Amanda. 'Just sensitive. Probably comes with the training. He's a policeman after all. And before you say anything else, he's got a girlfriend, so forget about him as a candidate for my hand and heart,' uttered Amanda with finality.

* * * * *

That evening, Thomas visited his former boss. They had dinner on trays on their laps, courtesy of the local Indian restaurant, and had chatted about the latest Test Match cricket until the food was delivered.

Michael Hogarth was a traditionalist in some respects, and was tucking into the UK's favourite dish: Chicken Tikka Masala. 'How was the funeral, then?' he asked.

Thomas spooned a helping of Lamb Jalfrezi onto his plate. 'Well attended.'

'I'm not surprised. Perran Cadabra was a kind and lovable soul,' Hogarth observed warmly.

'Yes.' Thomas piled on some rice and sat back.

'And how did you find the grieving granddaughter?' asked Mike.

'That's just it. She didn't look all that grieving — which is odd because they must have been very close. I'm afraid I sort of drew attention to it,' Thomas admitted ruefully. 'Sorry, I know what you said, but I think I reclaimed myself. I offered help if ever she needs it, gave her my card. And I meant it. Genuinely.'

'Hm. Did Amanda think you meant it, genuinely, in your opinion?' asked Hogarth.

'Yes,' Thomas said slowly, 'I rather think she did. At least, that is,' — his brow furrowed —,'I hope she did.'

They ate in silence for a while, savouring the spicy flavours.

'There was another strange thing,' said Thomas.

'Aha, now we come to it. It's the strange things that are the most interesting,' responded Mike.

'Well ... I think I .... when I was talking to Amanda after the funeral, there was no one else around, but I felt like ... I ... not exactly heard ... more sensed ... like a faint —'

'Voices?' suggested Hogarth.

'Yes. No. Not exactly. It was just ... like having thoughts that I know weren't my own.'

'Well, now. That is interesting,' remarked Mike.

'But not surprising to you,' observed Thomas.

Mike smiled a trifle mischievously. 'Not entirely.'

'Surely, it wasn't ...?'

'Wasn't it?'

'Not ghosts!' Thomas exclaimed uncertainly.

'You sure about that, lad?' Mike asked gently. He waited for a response, then filled the silence. 'Here, have some more lamb. You've told me everything that you can, so let's put in on the back burner for now.' He smiled encouragingly. 'You've done well, Thomas. I think you may turn out to be a natural at this.'

'Erm … what is "this" exactly, Mike?'

'For now, let's just say,' — Hogarth paused, choosing his next words carefully —,'relating to dimensions.'

Either in accordance with Amanda's wish or coincidentally, the three Cadabras did, at least to some extent, forget about Detective Inspector Thomas Trelawney. Amanda settled into the new version of her life where she dealt with all of the clients by herself. The grandparents were present when they wanted to be, or at Amanda's request. At other times, when they felt like it and were not needed they wandered off, not saying much about where to.

Amanda was content. She enjoyed brief chats with the villagers, customers came and went, she made visits to houses from ordinary to grand, repairing and restoring. Sometimes she lay in the bath and watched the world through Tempest's eyes, whether hunting or trysting. She had occasional protracted evenings of romance, but more often she was with Claire, having nights out in town, and nights in, with fish and chips and classic James Bond on DVD.

Life flowed smoothly until, after 350 years of their family living there, the Dunkley-McVittys sold Sunken Madley Manor, and the Poveys moved in

Chapter 20

❧

NEW MEN

The less charitable members of the village were doomed to disappointment. They had been looking forward to castigating Mr and Mrs Povey for being a couple of plutocratic philistines, hell-bent on ravaging Sunken Madley's beloved Elizabethan manor and turning it into a themed playground for the rich and indolent.

However, it was impossible not to like the pleasant, retired couple. Hugh Povey, pepper-and-salt-haired and of average height, had an eager, friendly manner. Diminutive Sita, with a single, long, glossy black plait, was youthful, stately and merry.

Their children had gained financial independence, so Hugh and Sita now had money to spend on themselves. Their imagination had been fired by the inspired amateur renovators, architects and builders in the television series Grand Designs. Consequently, they had chosen to invest in a property in need of love and care. And where better than in the village where Hugh's grandfather had been born?

Before embarking on any significant plans for the

restoration of the house to its original glory, Hugh and Sita had decided to spend their first year getting a feel for the Manor's position, setting and surroundings, and how it might enhance life in Sunken Madley.

In the meantime, the Manor needed a little cosmetic sprucing up, and Hugh and Sita, eager to become part of the village, were determined that the tasks should be given to local craftspeople. They found Amanda — Cadabra Restoration and Repairs — in a local online directory and both Mrs Sharma, co-owner with her husband of the corner shop, and Frank, the proprietor of the local pub, had recommended her. Mrs Povey telephoned Amanda and explained who they were and what services they were looking for, and Amanda made an appointment for the following day.

It was a clear, if rather chilly, May morning. The wind was busy scattering the fat candyfloss heads of the cherry blossoms in a pink snow of petals. Amanda had planned to do her local errands on the way to the Manor.

Amanda opened her front door, as Joan the post-lady was about to push a Jiffy bag through the letterbox. Buxom, bright-eyed and a walking Neighbourhood Watch, she was the backbone of the local grapevine, or an incorrigible busy-body, depending on the individual villager's point of view.

'Oh! Good morning, Amanda. Here, you can take it,' Joan said, handing her the padded packet. 'You on your way out? Going to the liiiiibrary?'

Joan's suggestive tone alerted Amanda.

'Why the library?' she asked suspiciously.

'There's a new librarian. Very nice. Buff, as they say, these days, well-spoken, librarianship more of a hobby, they also say, so he must be, you know, all right for the readies —'

'OK, well, thank you, Joan, I'm sure I'll bump into him at some point,' Amanda replied discouragingly, in an effort to nip the conversation in the bud.

'Well, if you don't fancy him, there's a footballer moving

into the village. And he's single too.'

'And therefore "must be in need of a wife?"' quoted Amanda, 'Must be off!' she insisted and made her escape into the street.

'Don't wait too long,' Joan called after her. 'You're not getting any younger ...'

Amanda suppressed a groan. No doubt the post-lady meant well.

She glanced back at Joan to wave goodbye politely and cannoned into the milkman. Granny had disapproved of cartons. A bottle was the only safe container for milk, in her view, and she had had a pint delivered daily. Amanda, who usually avoided milk products for the sake of her asthma, had asked Joe from the Madley Cows Dairy to bring a couple of cartons of coconut milk and half a dozen eggs once a week, to keep up his traditional visits. Joe was short, jaunty, and his speech was more inclined to volume than wit.

'Mind yourself, love!' He set her back on her feet. 'You on your way to the library?"

'Yes, I know. Joan told me,' Amanda forestalled him.

'Then there's the rock star, I think he is, who's bought Madley Towers. Single they say.'

'Yes, I know.'

'Well, it doesn't do to let the grass grow,' the milkman advised, waving an admonitory finger. 'Not at your time of life.'

'Right.' Amanda hurried to the corner shop post office to return a cabinet handle she had ordered that was the wrong size.

'Hello, Mrs Sharma. I'd like to send this second class, please.' Mrs Sharma's neat, willowy form was sailing gracefully towards the counter at the sound of the shop doorbell.

'Of course, dear, put it on the scales. Have you seen the new librarian? Very comely and then there's the cricketer who's bought the Towers.' There seemed to be some disagreement as to the millionaire's occupation. 'Broke up with his significant other a while ago. It was in the papers.'

'Uhuh', said Amanda, listlessly. 'How much will that be,

please?' She paid and made for the door.

'The clock is ticking,' Mrs Sharma said, significantly.

'I certainly hope so,' Amanda replied, dryly.

The last stop was the doctor's to collect a repeat prescription for her inhaler.

'Amanda. You're looking well,' said the receptionist, who was pink-cheeked, efficient and 25. She was also engaged and enjoying the status that was considered, among some of the Sunken Madleyists, due to a woman who had 'got her man'.

'I am well, thank you, Penny,' Amanda smiled.

'I've got your prescription right here for you, but the doctor's not busy and would like a word,' she said brightly.

That was rare. Amanda went down the passage, past the nurse's room and Dr Karan Patel's office, to his wife's door and knocked.

'Come in, Amanda. Sit down. How are you feeling?'

'Well, thank you, doctor.' Amanda's General Practitioner, Neeta Patel was nearing 60 and looked nearer 40, a good advert for the efficacy of her medical recommendations.

'That's fine to hear,' Dr Patel responded. 'I have some news to share with you. It's not public yet, but I had a letter from a colleague saying that plans are afoot to build a suite of labs on the site of the derelict row of cottages between here and Madley Humming.'

'The abandoned village of Lost Madley?' asked Amanda, distracted.

'That's right.'

'It was destroyed in the war, wasn't it?' she said slowly. It was all coming back to her. Amanda hadn't thought about that story in years, and yet, at the time she'd heard it, it had made a deep impression and played on her mind for days. 'I remember Mr Jackson, my neighbour, saying the Luftwaffe were trying to bomb Salisbury Hall, where the Mosquito bomber design team was based. But they hit that village and it was never rebuilt. Such a sad story …,' she murmured.

'Well, it's going to be rebuilt now,' said the doctor briskly, bringing Amanda back to the present. 'At least, part of it is. And healing will come out of the harming. You see, the labs will be expressly for studying allergies from every possible angle. The staff will be investigating the validly of treatments from your inhaler there to homoeopathy, acupuncture, Chinese medicine, you name it.'

'I thought the mainstream medical opinion is that alternative methods are all voodoo,' interjected Amanda.

'This is a private enterprise,' explained the doctor. 'Once the go-ahead is given it could be a matter of months before they launch, and they'll soon be looking for volunteers to participate in the programme. So I want you to think carefully about it. It could be a chance to improve things for you. On the other hand, you must consider any disadvantages.'

But Amanda's mind was racing ahead with the possibilities. A cure. A chance for a normal life. Well, more normal, at least. And new interesting people. Scientists.

'I think it's great,' she answered eagerly. 'Yes, I'm all for it, of course.'

'Well, give it careful consideration. I'll keep you updated. In the meantime,' Dr Patel said, as she wrote in a remarkably legible hand on the back of a form, 'here is a website that explains what can be involved in clinical trials.'

'Thank you, Dr Patel,' Amanda said, with enthusiasm and stood up.

'You're welcome, Amanda.'

She went to the door and, hand on handle, turned back to say, 'And thank you for not mentioning …'

'The new librarian and the sports idol?' suggested Dr Patel.

'Yes.'

They laughed.

'Whatever they say,' said the doctor, 'you have plenty of time.'

Back in reception, Penny told her about the librarian and the human rights lawyer who had taken the Towers. Amanda inwardly sighed but outwardly thanked Penny, when she warned Amanda about being left on the dreaded Shelf and added,' Don't get me wrong, you look really good for your age n' all but, you know …. once you've hit 30 ….'

On the last leg of what was becoming her arduous journey to the Manor, Amanda was intercepted by Jane, the church rector, who described the new men as the librarian and the man from MI5.

'Oh, could you take a look sometime at the lych gate?' she added. 'Iskender backed into it. Poor man, he was in a right old tizzy about the food that was stolen from his kebab shop last night.'

'Yes, of course, Jane,' said Amanda, taking a step away to continue her trek. 'I'll be in tou—.'

'Oh, and do you think that there might be some way of keeping Tempest out of the vestry? He's left grey cat hairs on my best surplice again.'

'I'm sorry, Jane, it's the gold candlesticks and the embroidery on your stole. He's just drawn to what he regards as luxurious things. I'll have a word with him though.' She added placatingly, 'Well, at least he was in church.'

'Only,' replied the rector, 'because he has a god complex, dear!'

'— Amanda-a-ah! Ja-a-ne?' came a piercing and familiar voice from their right. Nonagenarian Miss de Havillande of The Grange, still impossibly spry, was striding along the pavement. She was followed in meandering fashion by her terrier, whom she encouraged with ringing exhortations of, 'Churchill! Heel!" The ladies waited politely while Miss De Havillande and her canine companion crossed the remaining space between herself and her hapless quarry.

'Hello Cynthia,' said Jane, turning a friendly pastoral face toward the oldest of her parishioners.

'Hello, Miss de Havillande,' Amanda greeted her formally.

'My dears!' exclaimed Cynthia, 'I am so glad I caught you

both. Jane! I simply must request that you, in your capacity of spiritual leader of our community, instruct that demon driver to abate his godless style of circumnavigation of our village!'

'You mean, Mr Hanley-Page?' enquired Jane, knowingly. This was likely to be a protracted discussion, and Amanda began edging in the direction of the Manor. But her movements were spotted by the eagle eyes of Miss de Havillande.

'Dear! Before you go: a respectable man of presentable aspect and means has acquired Madley Towers. I think he would do very nicely for you. Now if, —'_

'— thank you, Miss de Havillande, but I really don't wan—'

'— Oh, if he doesn't suit you, there's the new librarian, who I hear, is of independent means, so goodness knows what he's doing working away — but that's neither here nor there. You have a choice of — oh good heavens, child, you'd better get along to the Manor or you'll be late for your appointment!'

Amanda narrowly prevented herself from rolling her eyes. Had her appointment been posted on the green?

'Yes,' said Cynthia, observing Amanda's expression, 'I know all about it. I gave you a splendid reference, so there's no need for you to worry.'

Amanda smiled gratefully. 'Thank you, Miss de Havillande, that was very kind of you,'

'Never mind that now. Off you go. And give my regards to Mrs Povey, a thoroughly estimable woman. And mind you take care while you're alone in that house. I remember in my younger days, hearing tales of ghostly comings and goings there, lights, shadows flitting around the house.'

'Yes, well, I expect old mansions do build up a reputation over time,' Amanda replied bracingly.

'Ah, but then about a year ago they said it had started again. Still, the spectres of Dunkleys past will have nothing against you, helping to restore their home.' Having thus discomforted Amanda, Miss de Havillande concluded, 'So don't you worry, my dear — Oh, look at the time! Off with you!'

Amanda hurried out of earshot, avoiding any more local nonsense and feeling lucky to have escaped any comments from the rector or Cynthia on Amanda's advanced stage in her life-cycle.

Yards from the Manor, Sylvia the lollipop lady accosted Amanda. Sylvia was returning home from her weekday morning duties shepherding children safely across the road to the school. Her job took its name from the circular sign she carried bearing the word 'stop'. It was mounted on the end of a pole and so looked like a piece of oversized confectionary. Sylvia took Amanda's arm in a kindly fashion, told her about the librarian and the astronaut who'd acquired The Towers and reminded Amanda of her age.

'I'm 78 and on my fourth husband. Time you made a start, dearie!'

Senara appeared semi-solidly at Amanda's side. 'Why are so many jobs in this village done by women?' demanded Granny disapprovingly. 'Is the War still on? Have all of the men gone to the Front?' Having made her point, she promptly vanished. And Amanda reached the front door of the Manor.

Chapter 21

෨

THE BANISTER JOB

Amanda stood before Sunken Madley Manor and tried the bell pull. Inevitably, it was broken. She banged on the iron-bound oak with her knuckles.

This was the closest she had ever been to the house. She stepped back and had a quick look at the façade. In front of her was the portal under a shallow porch. To her left, was a smaller door set in a circular roofed entrance. It went some way to balancing the incongruous turret, that was, seemingly, bolted onto the right wing of the building. Amanda guessed that the Manor was probably of brick behind the curtain of ivy, clinging to the walls.

Mrs Povey answered, with Hugh close beside her. Amanda introduced herself, and they shook hands. She looked wide-eyed at Sita. 'Sorry for staring,' she said, collecting herself. 'You look just like an older Jasmine out of Aladdin,' she explained naively. Sita was enchanted.

'Would you like tea or a trip around the house first?'

'House first, please,' replied Amanda, looking up in awe at the coffered ceiling. 'I've never been inside here before.'

'Let's start here in the entrance hall then,' said Hugh. 'The main job we would like done, is the banister rail polished.'

Amanda peered at the section at the bottom of the stairs. 'It would have to be stripped and sanded first, *then* polished,' she elucidated.

'Yes, all of that,' he agreed.

'Top and sides?' Amanda asked.

'Yes, for now, please,' Hugh confirmed.

The Poveys also had a list of items of furniture that were scraped, cracked or had pieces missing. The banister had scratches and gouges, and most of the polish was long worn away.

The house was a modest one by manorial standards. The main entrance led straight into a grand hall. Amanda could now see that the side entrance that she'd noticed from outside, was for leaving dirty shoes and possibly cleaning muddy dogs, judging by the two pairs of Wellington boots and roll of paper towels.

Leading off the entrance hall, to the left, was a library. Straight ahead, under the gallery above, was the kitchen, from where there was a door to the cellar. Next to that was a dining room and, to the right of that a drawing room. A bathroom had been squeezed in under the stairs.

The grand staircase was lined with a half panelled wall, topped by a dado rail serving as a handhold. It went up to the bedrooms, a bathroom and more stairs to what was once the servants' rooms, and to the attics.

'The bedrooms are named after colours: Scarlet, Peacock, Emerald and Yellow,' Sita explained pointing to the plaques on the doors. 'We only use Scarlet for ourselves, of course, but prepared Emerald in case the children want to visit and see a "before" and "after" of our renovations.'

Suddenly, Amanda sharply turned her head. Banging was coming from Scarlet.

'Oh, it's that loose casement again,' said Hugh, going in to shut the window. 'It keeps coming open. Yet another thing on the to-do list,' he added, cheerfully.

'It's a noisy, creaky old house, I'm afraid. But you don't look like the nervous type,' Sita observed.

Hugh chimed in, 'I hope you're not afraid of mice, Amanda. We have rather a rodent problem in the kitchen. They take anything that's not nailed down!'

'I'm sure they won't bother me,' she reassured him. Not if Tempest decides to honour me with his presence, she added to herself.

Amanda examined the damage to the banister and furniture, and assessed the time and materials needed to make the repairs. The Poveys conferred while they watched her carry out her inspection. By the end of the tour, over tea and ginger nut biscuits, the Poveys were ready to commit themselves to a decision.

'You are very professional, my dear,' Sita complimented Amanda. 'Hugh and I are agreed.'

'Yes, provided the price is reasonable,' confirmed Hugh, 'you have the job,'

Amanda smiled as Sita handed her a print-out, saying, 'This is a list of everything we've shown you.'

'You're very organised,' Amanda marvelled.

'Well, we want to get it right, to make a good start at restoring it to what it once was. It's all very wonderful and splendid to people from humble beginnings.'

'Darling,' said Hugh with amusement, ' you grew up in an Indian palace in —'

'— in a village —', his wife interrupted him.

'You own the village,' he bantered.

'My family owned it,' she corrected him, 'and they had to sell all of the land before I was born. You are giving entirely the wrong impression to this nice young lady.' She waved a playful finger at her husband. 'We had very little money when we first married,' she said, seriously, to Amanda. 'But we were in love. Yes …' she patted Amanda's cheek. 'You will find out. Your time will come. We are not the only new arrivals in the village,' she added, knowingly.

'Well!' interpolated Amanda, to forestall any matchmaking comments, 'thank you for the tea. I'll get straight back and make out a quote, and email it to you later today,' she said with bright efficiency, keen to make her exit.

Amanda walked home quickly across Sunken Madley, wondering if there was a village conspiracy to get her married off. She managed to avoid everyone except Pawel, the cherubic-faced Polish driver of the Royal Mail delivery van, which halted at the crossing for her. 'Hey! Amanda … have you heard about the …?'

Amanda sent the quotation for the restoration; the Poveys accepted. They booked a two-week holiday to Provence to be away from the smells and mess. From the 8th May, the Manor would be empty. Amanda would be left in peace to work.

At least … that was the idea.

Chapter 22

❧

FOOTSTEPS ABOVE
AND SOMETHING ON THE STAIRS

The Poveys left early on Saturday morning, and Amanda, eager to make a start, arrived at 9 o'clock. She drew up outside the Manor in her grandfather's legacy Vauxhall Astra. It was in British racing green, bearing the legend in gold script: Cadabra Furniture Restoration and Repairs.

Amanda parked in the driveway and unloaded. Once inside, with the door closed, she unearthed her lunchbox and smoothie flask and headed for the kitchen. The Wiltshire ham and Piccalilli sandwiches would probably remain fresh in her bag, but she preferred the Scotch egg and ginger beer to be kept chilled, so she put all of her lunch in the Poveys' fridge.

Amanda donned her boiler suit, but left her ordinary shoes on. Out of habit, she quickly scanned her surroundings, then drew her initialled Ikea pencil out of her overalls. She flipped open the end and drew out her Pocket-wand. Directing it at her materials, she enunciated:

'*Ymelyrol, arcofaras. Aereval, foglia.*'

Amanda's roll of polythene sheeting and two boxes hovered

then obediently followed her up the stairs. She paused for breath halfway for a moment, then took the summit.

'*Sedaasig,*' she said, and the boxes and roll landed gently. Amanda sat down on the carpet and poked around the equipment to find masking tape, scissors and a damp cloth. She took a moment to rest, and felt she needed to stop and get a sense of the atmosphere of the house.

For some reason, Amanda had the sensation that she was not alone. The air felt tense. Her ears fizzed. Suddenly the silence of the house was broken like a twig snapping in a deserted forest. She stiffened.

Was that a creak below? Amanda listened motionless, holding her breath. Probably the wind opening a door, she reasoned. The Poveys had told her to expect that. But the unexplained noise had turned her senses onto amber alert. And so it was that she heard the barely … audible … padding coming up the flights of stairs below her.

Tempest appeared around the newel post looking pleased with himself.

'Fine!' Amanda was both annoyed and relieved. 'That round to you, brat cat. Yes, you made me nervous. Now to make up for it, go and catch the mice invading the kitchen, and do something useful.'

Tempest promptly turned his back to her, settled himself on the lowest step of the flight, in a shaft of sunlight, conveying that making himself useful was at the bottom of his current agenda. Amanda smiled at his performance, but she had to admit that she found his presence comforting.

Up on the first floor, the banister rail ran along the side and length of the gallery then turned down the stairs to a broad landing. From there it made its final stately descent to the grand hall. The rail was supported by ornate barley twist posts, spindles that were not to be polished yet and had to be protected. So began the repetitive task of wrapping the top of each one with masking tape, where it met the underside of the handrail.

Masking tape will not stick to dirt and dust, so there was plenty of wiping to do, and soon Amanda's cloth needed a rinse. Removing her mask, she went down to the kitchen.

Amanda was wringing out the rag when she stilled her hands, and looked up at the ceiling. It sounded like the floorboards were creaking to the rhythm of a slow, careful walk. Her eyes followed its progress.

'Old houses!' Amanda remarked to Tempest and began to sing to reassure herself. Instantly the sound stopped.

'Well! Either the ghost isn't musical or doesn't care for my vocals,' she said, more robustly than she felt.

Amanda resolutely fixed her iPod to her earphones and fitted them into her ears. But even through them, before the first track of 50 Reggae Party Hits began playing, she was sure she heard the sound again, moving away.

Taping the tops of the spindles was not challenging work, but it did require concentration and precision that would pay off later. At the landing, Amanda pulled off her earphones, took out her water bottle and spent a few moments stroking Tempest, who accepted it as tribute.

'No, Pwecious, oo is not a foul-tempered, old rat-bag, is oo?' The milkman had thus apostrophised Tempest that morning for climbing onto the float, and trying to push a bottle off to smash on the pavement. Tempest allowed no one else but Amanda to address him in endearments. He purred with self-satisfaction at her reference to his dastardly exploits.

The house was quiet. Amanda sighed with relief. After her break, she returned to the top of the flight and pointed her wand at the three-foot-wide roll of polythene.

'*Ymelyrol, aereval.*'

It rose.

'*Saaetstendee.*' It hovered motionless while Amanda pulled out a length and wrapped the spindles, from the handrail to the treads, all down that section of the stairs, and fastened it in place with masking tape.

Amanda climbed back to the top, to apply more tape and polythene to protect the wall and panelling supporting the rail.

She was near the landing when she heard a faint rattle and whine from below. Amanda leaned over the banister. But she could see nothing strange.

Then there came another rattle, a clutter, a soft thunk, a pause, then a whine again.

'Must be the draft coming through that door I heard earlier. It's moving things around on the ground floor,' Amanda said decisively. It was windy outside after all.

Her heart rate was up, but Amanda made herself complete her task. She was tucking polythene around the bottom of the wall seven steps down the last flight to the entrance hall, when a panel came loose.

'Something else to repair — oh, my word, the dust!' It slid out of its place and dropped onto the treads below.

'*Saaetstendee,*' she ordered it, to stop it falling further.

'*Visgrim, cumdez!*' Amanda's mask rose off the newel post where she'd hung it and floated up to her. There was nothing for it; the panel had to be taken down and fixed back in place later. She put on the mask, peeled back the polythene and moved the section of wood to the landing, trying to remember what Grandpa had said about removing things from walls in old houses. Amanda suspected it was: 'don't'.

'Come on, Tempest, lunchtime. Maybe I can find something for you.' He followed her with studied nonchalance.

In the kitchen, the cellar door was slightly ajar. But it had been before ...., hadn't it? The fridge door wasn't properly closed. Surely she'd shut it? Maybe it was yet another item in the house that was broken, and came open of its own accord.

Her lunch box was open. One ham and Piccalilli sandwich was missing.

'Mice?' she asked Tempest. She had limited experience of animals other than her familiar, having to stay well clear of them for the sake of her asthma. 'They're highly intelligent, right?

Could I have been careless with the lid? Would a mouse take a whole sandwich?' she asked, incredulously.

Amanda wanted to eat in the garden, but reading through Mrs Povey's guide to unlocking the back door was a bridge too far in her current state of unrest. Instead, she went into the big, warm-hued library with its moth-eaten red velvet sofa and curtains. It smelled of leather, cigars and mustiness.

Amanda sat on the window-seat and began eating her remaining lunch while Tempest outstared a robin on the sill. She looked out at the once ornamental, walled garden at the back of the Manor, with its low, straggling arrangements of untended lavender, thyme, sweet cicely and wild marjoram. It has a seasoned, untidy beauty that somehow calmed Amanda's unease.

After a soothing cup of tea, Amanda invited Tempest to accompany her back up the stairs. She summoned her box of materials and began masking the tops of the spindles on the flight leading from the landing down to the ground floor.

She had just put the polythene in place and sat on a step for a rest, when Tempest became very still and looked intently to her right. After a moment he relaxed and went off in search of sunshine. She sat and hugged her knees. What a strange house! Then, distinctly, she saw the polythene sheet wave. It rippled out from where the loose panel had been. The air grew cold, though there was no draught. The plastic was quite still one moment, and moving the next. Goose pimples swept her body.

That was enough of being grown up. 'Granny! Grandpa!'

Senara and Perran appeared at her side.

'All right, love?' Grandpa asked her.

'No!' she whispered. 'This house is infested with ghosts and rodents!'

'Now don't you worry, love. Whatever it is, you can handle it,' said Grandpa, steadily.

'We're frightfully sorry, darling,' said Granny, 'but someone has just crossed over, and we have a lot on our plates at the moment.'

AMANDA CADABRA AND THE HIDEY-HOLE TRUTH

'What?' expostulated Amanda in astonishment.

'Tempest will look after you. Won't oo, big man?' Tempest snarled and flailed an ineffectual paw as Granny and Grandpa faded and disappeared.

'Well! That's a first!' Amanda exclaimed indignantly. 'So I'm on my own, am I?'

Tempest growled.

'All right. We're on our own. Fine. I'm a big girl now, and you're a …. a cat with attitude, and we can handle whatever it is that's going on here … hm!'

Amanda got to her feet, and worked her way to the ground floor, feeling somewhat tense. The light was going. She still had the dustsheets to lay on the stairs and fix at the sides. It was a quick and clean job, which could be done without overalls.

'I'll come back tomorrow,' she announced. Sunday. Amanda had nothing planned except to visit the playing fields, to see the Sunken Madley cricket team pit themselves against the formidable Romping-in-the-Heye eleven. It promised to be an exciting match. She'd thought it might be nice to dress up a bit and take a picnic to a spot beyond the boundary, by deep square leg, where she could watch and read in peace.

'Ha! In peace,' Amanda said out loud. Wasn't that what she'd expected at the Manor?

Chapter 23

❧

CLAIRY GODMOTHER, AND AT THE TOP OF THE STAIRS

'This,' Claire announced portentously, 'is your May Day present!' Amanda's best friend and neighbour proffered a brown-paper-and-orange-raffia-wrapped parcel.

Amanda was sitting on the dressing table stool in Claire's bedroom, which was freshly painted in Oval Room light blue. She accepted the package and smiled with delight and embarrassment. 'But … er … I don't have anything for you!'

'You fixed my table,' answered Claire, plumping herself back on the bed and getting into a half-lotus position.

'All I did was to wedge a piece of cardboard into the joint underneath. And that was last month,' said Amanda matter-of-factly, unpicking the string.

'No matter,' Claire dismissed this grandly. 'You so need this, darling,' she said gleefully. 'Go on, open it!'

Amanda pulled apart the paper. She could see fabric.

'I don't need any more clothes!' she exclaimed.

Claire was definite. 'Trust me. You need this.'

Amanda unfolded it and gasped as she shook it out.

'Cream. How lovely,' she admired.

'Buttermilk, darling,' corrected Claire with mock pretentiousness. 'Put it on.'

The under-dress was of ivory satin. It was covered with a layer of transparent silk that was self-patterned in a light matt gold. Claire tugged Amanda out of her dark t-shirt and jeans and threw the dress over her head.

The scoop neck flattered Amanda's jawline. The cut fitted her neat waist like a glove, and the flared skirt flowed out and down, floating flirtatiously around her knees. The colours somehow warmed Amanda's pale skin and brought out the bronze lights in her brown hair.

'See? You're a pretty girl, poppet. "And you shall go to the garden party."'

Amanda smiled in amazement at her reflection 'Wow,' she murmured. Then came to her senses. 'It must have cost a fortune. And I have going-out clothes already.'

'For the evening. This is for a summer's day. There's a change in the wind. New men are afoot. I feel it in my fingers, I feel it in my —'

'When would I wear it?'

'You'll know. Close your eyes, Ammy. Now imagine … you're standing on a beach,' Claire uttered dramatically, 'hot under a sky of blue. He rides towards you on a black stallion with flanks gleaming in the sunlight. The breeze blows his shirt against rippling pecs … and the surf crashes!'

Amanda burst out laughing. Her friend smiled. 'You may mock, darling mine. But you'll see. Now take it off and let's celebrate.'

'Celebrate what?'

'That I have a bottle of bubbly!' cried Claire, ever-ready to party.

* * * * *

That was ten days ago, and Claire's prediction had come to pass. After the previous day's unsettling events, Amanda needed to feel empowered. The spring day was unusually warm. Bright orange tortoiseshell butterflies were fluttering over the buddleia, and a song thrush was sending out a string of short musical calls. It was ideal weather in which to take her new frock for its first airing.

The dress emerged from its cover and went onto Amanda. Cream Falke holdups came out of the packet, and from their box, beige Manolo Blahnik heels. Claire had got them at half price and then decided she loathed them, but they not-so-miraculously fitted Amanda. They were utterly impractical but psychologically as uplifting as The Shard elevator.

Amanda applied delicate browns to her eyes and peach to her lips. She tonged a few twists into her hair, letting it fall around her shoulders instead of tied in her usual plait. Amanda looked at her jewellery collection for suitable earrings. Grandpa and Granny had given her some discreet gold-set amber drops for her 18th birthday. Today they were going to make it out of their case. Amanda took the top off the perfume that Grandpa had had made in France especially for her, from the plants in their garden, and rolled it onto her skin. She put on her shapeliest straw hat. Were beige gloves a little over the top? Why not?

Amanda picked up her Pocket-wand and realised that her dream dress was lacking in just one respect: no pockets. She had a jacket but no guarantee she would not take it off. Bertil had said she should always have the wand with her.

Where did the heroines of films secrete their weapons? She looked down speculatively at her neckline. No, the bodice was too fitted for that. However … the loose, flowing skirt would certainly conceal ….. Amanda lifted the hem and tucked the pencil into the top of her holdup stocking. She let the skirt fall back into place and studied the effect. Perfect. Amanda felt like an adventuress. It was a pleasant sensation.

Amanda slipped on her jacket. Finally, she grabbed Grandpa's old brown workshop coat and went out to the car, avoiding the purple streamers of the wisteria around the front door.

The 'colonel', who was a civilian and only a child during the war, but with the upright bearing and fine handlebar moustache that had earned him the nickname, was walking back from the corner shop with the Sunday papers. 'Amanda! I say!' he said admiringly. 'Looking very lovely today. Very lovely. See you at the cricket later?'

'Thank you, Henry. Yes, I'll be there.'

'Good show. Yes, indeed!' he confirmed.

Amanda arrived at the Manor in high spirits. Her thoughts had been turning to the new arrivals: the librarian and the astronaut-rock-star-sports-idol-spy. Tempest was sitting expectantly on the mat.

The house was quiet. Motes floated in the sunshafts through the hall windows. Amanda could hear her own short breaths as she listened cautiously. Assured that all was apparently well, she took off her jacket and hat, and put on the lab coat. At the bottom of the stairs, Amanda had left a box of clean, laundered canvas dustsheets. She didn't need a wand for this short, easy task and pointing to the top sheet, pronounced, '*Aaereval lytaz. Abrfraeddna.*' It lifted off the ground and spread itself out.

'*Sedassig,*' Amanda added, and it lay down on the bottom seven treads. She ordered the box to follow her and went up laying the protective coverings as she ascended the stairs, tucking each into place with a little masking tape.

Amanda paused on the landing. Just before the last flight, she sensed something was wrong. No, not 'wrong', just different. It was dark up there. Darker than yesterday. Yes, she'd opened the Peacock bedroom door at the top of the stairs to get the light from the window onto the landing, and now … she went up … it was closed. Wind? She hadn't opened the window. Then how…?

Chapter 24

❧

THE FLOOR OF PEACOCK

Amanda frowned suspiciously.

With raised heart rate she walked up the stairs, approached the Peacock room and put her hand on the black iron handle. Slowly, she pushed it down until she felt the latch release. At her push, the door hissed over the carpet, and she peered into the room.

The curtains were closed, but Amanda could still see that the furniture was under Holland covers, just as it had been the day before except … for an armchair … and something on the floor with one of the large cloths draped over it. That surely hadn't been there yesterday.

Amanda crossed the room and twitched open the curtains. Looking back, she saw that it was something long and low and … there was a red stain at one end … was that …? She knelt and whipped back the white cotton sheet, and there was the body of a man. With a sharp intake of breath, she recoiled. The eyes were closed. On the back of his head, the dark, grey-flecked hair was slightly matted with a small amount of blood. But it had been enough just to seep through the fabric.

The man was about 50 years of age, she guessed. Mid-height and slight, he was sallow of complexion and hollow of cheek. Amanda touched his bony wrist to feel for a pulse. The flesh was cold.

She dropped the hand in horror and stood up. She saw that within his navy- jumper-clad arm was a plate, a bread roll, a heel of Wensleydale cheese, a beef tomato and a bottle of Buxton Spring Water.

'What on earth?' she exclaimed. 'Police … must call p— police.' Amanda fumbled for her phone …. She jumped, as the bell had rung. The bell? The front doorbell was broken. It must be the side door. But she didn't know how to open the side door. And who was it? Never mind, she could ask them for help, whoever it was. Amanda hastened to the window. She couldn't see anyone. Dammit. The door must be below the next room. Amanda rushed into the Emerald chamber, threw open the window and leaned out.

'Hello!' she shouted, urgently.

A man looked up at her, showing the welcome face of Detective Inspector Thomas Trelawney.

'Oh, thank heavens!' she called out with relief. 'Come ….' But her voice was drowned out by car horns and shouts from the road running alongside the Manor. Mr Hanley-Page in his vintage Rolls and Miss De Havillande in her Range Rover had chosen that moment to engage in an altercation at the junction. They were beeping and hurling challenges and insults over right-of-way.

Amanda repeated herself but was out-decibelled. She tried gesturing, and finally succeeded in conveying to her welcome visitor, that she didn't know how to unlock the side door, so could he please go round to the front as quickly as possible.

She straightened up and closed the window. The thud seemed to echo in the next room. Odd. Amanda hurried back next door to the crime scene.

She gasped. The body had gone.

Amanda jerked her head from side to side as she searched the room. The man, the plate, the food and water had disappeared.

Tempest strolled in and sat on the spot where the body had been, and began to wash himself leisurely.

'I didn't imagine it,' Amanda insisted, 'I know I didn't.' Tempest paused in his ablutions to stare at her knowingly. 'He'll think I'm crazy. He'll think I'm making it up to get his attention. That I'm trying to distract him from investigating the family accident.'

Tempest blinked. Once for 'yes, you said it, sweetheart.'

'What am I going to say?' Amanda ran down the stairs faster than was good for her asthma. At the bottom, she took a moment to regain her breath and compose herself.

Thomas, meanwhile, stood on the mat, surprised by the enthusiasm of Amanda's welcome from the window above. Although she'd appeared rather stressed, she had seemed pleased to see him. In spite of himself, he felt a little gratified. It had been difficult to make out her exact expression from that distance, but her face had definitely lit up when she'd recognised him.

The door opened with a quick swing.

'Detective! How good of you to call!' Amanda's voice rang out a little too loudly.

'Miss Cadabra,' he greeted her with polite warmth.

She looked flushed, and her pupils were dilated. Thomas noticed the dress under the lab coat. He noticed other things too; her soft brown copper-lit curls — the first time he'd seen her hair down —, subtle makeup defining her eyes and lips, and the gold and amber earrings glinting through her tresses. The contrast with the stained baggy boiler suit, messy plait and glasses was so marked that he was momentarily distracted, but professionalism hauled him inexorably back into reality.

'Are you all right?' he enquired solicitously.

'Oh … yes … just so rushed. I have some things I must finish before … I ….' Well, thought Amanda, he has a girlfriend so why not? She continued '… my date?'

'You have a date?' Thomas thought she seemed uncertain.

'Er yes … I have a date …,' she nodded emphatically.

Amanda felt more was needed.

'With … a man ….'

He inclined his head noncommittally, offering a well of silence into which to drop her explanation.

'Who …,' she continued in search of inspiration.

He looked at her mildly questioningly.

'… I know… from …'

'Hm?' he encouraged.

'… the village,' she concluded feebly.

'Ah'.

'So,' she continued with new energy, and he let her ramble, 'I was eager to finish my work here and I was at the top of the house and I had to come all the way down so I'm a bit out of breath,' she finished in a rush. 'You see.'

He nodded. 'I do.' He wondered if her swain was in the house. But her tidily arranged clothing did not suggest that he'd caught her in flagrante. And she had seemed extremely eager to see him at first.

'So … I'd love to invite you in for a' —she narrowed the door an inch or two — 'chat but could we make it another time … do you think? Please?'

'Yes, of course. I'm in London for a long weekend. How about if I come back tomorrow?' he offered in a relaxed tone.

'Tomorrow. Evening,' Amanda stressed. She hoped to heaven she'd have this mess unravelled by then. 'Yes. Very nice.'

Nowhere where he might be able to smell magic though, she thought.

'Sinners Rue,' she said.

'I expect they do,' he replied equably.

'The pub.' Amanda pointed. 'Next to The Big Tease.'

He raised his eyebrows.

'Tea and coffee shop,' she elucidated.

'6 o'clock?' he requested. 'I'll have a 4-hour drive afterwards.'

'Yes. That's wonderful. Great. 6 o'clock, Sinners Rue. Thank you so much for coming over.' She pumped his hand. Something occurred to her. 'How did you know where to find me?'

'An elderly gentleman with a handlebar moustache was very helpful.'

'Ah, I see ... well' she said, brightly, 'must get on!'

'Till tomorrow then,' he replied with polite friendliness, turned, and walked away.

Amanda raced to the bottom of the staircase before she remembered. Ah. She'd left the front door open. As she wheeled, she saw it draw to ..., the knob turning, pulling in the latch. The door closed quietly. In the breathless silence, she heard the latch click gently back into place.

'What the ...?' She ran back. Wind? Wind didn't turn knobs? What else could it be? A ghost? Did it have something to do with that strange chill she'd experienced on the stairs. There had to be a ghost. Of whom? Whoever it was, she felt, that they had closed the door to keep her safe. Could it be the ghost of the dead man? Why would he want to protect her? Maybe he wanted her to help him, to find his murderer.

This flashed through Amanda's mind as she reached the door and wrenched it open in case some living, human hand wielding a key had been responsible. But she saw only Trelawney driving out onto the road. He looked back and waved. She closed the door, leaned against it and took a swig from her inhaler. Tempest regarded her mockingly.

Chapter 25

❧

THE VISION IN THE LIBRARY

Amanda tottered to the hefty wooden chest by the hall wall and collapsed onto it.

'His timing is impeccable,' she gasped out. 'Not.' She took a few slow breaths. 'How does he do it?'

Tempest cocked an eye at her, then strolled suggestively into the kitchen. The Poveys had insisted that she make herself at home saying, 'Help yourself to the contents of the fridge, cupboards, anything. Use the facilities and stay overnight if it makes things easier for you.' They'd asked around locally about Amanda and received such glowing reports that they trusted her implicitly with their house and possessions.

'Hugh and Sita had such faith in me. And now a murder has been perpetrated on my watch,' she chided herself. 'And a body stolen ... or was it?'

She followed Tempest thoughtfully, put the kettle on, filled a saucer with water for him and plonked herself at the table on a chair close to the window. Over tea, she recovered and pondered.

'I know what I saw,' she said with determination and

narrowed eyes.

Tempest finished lapping up the water and looked pointedly at the fridge. Amanda got up distractedly and found him some leftover ham. He turned up his nose at it then graciously consented to chew on a morsel.

This was supposed to have been a quick visit to the Manor, before hot chocolate at The Big Tease, followed by a leisurely Sunday lunch at the Snout and Trough. They were also known as The Other Pub but did the tenderest roast beef, the fluffiest Yorkshire puddings and the crispiest roast potatoes, parsnips and carrots in Sunken Madley.

However, Amanda didn't want to risk bumping into Detective Inspector Trelawney in case he'd stopped off there. She needed to gather her wits and her poise before she met him again.

'There must be something,' she insisted to the gourmandising Tempest. 'I'm going to search,' she announced resolutely. Amanda took the stairs slowly, aware of a little chill that made her pull her workshop coat closer by the lapels.

The bedroom with the shrouded furniture appeared to be just as she'd last seen it; white draped shapes and an uncovered armchair. She squatted on her Mary Jane heels and looked along the floor. She didn't want to get too close to the dusty carpet in case it set off her asthma. It had already been teetering on the edge of an attack. There were no marks on the rug. No damp patch that she could feel, but then there hadn't been that much blood. He must have been hit with a blunt object, enough to cause death by trauma without much exsanguination.

Tempest walked in, stroked past her legs and burrowed under the armchair. He liked dark places to tuck himself and lie in wait for hapless insects or a passing ankle. Amanda ignored him and toured the room, lifting the covers one by one, looking for anything that might be helpful.

She was distracted by the sound of Tempest rustling under the furniture. He was not given to kittenish behaviour. He must have found a mouse. Suddenly he emerged batting a round, light-brown-and-white object across the floor in front of him. It tumbled across to her feet, and she picked it up.

A roll. A bread roll.

'Ah! A clue! The dead man must have had two bread rolls on his plate. And this one ended up under the chair.' She felt and sniffed it. It was fresh. It was real. Immediately Amanda was energised.

'I knew I hadn't imagined it. Good boy, Tempest!' She ruffled his head heartily. He turned away with an air of 'Do I have to do everything myself?'

'Now why couldn't you have found this before the Inspector turned up? I suppose there was no time. Never mind. He'd probably still think I was mad if I presented just a bread roll as evidence. Hm.

'So.' Amanda clasped her hands together emphatically. 'There was a body, and now there isn't ... so ... someone moved it. But where?' She started tapping the walls, looking for joins, seams, anything that might reveal a hiding place. She looked in the other bedrooms and drew a blank.

Amanda felt momentarily foiled, but not defeated. She tapped her foot. 'Tempest. I think it's time I checked out the new talent at the library.'

Amanda returned to the ground floor, changed her coat for her jacket, and looked at her reflection in the downstairs bathroom. She was a little pale but not unusually so. She pinched her cheeks, put on her hat and arranged her curls at the sides.

'Not too shabby,' she decided.

Amanda locked up the house, 'for what it's worth,' she remarked, turning the front door key, and went out to the car.

'You coming?'

Tempest minced in and settled himself regally in the back seat. Amanda laughed.

'So I'm the chauffeur now, am I? Drive on, Cadabra!' she uttered imperiously to herself.

* * * * *

Trelawney drove south to Crouch End where he was staying with his mother for the weekend. He was torn between keeping his attention on the road and his two interchanges with Miss Cadabra. Try as he might, he was unable to reconcile her switch in manner. Had he only imagined her intensely relieved welcome of him from the upstairs window?

Fortunately, his mother was used to Thomas racing into the house and darting up to his old bedroom to make or take a work phone call.

'Lunch is at one, darling!' she called after him.

'Right. Thanks,' he replied, and closed the door behind him before he dialled the number. Mike Hogarth answered promptly.

'What's up, Thomas?'

'Not sure but ... something,' he replied not very lucidly. 'I called at the Manor where a neighbour said Amanda was working. The front doorbell was broken, so I found a way around to the side door — tradesman's entrance, probably, — and rang there. She appeared at an upstairs window.'

Hogarth thought of making a reference to Juliet at her balcony but thought better of it.

'She was obviously some distance away,' continued Thomas, 'but I could swear she was overcome with relief at seeing me. There was a lot of traffic noise in the street, so we couldn't hear one another but she communicated that I should go to the front door.' Thomas became aware that he had been speaking quickly and took a slow breath.

'And when Amanda opened the door ...?' Mike prompted.

'Her attitude had done a one-eighty. Unmistakeably flustered. Couldn't get rid of me fast enough. Made up a ridiculous story about having a date.' Thomas paused, calmed and half-grinned. 'In fact, it was almost laughable. But, something was definitely going on in there. Something she didn't want me to know about.'

'Serious in nature?' asked Hogarth.

'I believe so,' replied Thomas with certainty.

'Illegal?'

'Er, possibly.' He was less sure about that.

'Hm,' was Hogarth's response.

'Do you think I should go back there?' Thomas asked, ready for action.

'No. No, lad, I don't think you should do that. Whatever it is, for whatever reason, Amanda believes she must handle it herself. You won't get any more out of her than you already have. My gut feeling is that whatever is going on in that house has little or nothing to do with the case of the accident that you are investigating. Whilst I applaud your enthusiasm, Thomas, know this: that you are not going to solve the case overnight. You are in this for the long haul. And not all of the answers will be in the places where you expect them.' Hogarth let that sink in.

'All right. I understand, Mike,' Thomas said soberly. 'I made an appointment for tomorrow evening, at the local, to tell Amanda the news.'

'Good. Well, don't bring up your encounter today. Treat it as though you take whatever she said at face value.'

'Understood.'

'Enjoy your Sunday,' Mike adjured him. 'Do that thing people so often do on that day of the week.'

'Er?'

'Relax!'

Thomas laughed.

'Enjoy your lunch, and all the best to your mother,' said Hogarth.

'Thanks, Mike, will do.'

* * * * *

Sunken Madley library was mostly attended by volunteers on Sundays. It opened at 10.30 and closed at 1 pm, so the staff had time to have lunch before getting to the cricket match for its start at 2 o'clock.

The library was unusually full, and Amanda noticed that the ticket holders were predominantly teenage females. She saw the man behind the counter and comprehension dawned. Her eyes widened. He could have modelled for an old master, played Lord Byron or Rudolph Valentino. She had never seen a face so flawless, such perfectly molded lips, planes of cheek, such glossy black hair. He looked like he must be the product of sophisticated computer graphics. Yet, he seemed utterly unaware either of his appearance or the effect it was having on Olivia Mazurek, the milkman's daughter. She was gazing at him worshipfully, as he shyly scanned her reader's ticket and stamped the return dates in her borrowed books.

He returned Olivia's entranced smile politely, but uncomfortably, as he pushed her selections towards her across the counter. Amanda stood and watched as Hannah Byrne, next in the queue, had her moment with the vision and then gave place to Becky Whittle.

However, when Ruth Reiser, next in line, asked him a question, a change came over him. He looked into Ruth's earnest, bespectacled face. He nodded with lively interest and, talking quietly, led her to the reference section, taking a volume from the shelf. Ruth looked pleased, and they returned together to the counter. Interesting, thought Amanda.

On her way out, Ruth said 'Hi, Amanda,' and tilted her book to show the title: *Medieval Metallurgy: Alchemy*. Amanda smiled and nodded.

'Let me know if you need help,' she said.

'Ok. Thanks. Bye,' replied Ruth, with a quick answering smile.

Ruth was Amanda's favourite teenager in the village and

occasionally assisted with her history homework. Today it was Amanda who needed help, but she patiently waited until the mob had abated before she approached the counter.

'Hello,' she said, and careful not to frighten him with introductions or small talk, 'I'm looking for information on hidey-holes in old houses. I'm a furniture restorer working in a manor, and I'd like to know more about them and the ingenious features the original carpenters invented.'

His eyes lit up. Bingo, she congratulated herself.

'Yes, of course, Miss er ...?' he asked diffidently.

'Amanda, Amanda Cadabra'.

He paused as people usually did on being told her full name, then replied,

'Jonathan Sheppard.'

'Pleased to meet you. And welcome to Sunken Madley. So where do I look?' she continued smoothly to avoid an awkward interval.

'This way, please.' Jonathan led her to shelfmarks in the 900s in the non-fiction section, explaining animatedly, 'Priest holes, as they were called, were first created in the 1550s in Catholic houses to hide members of the clergy. Elizabeth I had something of a personal and political vendetta against Catholics in general and priests in particular.'

He pulled out *Hidey-holed Up* by Anna Cavity-Wells and opened it. 'Here's a photograph of a concealed entrance in a water closet in Courtnot Hall.' He put it into her hands, saying, 'And if you'd like to follow me just over here to the 600s ....' Amanda closed the volume and accompanied him.

Jonathan continued as they walked, 'Secret spaces, tunnels and stairways continued to be constructed for at least the next 200 years. Some group or other was often the object of persecution by the authorities: Catholics, Cavaliers, Jacobites, witches.'

He scanned the 600s until he found his quarry. 'I think you'll find this helpful; Mind Your Manors by Tim Berty,' Jonathan said, laying the book on top of the one Amanda was holding, 'and here …,' he went on as he took her round an aisle into a corner. Jonathan ran his fingers along the spines, searching for a particular title, 'Ah, yes,' he said with satisfaction, unwedging it from the crowded shelf, 'Secret Rights of Passages by T.U. Nelson. Oh, and of course,' he added, tugging at a tall, slim book until it came free, 'Manors Maketh Man by Joyce T Beamish.'

'Well! Thank you, Jonathan, you certainly know your subject,' Amanda said, with a mixture of surprise, suspicion and appreciation, as she gazed down at the pile in her arms. She looked up at him. 'I know you've just moved in, but do you know if the library has anything specifically on Sunken Madley Manor, where I'm working?'

'It might do,' said Jonathan hopefully. 'But old maps and plans for buildings in the area are in the stacks downstairs though, and I can't leave the lending library unattended. Can you wait until we close at 1 o'clock?'

'Of course,' Amanda responded. 'I can come bacTempest rarely found the library of interest but turned up outside the Snout and Trough to register his presence with her, before making for the pub's kitchen back door. Amanda took her literary swag inside the pub, checking for Trelawney, who in her mind had become ubiquitous, as she entered. She settled herself into a corner for a quick flick through the books, before her lunch arrived and required her full attention.

The high-backed settle on the opposite side of the table allowed her to duck out of sight when anyone who knew her might turn away from the bar and spot her. And worse still, want to engage her in conversation. She had a narrow escape with Penny, the doctor's receptionist, who took a bored look around the pub while waiting for her fiancé to acquire her white wine spritzer.

Half an hour later, Amanda was distractedly forking her way through spotted dick and custard and reading the contents page of *Hidey-Holed Up*. Out of the blue, the most beautiful woman in Sunken Madley swooped over Amanda in a breath of

Chanel Coco Mademoiselle and kissed her cheek.

'Darling! It's been ages!' cried the goddess.

'Oh!' started Amanda looking up in surprise. Quickly, however, she responded to the agonised plea in the famous pale blue eyes, saying with equal enthusiasm,' It's wonderful to see you too! I can't believe how long it's been!'

The model turned her head to smile regretfully at the would-be village Lotharios who, she managed to convey to Amanda, had been pressing their unwelcome attentions upon her. The acclaimed paragon of loveliness flung her Alexander McQueen cashmere sweater onto the settle opposite Amanda and sat down, announcing animatedly, 'Now. We simply must catch up!'

She leant intimately towards Amanda.

Chapter 26

༄

THE ICE QUEEN

Amanda was surprised that a nationally known model, who must be used to attention, couldn't deal with a couple of village lads in the local. She could only imagine that the lady lived a rarefied existence.

'You're welcome,' Amanda replied to her fervent thanks for playing along with the fiction of their friendship.

The model spoke in a low and unexpectedly friendly voice, leaning towards Amanda with an air of confiding girly gossip. 'I don't think we've ever formally met. I'm Jessica. Jessica James.'

'I know,' smiled Amanda, pleased to find that the Sunken Madley VIP didn't expect everyone to know who she was. 'I'm Amanda. Amanda Cadabra.'

'Perran and Senara's granddaughter?'

'Yes,' confirmed Amanda

Jessica looked at the books on the table.

'Research into old houses, I see? I expect you have a professional interest. You're working at the Manor, aren't you?'

Jessica asked brightly.

'That's right. No secrets in Sunken Madley,' Amanda replied wryly.

'Well, not many.' Jessica had become serious. She played with a cork-backed coaster advertising the local craft beer, Stinking Rich.

Amanda waited.

'I'm sorry we've never spoken,' Jessica said after a while. 'I knew your grandfather a bit. He came and restored an antique dresser at The Elms for my mother, Irene. A lovely man. Gentle.'

'Yes, he was.' Much as Amanda liked to hear Perran spoken of affectionately, she was wondering where all of this was going. There was a silence while she waited for Jessica to get to the point.

'And your grandmother was very ... respected, you know.'

'Yes,' agreed Amanda, wholeheartedly.

'The librarian — Mrs Pagely — speaks highly of you,' Jessica added. Amanda was amazed that Jessica borrowed books. She was more of the income bracket that bought them and then dispatched them to charity shops. Still, when she was a child perhaps?

Jessica correctly interpreted Amanda's expression.

'Oh, the library? I wasn't born with money, you know,' she said a trifle defiantly. 'I had to borrow more than books. My father opted out of family life when I was a toddler. My mother was in her 40s; I was a surprise. My parents' fortune, such as it was, disappeared in the stock market crash of '87, and daddy dearest decided to head for the hills.' The warmth of anger had entered her voice. 'My mother provided for us both; Gordon French, who was an old friend of hers, offered to help but she was too proud to accept. We had to move into a couple of rooms above the chemist. My mother worked nights developing film. I was determined that one day I'd get her out of that place, and set her up in the palace she deserved.'

Amanda nodded understandingly.

'Well,' continued Jessica, more calmly, 'my mother always

had great style, even on a charity-shop-clothes budget and, I think, largely to my outfit that she put together for me, I was talent-spotted while I was a student at Hertfordshire college. That's how I got my first modelling job. D'you know how I got my nickname, The Ice Queen?'

'Tell me,' Amanda invited her kindly.

'The cameraman on that first shoot told me not to smile. He meant just for those photographs, but I took it to heart, and after that, I made sure that I never smiled in public. I started becoming known for it. My agent advised me on how to capitalise on it, and we built my name as The Ice Queen.'

'I see. Well, thank you for sharing that with me,' replied Amanda. Flattering as it was to be acknowledged by Miss James, she did still want to get back to her books.

'You're wondering why I'm telling you all this, and I expect wanting to carry on with your reading,' Jessica observed accurately, touching the nearest book with faultlessly French-manicured fingers.

Amanda didn't want to be rude. 'I'm honoured by your confidences, of course, but well, … yes.'

'OK, please bear with me. There is a point to all this,' said Jessica.

'Sure.'

'I became very successful on the strength of my image.'

Amanda interrupted, saying with candour, 'You're also very beautiful, if I may say so, Miss James, stunning, out of the ordinary. And I'm sure you work very hard at your job and are very good at it.'

'Thank you for that, Amanda.' She seemed genuinely to appreciate the compliment. 'Please called me Jessica.'

'OK, Jessica.'

'As I say, I did well, made a packet, and I bought The Elms for my mother — for Mum. It has eight bedrooms, so she could rent out the top floor, turn it into a guest house, whatever she wanted. Plus use a room for a studio. She makes jewellery, you know,' Jessica added with pride, and stopped fiddling with the coaster. 'Really unusual. She has a great talent.'

Amanda nodded encouragingly.

'Anyway, after I bought her the house, and she set up her jewellery design business, I asked her to make something for the Ice Queen, not for her daughter, but for the model. So ... she made this amazing bracelet, made up of lots of fine chains of silver, connected together like a sort of delicate cuff, and studded with small diamonds and light blue topaz. I started wearing it all the time, and it became my trademark. Silver, diamonds — ice?'

'I get it,' Amanda smiled.

'And then about a year ago ... I lost it.'

Amanda was starting to see where she might come into the model's picture.

'You lost it somewhere that you think I might be able to find it?' she hazarded.

'Yes,' Jessica replied frankly. 'But let me go on. You see, I can't have a ... a romantic relationship ... the image, you know ... I've nearly made enough to "retire" on, to make Mum and me secure for the rest of our lives. Nearly. I need another year, perhaps. I'm at the very outer age limit for a model. I can't afford to compromise my persona.'

'OK.'

The model quickly scanned the room, checking no one was anywhere they might be able to overhear her next words.

'The thing is…..' The light blue of Jessica's eyes appeared to deepen. 'I fell in love.'

Chapter 27

❧

BLACKMAIL

Two mischievous brown eyes chose that moment to appear above the edge of the table. They were topped by a head of dark, fluffy curls. For some reason, two or three of the village toddlers were inexorably drawn to Amanda. In the intensity of the conversation, neither Amanda nor Jessica had noticed Amir Patel's knee-height approach.

Amanda smiled at the doctor's grandson, ruffled his hair and put a finger to her lips. 'Amir. Ammy's hiding. OK?'

The two-year-old nodded enthusiastically, and with a tottering run returned to his parents. Amanda turned back to Jessica.

'You fell in love?' said Amanda seriously.

'Yes,' confirmed Jessica.

'That must have complicated your life.'

'We had to meet in secret,' Jessica told her.

'Right,' agreed Amanda.

'Very secret. I knew a place. Somewhere I'd played when I was a child, with some other children. So we met there. We had to be very quiet and very careful, and, in the end, it got too dangerous. And so we agreed to leave it for a while. It was on the last time we were together that I must have dropped it,' — Jessica shook her head and shrugged — ' or mislaid it, I don't know but ... the next thing I knew, I received,' — her voice fell lower—, 'a blackmail letter. It said that if I paid up, then the bracelet would be returned to me. I did, a great deal of money — so much of what I'd saved; that's why I have to keep working — only the bracelet wasn't returned.'

'So what did you do?' asked Amanda, intrigued.

'Well, after that, there was never any opportunity to do anything about it, until now.'

'Was this place where you had ... your trysts,' Amanda asked delicately, 'the Manor, by any chance?'

'Yes,' Jessica admitted.

'You were friends with Nicola and Simon Dunkley-McVitty?'

'Yes. You know what children are: into hiding places, pressing and pushing and playing with everything. So I knew a secret way in when .... he and I needed somewhere we could be together. Dunkley, the father, was sometimes out all night. We'd watch for his car. Usually, if he wasn't back by midnight, he wouldn't be home 'till the next day. His wife had a champagne habit the whole village knew about. She'd be out cold by 11 pm. We just had to wait and watch, and then — oh I know it was wrong, we had no right to be there, but — we would meet in the house ... in one of the rooms ...'

There was a pause, during which Jessica struggled with the embarrassment of having confided so much personal information to a stranger. Amanda thought about the blackmailer.

'Did anyone else ever stay there? Or could any of the staff have found it?' she asked.

'They had a cleaning lady who came in about three times a week,' replied Jessica, 'though I don't think it was her because she seemed a very honest person. But Mr Dunkley's cousin Vernon used to stay sometimes. He could have found it. Only, soon after I paid the ransom, he got knocked down by a London Genuine Tour Bus.'

'Well, that's something,' said Amanda looking on the bright side.

'But what if Cousin Vernon told someone or gave it to someone?' Jessica continued. 'They could come back for more money or break the story to the papers, who'd pay a fortune for it, and my career would be over!'

'Are you sure?' Amanda was sceptical. 'Surely no publicity is bad publicity?'

'I can't take the risk,' Jessica insisted. 'Not when I'm this close to everything I've worked for since I was 18.'

Amanda exhaled and thought. 'So we think Vernon maybe hid it in the house?'

'Yes,' Jessica agreed, 'but how could I search? The Dunkleys never left the house, not both of them, not when I or ... anyone else who might have helped, was around.'

'Did you tell your mother?'

Jessica blushed under her flawless foundation. 'No. I thought she'd be so disappointed in me. I've always just wanted to make her proud.'

'OK. So ... then ...?' Amanda said, moving her off what was manifestly a sensitive subject.

'Then the Dunkleys sold to the Poveys. But they've been there all the time until yesterday and then you...' Jessica trailed off.

'Yes, I see,' said Amanda understandingly. 'You had a two-week window in which to try and get into the Manor and find the bracelet. But you didn't know when I'd be there, or if I might find it?'

'Yes,' Jessica confirmed. 'And I decided, through one thing and another, that my best bet was to trust you.'

Amanda laughed knowingly, 'I am Village, after all.'

Jessica allowed herself a small, glimmering smile. 'You are

Village, yes.' She continued, grave once more, 'So … have you seen anywhere in the house, where you think my bracelet could have been hidden. You're repairing the furniture, aren't you? Could there be a secret drawer or concealed compartment in a …. secretaire or … tallboy or something?'

'There could. I'd like to help and will keep my eye open, but I do have a schedule. I can't spend every day searching the house.'

'Yes, I understand. But please, Amanda,' Jessica entreated, 'will you try?'

'Yes. I'm researching old houses anyway. If I find any leads or the bracelet, I promise I'll let you know. Oh, which room did you and er … your er … meet in?'

'Scarlet,' Jessica replied ironically.

Of course, it was, thought Amanda. 'Could you have dropped it in the secret passage you used to get into the house? Er, where is the passage?'

'I can't tell you that,' immediately stated Jessica.

'Why not?' asked Amanda, taken aback.

'I took a blood oath not to tell,' Jessica said staunchly.

'But you must have told your er … boyfriend,' Amanda queried, reasonably.

'I didn't *tell* him, I *showed* him,' Jessica countered.

Amanda was beginning to feel indignant. The model had asked for her help and was now refusing to give her information vital to the mission.

'Well, then you can show *me*.'

'No, I can't be seen near the Manor, it's too risky.' Jessica was adamant.

'But you were planning to break in!' objected Amanda.

'Well, I've lost my nerve now. I realise how foolhardy that would be. No, I can't go there with you. I'd have to show you by night, and there are people with eyes in the back of their head in this village, even after dark. I have to stay right away from that house.'

It sounded like paranoia to Amanda. Nevertheless, she had to accept Jessica's position.

'All right,' she agreed, 'I'll look for it as best I can.'

'Here's my card,' Jessica slipped it covertly under *Secret Rights of Passage*. 'Thank you just for trying. I owe you a favour. And if I can send work your way I will and when this is all over, and my life becomes more normal, and I'm spending more time here with Mum … I hope maybe we could be friends. I'm not nearly as horrible as I'm portrayed in the press.' Amanda got a glimpse of a smile of surprising sweetness.

She grinned, won over. 'OK.'

'I'll go now and leave you to your reading.' They'd had their heads close together, and now Jessica straightened up and raised her voice to public address level.

'Wonderful to see you, Amanda!' She stood and picked up her top. 'So good to catch up.' Mwahh! Mwah! came the perfumed air-kisses 'Ciao!'

'You too, Jessica!' said Amanda. 'Take care.' The model slinked gracefully through the crowded pub and was gone, leaving behind her secret and her scent.

Chapter 28

∾

GOING UNDERGROUND

Amanda was back at the library promptly at five minutes to one. The last readers were filing out, with backward glances at Jonathan. When he saw Amanda, Jonathan smiled, showing perfect white teeth between generous lips, his brown eyes sparkling.
'Hello, Amanda.'

'Hello, Jonathan.'

The door swung to, and Jonathan locked the two of them in, and the public out. The library was eerily quiet now, the toys in the children's section stacked neatly in their primary coloured crates, the leaflets on the counter precisely piled.

'This way,' he invited her, weaving around the magazine display and two desks, with user terminal computers now powered down. Their feet padded on the carpet. Jonathan rounded the far end of the information counter and unlocked a green metal door, the bunch of keys clattering against it as the tumblers fell. Cold air mushroomed out. Jonathan reached in and pressed a wall switch, and an overhead lamp illuminated a narrow stone staircase leading to the basement.

Amanda felt a touch of claustrophobia. She suppressed it and followed him down. Turning the corner of the final flight, Amanda saw the light of the last bulb swallowed up into blackness. She drew back then heard a click. Fluorescent tubes flickered on, revealing a large area. It was windowless and cool with cement underfoot, on which their feet tapped and clacked loudly in the otherwise silent space.

Amanda followed Jonathan through a maze of high shelves filled with tall reference works, fat volumes, hardbacks with broken spines and decayed covers, ring-binders and boxes for which the lending library had no other storage facility.

'So many of the local libraries are closing,' Jonathan's regretful voice joined their lonely footfalls, 'but they've kept this one open thanks to the archive space.'

Amanda was beginning to feel a sense of panic at the locked library door, the narrow staircase, the underground book bunker. Was it Jonathan or this place or both? She felt trapped and disorientated. Her head was aching but her mind was racing. She wanted to run. Amanda wished she hadn't had the spotted dick for pudding. She felt heavy. What if she had to escape from whatever down here was inducing this nebulous sensation of alarm? Amanda put her hand on her thigh and felt the comforting shape of her Pocket-wand. She could probably use it to bring at least one of these high shelves crashing down between her and her pursuer, if she had to. But that would mean risking exposure of her magical power. Amanda brought her imagination skidding to a halt.

What a ridiculous train of thought! she chided herself. He is perfectly harmless and is being very helpful.

They emerged into a small open space. Jonathan gestured towards a chair at a sizeable table next to an A3 photocopier, then disappeared into the stacks. Amanda waited in silence, aware of the dust, the artificial atmosphere, the chill. She heard his approaching footsteps, then came his appearance with rolls of paper in his arms.

'This is a map of the area made in 1769 by Dr Indigo Jones.' He leaned across the table and spread out the large sheet of paper. She helpfully held down one corner to stop it scrolling back up.

'He was something of a local explorer and cartographer.' He pointed. 'This is Sunken Madley. Here's the church with the graveyard to the north and, above, the Manor house here, at the edge of the forest. The trees came right up to the back of the knot garden then.' His finger moved to the top of the map and accidentally touched hers. Instantly they both moved their hands apart.

His had been icy cold. Like the dead man's in the Manor bedroom, Amanda thought.

Jonathan unrolled the second map on top of the first. Amanda was careful to hold the corners at the very edges.

'This is an architectural floor plan of the Manor. It is the sort of thing you're after, isn't it? ' His eyes were bright and intense.

'Yes,' Amanda replied in an unintentional whisper. She cleared her throat and repeated clearly, 'Yes.'

He was smoothing out the paper lovingly. 'Look at these exquisite sketches of architectural details. This is from much later though: 1856.

'Now, about hidden passages and spaces,' he continued. 'One way that historians, and indeed treasure hunters, use to find them, is to count the windows from the outside of the house, and then count the windows from the inside and see if the number totalled in each case is the same. Extra windows mean extra, hidden rooms. Back in the 16th century, the priest-hunters worked that out. So architects and builders had to become more ingenious about making secret places. They would look for any structures that could be hollowed out, or spaces that could be utilised for their employers' purposes.'

Jonathan ran a pale, delicate finger along the side of the Manor on the drawing. 'Walls were thick; chimneys were deep. As for ways in, there could be tunnels leading from the house and opening up in the forest. Some secret spaces were so cramped that the occupants died from lack of air ….' He seemed to emphasise the last phrase. Amanda was finding it harder to breathe.

'Would you like photocopies of these?' Jonathan offered.

'Please!'

The machine whirred away while Amanda coughed into her handkerchief.

'Are you all right?' Jonathan asked.

'Dust,' she wheezed. 'Look, my interest is purely academic,' she felt the need to add. 'Or I've watched too many period films about smugglers!'

Amanda suddenly wished she hadn't said that. But Jonathan didn't react. He rolled the photocopies, sealed them with elastic bands and handed them to her.

'Thank you,' Amanda said, breathlessly, 'What do I owe you?'

'That's all right. I've closed the till.'

'I must give you something,' she insisted, aware of the library's slender budget.

'Well … if you like — if you're not too busy, that is — I may be able to find more information on the old microfiche system, and I could bring it to the Snout and Trough one lunchtime. If you could spare the time and if you would be interested …, I would enjoy that.'

'I'd be very interested,' confirmed Amanda. If she had any real reason to feel wary of Jonathan Sheppard, then meeting in the pub was safe enough.

'I'd like to hear more about your craft and the house that you're working on,' he added earnestly.

'Of course,' she answered, 'That would be very nice.' Would it? she wondered. Amanda stood up and gestured away from the desk. 'Is this the way out?'

'Yes. I'll just put these away, and I'll be right behind you.' Amanda wasn't sure she wanted Jonathan Sheppard right behind her.

'I'll find it. Thank you again.'

'The front door key's behind the desk,' he called. She resisted the temptation to run but reached the open air with relief.

Amanda collapsed into the driver's seat of her car and used her inhaler. I'm getting as paranoid as Jessica! she reprimanded herself. He's nice. He's helpful. He's everything a librarian should be. And attractive.

Not nearly as attractive as she'd first thought him, though.

Chapter 29

✍

RYAN FORD

Amanda collected her picnic rug from the boot of the car, and walked down the path onto the playing fields behind Sunken Madley School. There were a few early arrivals getting the best seats in front of the pavilion, or collecting cups of punch or Pimm's from the refreshments stand: the Kemps, the Mazureks and the Whittles. Amanda noticed Miss De Havillande and Miss Armstrong-Witworth, finding seats as far away from Mr Hanley-Page as they could get. Not surprisingly after the altercation in the road by the Manor that morning.

Next, the Patels arrived, the doctors each holding a hand of little Amir while the rest of his family brought up the rear. Here was Mrs Pagely, the librarian with the Sharmas. Joan the postlady and her partner and the Pickersgills had turned up, and Jessica James, enigmatic of expression behind Gucci sunglasses. Clad in cream capris and silk shirt, she was elegantly draping her exquisite form over a lounger next to her mother, Irene James.

Ruth Reiser was the only one who saw Amanda at the edge of the trees, and, knowing she would want some seclusion there, gave her only the most covert of waves.

Amanda had just spread out her tartan rug and was taking off her shoes, when a voice behind her issued a greeting.

'Hello.' She looked up into the face of a tall, sunny-haired stranger, standing beside her, Raybans in hand. He wore a blue t-shirt with beige trousers, and his left middle finger was hooked into the matching jacket slung over his shoulder. Whatever his identity, he was definitely upping the standard of good looks in the village, if only for the day.

'Excuse my forwardness, but may I introduce myself?' he said, with humorous ceremony, 'I'm new to the village.'

'Aha, you're the new Madley Towers owner, the astronaut-rockstar-James Bond we've been hearing so much about,' Amanda replied in the same tone.

He threw his head back and laughed. 'Much more mundane, I'm afraid.' He held out his hand. 'Ryan Ford.'

'Amanda Cadabra.'

'Really?' He reacted as most people did to her uncommon nomenclature.

'Yes, let's not go into it,' she appealed.

'Perhaps not at this moment,' he agreed. 'You see, I'd like to enlist your help. Away from the audience at the pavilion.'

That sounds a bit dodgy, Amanda thought. Aloud she said 'Oh?'

'I wondered if you'd be so kind … as to explain this game to me?' Ryan entreated.

'Cricket?' she expostulated in disbelief.

'Exactly,' he responded earnestly.

Odd, thought Amanda, regarding him carefully. He looked fit and tanned. Maybe ski-ing, rather than field sports, was his thing. Or sky-diving or something equally exotic, as befitted the purse of anyone of sufficient means to afford the outrageous price tag of Madley Towers.

Still, Ryan Ford was charming, in her view. Attractive and with an air of cheerful modesty that Amanda found rather taking.

Her reading was not so urgent that she could not while away a few minutes in his company, giving some tuition on the village's favourite sport. Besides, it might be the only polite way to get to him to leave so she could get her privacy back.

'All right.' She remembered her manners and said, 'Do sit down.' She moved herself and her books to one end of the blanket to make room, and allow for a proprietous gap between them.

'Do you see that well–kept strip of grass there?' said Amanda, pointing.

'Yes,' he nodded, following her finger.

'That's the "pitch". When it gets near the time for the game to begin, an umpire, that means referee, Gordon French, will bring out the stumps. A gate-like thing?' Ryan Ford looked vague. He must have seen ... oh well ... , thought Amanda and continued, 'Three upright poles with slots in the top for two short turned pieces of wood to fit onto. They're called the bails.'

'The bales?' queried Ryan 'As in hay?'

'B-A-I-L-S,' Amanda corrected him, patiently.

'I see. Do go on. There will be a set of stumps at each end of the pitch, you were saying,' he recapped.

'There are — did you really not play this at school?'

He gestured toward the pavilion. 'Not everyone here grew up in England, did they? '

Oh dear, was she somehow being discriminating? Amanda wondered anxiously.

'And some children have health conditions that limit the sports they can participate in,' he added.

Well, Amanda certainly knew that first hand.

'I'm sorry, yes, of course,' she agreed, flushing lightly. She continued 'There are two teams of eleven players.'

'Men?' he offered.

'Well, that's a sticky subject! Madeleine Fleetfoot is playing today because her brother has twisted his ankle, and that has one or two of the old guard in a tizz, but she's every bit as good as he is.'

'I'm sure. The teams …?' Ryan prompted.

'Oh, look!' She pointed towards the pavilion where the visitors were greeting their hosts. 'There's the Romping-in-the-Heye eleven turning up now.'

'Ah, I see,' he said, following the direction of her gesture.

'Well, anyway,' she resumed, 'the two teams take it in turns to bat. The team that is batting will have two batsmen — er, batspersons! — on the field at a time. One standing in front of each set of stumps.'

'Got it,' he said, frowning with effort.

Amanda looked at him incredulously. 'Are you *sure* you've never seen a cricket match?'

'I've been abroad a good deal,' Ryan explained.

She looked at him out of the corners of her eyes. 'Places with no television?'

'Working,' he replied, looking down sorrowfully at the blanket. She supposed uncertainly that, that could account for it. His eyes caught the title of one of Amanda's books. He looked up as she continued, 'The team that isn't batting will have a bowler who throws the ball towards one set of stumps, which is called the "wicket".'

'Wicked?'

'Wick-*et*,' she enunciated.

'OK. Hm, I wonder if I should take notes?' Ryan searched his jacket pockets. 'Oh dear, no paper,' he said with mild frustration.

'Well, I'm sure someone can explain it to you again later. And don't worry if you don't understand it all, first time round. Cricket is complicated. Anyway, the batsman's job is to stop the ball from hitting the wicket by knocking it away.' Her hands grasped an imaginary cricket bat, and she gestured the stroke. 'Once he's fended it off, his next job is to run to the other set of stumps, while his teammate runs across to the wicket.'

'So the two batsmen run towards each other, cross and end up at each other's wickets?' Ryan checked.

'Er… yes, except … well anyway, if they manage to do this without any of the fielders …'

Ryan gestured at the grassy expanse before them. 'They are on the same team as the bowler, I take it?' he interpolated.

'Yes … without the fielders catching the ball or throwing it at the wicket, while the batsmen are running, then the batting team gets a point. It's called a "run",' Amanda finished.

'I see. And at the end of the game, I suppose the team with the most runs is the winner?'

'That's right,' she nodded, approvingly.

'Well, I think I've got it,' Ryan said. looking up at the blue unclouded sky as though trying to see it all his mind's eye, and, at the same time, affording her a view of a handsome profile.

'Oh, and just a couple of other things,' remembered Amanda, returning from her student's distracting appearance to the lesson in hand. 'From when the opening batsman bats to when the last one is out, that's called an "innings". So everyone decides whether the game will consist of one or two innings per team, or a set number of overs'.

'Overs?' queried Ryan, looking mystified.

Good grief! Had the man never heard a cricket score on the news?

'Never heard of overs? Not even on the news? "Middlesex are 174 for 8 and only 3 overs to go" and that sort of thing?'

'Sorry,' he shrugged helplessly.

'Oh, OK, well the bowler bowls six times towards one set of stumps before he changes direction. That's an over,' Amanda explained.

'My goodness, it's very technical,' Ryan remarked, bewilderedly, pushing a hand into his thick straight hair and rubbing his head.

Amanda regretted her scepticism regarding his ignorance of the game. She couldn't hold it against him. It wasn't his fault that he'd gone through life without contact with England's national sport. She said sympathetically, 'Not really. You'll get used to it.

And if you take to it and spend some time at the practice nets, I'm sure the team would love to have another reserve one day.'

'You're very encouraging, Amanda,' he said, but looked doubtful.

Much as she was enjoying Ryan Ford's company, the library volumes were her priority.

'Why don't you go and introduce yourself to the locals at the pavilion?' Amanda suggested.

'I'll do that.' He got up. 'Thank you for the lesson. You're a lucid and engaging teacher, if I may say so.'

'Thank you,' she smiled, enjoying the compliment.

'I hope to see you later,' Ryan said, with every indication of sincerity, returning her smile. 'Oh, by the way, interesting title.' He nodded towards her books. 'Hidey-holed Up.'

'Yes,' she agreed, noncommittally.

'Well, bye for now.'

'Bye,' she said with brief wave. Amanda couldn't help watching him walk nonchalantly towards the pavilion.

'Hmm' said Amanda, thoughtfully. Well, she remarked to herself, he seems nice. Very nice.

He disappeared from view as the trees at the edge of the field obscured his progress. Tempest stalked out from behind a shrub to see if the sandwiches contained anything of interest.

'Probably charms every female he meets,' said Amanda. 'And there's something about him that I can't put my finger on …..'

Tempest twitched his nose at the place where Ryan Ford had sat. Then he planted himself and stared piercingly in the direction the man had headed. Amanda looked at her familiar closely, but Tempest's contempt for humans was so universal that it was difficult for her to judge his opinion.

Amanda, in fact, was not at all sure what to make of Ryan Ford.

Chapter 30

༏

REVENGE

With Ryan Ford out of sight, Amanda was soon so immersed in *Manors Maketh Man* that it took the patter of applause from the pavilion, to bring her attention to the match. The players were walking onto the field. Sunken Madley had won the toss of the coin, and had elected to bat first. The umpires, and Pamela Whittle on the scoreboard, were already in place.

The Romping-in-the-Heye fielders were spreading out into their allotted places. Amanda identified Ashlyn Seedwell, captain of the Sunken Madley eleven and, striding out beside him ... his fellow opening batsman.

Amanda felt her face go red with embarrassment and indignation.

The perfidious wretch! She looked in outrage at Ryan Ford, now in cricket whites and carrying his bat. That comment he'd made, about some children being too ill to do sports, stung. It was as though he'd mocked her. Good thing I'm not a Darkside witch! she thought furiously, or I'm sure I could turn him to ashes with a single glare! — Ashes!

'The Ashes' was the famous prize for the bi-annual Australia-England matches.

'How appropriate would that be?' she said aloud.

Amanda ran over to the scorekeeper.

'Pamela, who is that walking out on our side?'

'Surely you know the captain?'

'No! The other one,' she asked, urgently.

'Oh, that's Ryan Ford. He's a county team member, plays for Middlesex, actually,' Pamela added proudly.

Amanda flushed an even deeper shade. She had just been duped into teaching one of the top cricketers in the country the basics of his game!

'Thanks, Pamela,' she said between gritted teeth.

Amanda concealed her wrath and returned to her blanket. She hugged her knees and stared until ... a mischievous glint appeared in her eyes. It would be easy. So easy. Just the tiniest of spells, the gentlest of nudges. On the first ball being bowled to Ryan to just ben-n-n-nd the ball around his bat and into the wicket. Imagine that! Middlesex's finest, out for a duck, returned in shame to the pavilion without a single run to his name. Sooo easy. She fingered her Pocket-wand.

* * * * *

Ten-year-old Amanda stood in the corner shop. Skinny, spiky-haired, blonde Kevin Buttal, her peer but not her friend, was running his incongruously fat fingers over the chocolate bars, while Mrs Sharma was rustling around in the back, collecting Mrs Buttal's special order case of gourmet mushy peas. He picked up a Milky Bar and put it in the pocket of his combat trousers, looking at Amanda challengingly.

Amanda looked significantly towards the doorway to the rear of the shop. Kevin put the bar back.

'You're a weirdo,' he said venomously.

Amanda raised her chin and looked straight ahead. She chose to regard the word as a badge of her unique intelligence. Kevin looked at her speculatively and tried another weapon.

'My mum says your Granny's just a busybody.'

Amanda's head slowly rotated towards Kevin, as Mrs Sharma came back to the counter.

The children locked eyes.

'Kevin!' said Mrs Sharma sharply. The boy looked up at her with a cherubic smile.

'Yes, Mrs Sharma.'

'Here is your mother's order. Be careful. It's heavy.' Kevin took the bag full of tins from her.

'Thank you, Mrs Sharma.' he said with sing-song politeness, and she turned away to the shelves behind her. Kevin took advantage of her lapse in surveillance to put his tongue out at Amanda and cross his eyes. At that moment Amanda saw that the wedge keeping the shop door open was at the very edge of the wooden frame, only just holding it place. Mindful that she must never use spells against any living creature, Amanda muttered under her breath. The wedge moved forward half an inch, freeing the door. Kevin turned to go and walk through the entrance gap he believed to be still there.

He collided with the heavy wooden door frame with a yelp, dropping his bag and spilling the cans on the floor with a crash and a clatter. Kevin had not been moving at speed, and the damage to his nose was slight. The damage to his esteem, however, was critical. He whipped round to see if Amanda had witnessed his mortifyingly failed exit. She didn't laugh or even smile. But her look of satisfaction was palpable.

'Karma,' said the shop owner succinctly. 'Pick up your tins, and don't come back until you can treat other customers with courtesy.'

Kevin rummaged on the floor, banged the mushy peas into the bag with fury, and ran out of the shop. Amanda felt ripples of empowerment flowing through her veins.

Three days later, Granny came back in from an errand and found Amanda reading an entry in a volume of the *Encyclopaedia Britannica*, on the dining room table.

Amanda looked up with a smile. 'Hello, Granny.'

Granny did not respond in kind. 'Mrs Sharma has been talking to me about Kevin Buttal.'

Amanda became very still.

'I understand that he was rude to you the other day.'

Amanda gazed down at the book 'Yes,' she answered, with a spurious air of preoccupation.

'I also understand that he had an unfortunate accident with the door,' remarked Granny.

Her granddaughter pretended to be absorbed in her reading.

'Amanda, dear,' said Granny seriously.

'Yes.'

'Amanda. Look at me.'

Amanda met Granny's eyes and held her gaze steadily.

'How did the wedge come away from the door?'

Amanda could not lie. She folded her lips then came clean. 'I moved it. Just the tiniest bit!'

'Hm.'

'He wasn't hurt, I promise! I just wanted to teach him a lesson, and Mrs Sharma agreed. She said it was karma because she'd actually heard him being so rude! I didn't use magic on him. I know not to do that, but you never said anything about not using it on door wedges,' Amanda claimed logically.

'That's true,' acknowledged Granny fairly. 'But did you cause harm?'

'No, he just got embarrassed.'

'Did you cause emotional harm?'

Amanda thought. 'Well, it did him good,' she excused herself.

Granny modified the question. 'Did you cause emotional

harm in the short term?'

Amanda sighed. 'I s'pose so.'

'Do you feel good about that, dear?'

'I did at the time,' she replied wistfully.

'Do you now?' asked Granny.

'No,' Amanda admitted quietly.

'Why don't you feel good now?' Granny asked her gently.

Amanda considered then replied regretfully, 'Because I used my power to make someone feel bad.'

'"And with power…",' began Granny.

'…"comes responsibility,"' finished Amanda resignedly.

'Would you do something like that again?'

'No, Granny, I wouldn't.'

'Then it has been a worthwhile lesson. But before we move on … what was it exactly that made you feel so upset?'

'He said something rude about you, Granny!' Amanda said passionately.

'And do you think I would be affected by the opinion of this child and his mother?' asked Granny, making it clear that Mrs Sharma had told her exactly what had been said by Kevin.

Amanda considered. Then shook her head decidedly.

'But you were defending my honour, is that it?'

'Yes,' answered Amanda, relieved that Granny understood. 'And I avenged you,' she added simply.

'I appreciate the sentiment, my dear. Kevin wounded your sense of family pride, and you retaliated. But is that a good reason to use your magical gifts against a Normal?'

Since Granny put it that way … Amanda shook her head. 'No. No, it isn't,' she said levelly.

'Remember this then: A witch does not take revenge.'

Granny had invited the Buttals for tea that Sunday and asked Amanda to bake a cake for the occasion. Mrs Buttal and Granny had a private talk in the kitchen, and, after that, Kevin grew a lot kinder. He ended up owning a home-style accessories shop in Cockfosters a few miles away, and Amanda had repaired a couple of pieces for him. They'd even laughed over the corner shop incident.

But Amanda never forgot Granny's words about that day.

* * * * *

'A witch does not take revenge.' She heard Granny's voice in her memory. Amanda stared longingly at the wicket. Sooo easy to send the ball into the stumps. But alas, she was both too much a Lightside witch and too British to do something that, in every sense, was just not cricket. That did not prevent her from taking impish delight in the thought, however.

As the match began, Amanda's irritation cooled, and she went over their conversation. She had to admit that at no time had Ryan stated ignorance of the game. But he'd grossly misled her. He'd given her an intensely embarrassing moment. On the other hand, it had been entirely private. It was not like he'd made a laughing stock of her in public.

By the time Sunken Madley had got their first fifty runs on the scoreboard, and the captain had been caught out from an overconfident stroke of the bat, Amanda's good nature had won out. At least, to a great extent. It was difficult to suppress an oh-so-secret desire to turn the tables on Ryan Ford if she got the chance. In an entirely Normal way, of course.

Chapter 31

☙

HISTORIES

By the time that Dilip Patel, Neeta and Karan's athletic son, left his family's side to join Ryan on the pitch, Amanda had long felt she was sufficiently recovered to return to her studies.

Amanda unfolded the copy of the map of the village Jonathan had made for her. She saw that the woods had retreated from the back of the Manor since it was built, but there was a still a copse nearby that could shelter an entrance to a tunnel leading into the house.

Next Amanda opened the plan of the Manor house. What about the bedroom to the left of the disappearing-body room? Didn't that seem narrow compared with the other two bedrooms? Could there be a secret room or passage concealed there? Resolving to inspect that chamber, she flicked from book to book, reading about various devices for opening hatches, latches, panels and trapdoors.

Amanda's deliberations were interrupted by a familiar voice.

'A peace offering!' Ryan called ruefully. He was bearing a

cup of Pimm's and a paper plate with cucumber sandwiches on it.

Anything but a bread roll! thought Amanda, remembering the last meal of the cold body on the floor of Peacock.

'I most humbly apologise,' said Ryan inclining his head in a bow then looking at her appealingly. Having earlier noticed the books on the blanket, he gathered that Amanda was of literary bent and hoped she might be placated by a little of the Regency romance hero. 'I do hope you see that it was impossible to resist!'

Amanda recognised his ploy, was unimpressed, but willing to play along. 'Very well,' she said with mock grandeur. 'I accept your apology. However, I shall only concede that it was a *challenge* to resist, rather than impossible.'

'Ahhh, I see; only a lesser mortal would give into it. May this morally inferior specimen be permitted to join you?' He proffered the olive branches of food and drink.

'He may,' she inclined her head, graciously, in a fair imitation of her grandmother.

'Truly, I am sorry,' said Ryan penitently as he sat down, 'but you only get one chance at that sort of thing when you're the new boy. And your tuition was so expert, I couldn't help but be drawn into the lesson, Miss Cadabra. Is it Miss?'

'It is. As befits a schoolmarm!' Amanda replied acerbically, as she selected a sandwich from the plate between them

'I wish my teachers had been like you,' he replied winningly, still trying his best to appease her.

'I expect they were masters, rather than teachers, and it was an all-boys boarding school,' Amanda countered, unmoved, having decided he had been privately educated. Not Eton or Harrow, but the next level down. She bit through the artisan brown bread, soft with the sun-melted butter, and into the crisp, sliced cucumber, savouring the textures and flavours, for a moment transported. His reply brought her back to the blanket.

'No, as a matter of fact, I attended Sunken Madley Primary,' he replied with aplomb. 'My family moved away when I started senior school. And it was neither private nor boarding, I assure you.'

Amanda swallowed her bite of sandwich. 'You lived here?' she asked, amazed, managing not to spray crumbs.

'Yes. And where do you hail from?' he returned.

'Here.' Amanda sampled the Pimm's.

It was Ryan's turn to manifest surprise. 'Either you're much younger than I am, much older — although that seems highly unlikely given your youthful appearance — or wore an invisibility cloak throughout your primary school years.'

Amanda smiled and took her time over another drink from her white plastic cup. 'Not exactly. I was home educated. Not very healthy either so I didn't get out and about all that much.'

'Nothing serious I hope.'

Amanda shifted position, stretching out her legs momentarily then curling them under her. 'Just asthma,' she explained, playing it down. 'More of a nuisance than anything.'

'Amanda Cadabra … Cadabra … your father …?'

'Grandfather.'

'… owns the furniture restoration business.'

'Owned.'

'I'm sorry,' he condoled.

'No, don't be. I feel he's still with me as much as ever.' Until he and Granny ratted! she remembered with annoyance. The wind played with her skirt. She smoothed it back into place.

'So what happened to the business?' Ryan asked.

'I'm it now,' Amanda replied, proudly, inspecting the sandwiches again.

'Well done you,' he said with appreciation. 'Any exciting objet d'art passing through your delicate but skilled hands at the moment?'

'Actually, I'm working on the banister at the Manor.'

'The Manor? Oh, my word. The Dunkley-McVittys?' Ryan asked.

'They sold it a few weeks ago,' Amanda told him.

'Really? I used to play there as a boy. With their son,

Simon. We'd be all over the family pile playing hide and seek in every room, forbidden and otherwise, or out in the garden playing cricket and periodically breaking the windows.'

Amanda's interest was now sharply focused on Ryan's relationship with the Manor. However, she did not want to appear openly curious. She grinned. 'Now that last bit doesn't in the least surprise me!'

Ryan continued, enjoying reminiscing, 'We used to dragoon Nicola too, Simon's sister. She was chums with Jessica James, sitting over there under the yellow and red parasol by the pavilion. Never dreamed when she was all dark frizzy hair and skinny legs that she'd end up as a Burberry model.'

'So you know the house?' asked Amanda, in a casual tone of voice.

'Knew. I expect a lot of changes have been made over the years and the new owners will make more,' he said regretfully. The wind rose unpredictably, seized Amanda's hat and cast it at the foot of the nearest tree. Ryan gallantly retrieved it, but their conversation was at an end.

'Thank you,' she said, receiving her millinery.

'Well, I must get back and mingle with my teammates,' Ryan admitted reluctantly.

'You're doing very well,' Amanda said supportively, with a surreptitious look at the scoreboard.

'Not bad. Doesn't do to be overconfident though.'

Ryan hovered, as though there was something more he wanted to say but was hesitating.

'If you're keen … it would be rather nice if you could make it to the next county match that I'm playing in. Got a couple of spare tickets if you and your partner …? boyfriend …? would like to come along.'

Amanda smiled. 'I have none of either but my best friend Claire might like to keep me company.'

'It's Saturday week. If you're free. My way of making it up to you for … you know.'

'Thank you.'

'I'll be in touch. Word of a cricketer!' he ended merrily.

Ryan Ford walked away, and Amanda put a hand on her chest to calm her heart and breathing. She'd been shocked, embarrassed, charmed and educated in too short a space of time. But her mind was quick to clear, and she saw, above all else, that there were two people, Ryan and Jessica, who were intimately acquainted with the Manor, and that probably Ryan, as well as Miss James, knew a secret way in. Either of them could have gained access to the house, murdered the man she'd found on the floor of the Peacock room and then hidden the body and themselves.

Was either of them the type to kill? Not on the surface. The man was struck on the back of the head. It wouldn't have needed strength, just surprise and resolve. Either of them could have done it.

'Surely not,' Amanda said aloud. 'They both seem so nice … *seem* …'

Chapter 32

૭∼

WARNING

Amanda looked towards the pavilion where Ryan was chatting to Jessica. They made a striking pair, standing together, with his short golden hair close to her raven coiffure.

Jessica, Amanda reflected, had admitted to visiting the Manor recently, and by covert means. Ryan had played there as a boy. And even Jonathan, the lush librarian, had extensive knowledge of the secrets of old houses. Amanda had found their basement meeting creepy but that was probably, she told herself, down to her imagination and asthma.

None of the three seemed the homicidal type. Amanda couldn't picture any of them wielding a heavy object against a defenceless man. Probably they all had alibis anyway. No. It had to have been someone else.

But where did the murderer disappear to? The blood on the man's head had looked quite fresh, even though he was cold to the touch. He couldn't have been dead all that long. And where did the body go?

Amanda's cogitations were interrupted by a new visitor.

Honestly, her quiet boundary retreat was turning out to be busier than Oxford Street on Christmas Eve!

It was Gordon French, the umpire, walking tall even with his stick, grand in stature, with shrewd, kindly eyes, and clad in cricket whites. Although long retired from his headmastership of Sunken Madley School, he still kept a proprietary eye on his village.

'Well, Amanda,' he said by way of friendly greeting, taking off his Panama hat.

'Hello, Mr French,' she smiled, putting aside her Pimm's.

'How do you like the match?' he asked, gesturing towards the pitch.

'It's promising for our team, I think,' answered Amanda.

'Should be, with a county player on our side,' he observed.

'Yes,' she agreed, wryly.

'I noticed that he came over to talk to you a couple of times,' said Mr French.

'Yes, he seems an amiable addition to our community,' she replied, carefully picking her words.

'Indeed, but it's early days, isn't it?' he cautioned. 'It takes time to get to know what people are really like, doesn't it?'

'That's true,' she agreed, wondering where all of this was leading.

'You know, I've always kept an eye on you. And all the more so since your grandparents passed away.'

'I know, and I appreciate it,' Amanda said, sincerely.

'Yes, and I wouldn't be serving either of them,' he said slowly, 'if I didn't put you a little on your guard against … strangers.'

Amanda felt put on the spot and perversely found herself defending Ryan, 'He's not exactly a stranger, though, is he? He grew up here, after all.'

'Not quite.' French tapped his cane on the ground for emphasis. 'He was born in Portsmouth. He only moved here with his parents when he was 9 years old, and when he was 11, they left. We don't know what sort of a person he is now.'

'What do you mean, exactly, Mr French?' she asked,

respectfully.

'Well, for one thing, I don't care for the way that he's been patrolling the village.'

She frowned in bewilderment. 'Patrolling?'

'I saw him only this morning,' enlarged Mr French, 'standing in the side road by the Manor, looking up at it. It seemed very early for a celebrity to be up on a Sunday morning.'

Fancy that, thought Amanda, but diverted French with, 'Maybe he was just reacquainting himself with places he remembers from childhood. He was a friend of the Dunkley-McVitty children.'

'Hm, told you that did he?' he said suspiciously.

'Yes,' Amanda insisted.

'Well, he's not the only one who was wondering about this morning. I saw Jessica James,' he continued, pointing his stick towards the centre of the village, 'walking towards the green at half past six. I wouldn't have thought a model would get out of bed before lunchtime.'

'Oh no, Mr French,' Amanda objected, 'models lead very demanding lives. I know this from my neighbour, Claire, who comes across them in the course of her work. They get up early to exercise, train rigorously. They have to keep in shape. She could have been out for a jog around the green. And Jessica lived here as a child too.'

'And moved away,' French added, as though this were an act of treason. 'I just hope she hasn't got into the wrong crowd. It would break her mother's heart, and goodness knows Irene has had enough to contend with over the years. And that Sheppard fellow, the new bookworms' heart-throb,' he continued, 'what was he up to betimes near the spring? The locals would say you have to be very careful of foreigners.'

'Foreigners? Then what about the Patels? And our spin bowler, who was born in Jamaica? And Iskender who owns the kebab shop? Am I supposed to be on guard against them as well?'

Mr French's eyebrows beetled, and he drew in a portentous

breath. 'The Patel family, Mr Reid and Mr Demir are not Foreigners, Miss Cadabra. They … are Village,' he said severely. 'I'm sure your grandparents would be disappointed to hear you say otherwise.'

'Indeed,' Amanda said hastily, 'Mr French, I didn't mean to imply otherwise in the least. It's just that … well… we can't be suspicious of *everyone*; there must have been plenty of people up and about this morning. It's such a lovely day.'

'Yes, Miss De Havillande was out with her terrier, and so were the other dog walkers, naturally. People who had a *reason* to be out.'

'What about just a nice walk?' suggested Amanda.

'I suppose it's possible,' he conceded unconvinced. 'I saw you at 10 o'clock off in your car to the Manor, but I expect you had a few odds and ends to do. And looking very pretty if I may say so, Amanda. You have a look of your grandmother at times, you know. She was a very handsome woman.'

'Thank you,' said Amanda, happy to see him thawing.

'And I wouldn't be doing less than her memory deserves if I didn't caution you regarding Certain People.'

'I understand.' Amanda nodded. 'And thank you, Mr French.'

So, thought Amanda, means, motive and opportunity. That morning Ryan Ford, Jessica James and Jonathan Sheppard all had the chance to enter the Manor, if they knew how to, which they probably all did, which meant that they had means too. But motive, what motive would they have for laying low the man in the upstairs room? What had the librarian said? …. Treasure-hunters? … Did any of the three need money? Or was it something else in the house? Something incriminating, perhaps? Had the dead man tried to stop them? Was he the 'something incriminating'?

Amanda's presence had been noted by too many people for her to go off before close of play. Finally, the last round of applause signalled time for stumps up and hand-shakes with the inevitable losers. The players were mingling, reviewing, congratulating and commiserating. Amanda glowed with affection for her village, watching the gracious crowd of its inhabitants and their visitors around the pavilion. Then the memory of the body on the floor of the Manor bedroom gushed over her mind like a bucket of iced water.

However strangely Normal and occasionally irritating her fellow Sunken Madleyists seemed to her, they did not deserve to have the stain of murder on their little community. She reached a decision. She went home for a change of clothes, overalls and sponge bag. Amanda Cadabra was planning for a long night.

Chapter 33

❧

LUKE

Amanda, now in dark jeans, trainers, t-shirt, jumper and jacket, returned to the Manor. Tempest appeared promptly from under a hydrangea bush. The light was fading out of the sky, but there was still enough for what she needed to do before nightfall.

Amanda dropped off her supplies just inside the door, checked she had her Ikea pencil, and pocketed the workshop torch. Tempest accompanied her on a tour of the exterior of the Manor, as she counted windows and looked for trapdoors in the adjoining ground. They went further afield, covertly checking neighbouring gardens, discreetly inspecting utility covers in the pavement, going as far as the copse at the edge of the village.

But no joy.

Tempest led the way back to the house. Again, Amanda tapped walls, counted windows, estimated room sizes, inspected the attics, and pressed every knob and boss. She tried twisting each newel post on the stairs, opening every window seat, pulling forward significant-looking books on the library shelves, and peering at chimneys …. Nothing.

Amanda stood leaning on the gallery rail looking down on the hall below, feeling for inspiration. Letting out an impatient huff, she went and sat on the stairs, tired and discouraged. Tempest was walking down past her with his slow dainty gait almost certainly towards the kitchen.

'Look!' demanded Amanda, 'I need help, not food, right now ….' The last word faded to nothing, as she sat very still. The polythene sheet protecting the wall to her left rippled up from the bottom of the stairs, and stopped right next to her.

She felt a distinct chill.

Tempest halted and turned, staring at a spot directly in front of her. At first, there was nothing. Then the air fizzed and broiled until something began to condense into a vague mass. A shape formed before her eyes …. A short figure ….. A child.

It was a boy of about 8 years of age, dressed in ruff, brown velvet doublet and breeches that matched the colour of his hair, and stockings.

He was not entirely opaque but solid enough for Amanda to observe that his rosebud lips were countered by a determined chin, and his grey eyes were regarding her with interest.

'Another ghost!' he said, surprised and less than pleased. 'T'is my hope that you shall be of more use than the others.' He nodded scornfully and put his hands on his hips.

Amanda was taken aback, but Granny and Grandpa had accustomed her to the spirit form of existence.

'Hello,' she managed, in a friendly voice.

'Who are you?' he demanded.

'Amanda,' she replied succinctly. 'Who are you?'

'You know,' said the ghost-boy.

'No,' Amanda contradicted him, 'I don't.'

'Forsooth, you do,' he insisted. 'You called upon me. You said "Luke. I need help."'

'No, I said ….' 'The dead can only help the living if asked,' Granny had told her. 'Yes, you're right,' Amanda hurriedly corrected herself, 'I did. Hello, Luke. Thank you for er …

appearing.'

She moved over, and Luke sat down beside Amanda, still studying her, assessing her value to him.

'Your costume is passing strange, just like unto the others,' he observed critically. 'They weren't of much use.'

'The others?' queried Amanda

'Yes,' Luke stated emphatically. 'Have you seen my Papa and Mama?' He pronounced it 'p-paa and m-maa'.

'I'm afraid not,' answered Amanda, apologetically

'Perhaps you have seen ought of Wilkin?' Luke suggested.

'Your dog?' she hazarded.

Luke looked at her as if she had a screw loose. 'Papa's groom.'

'Oh, I see. Sorry, no, I haven't,' she said, regretfully.

He sighed. 'Neither have I. Not for an age. Papa and Mama are always having accidents. It would surprise me not at all if they had fallen into the Thames. They are most dreadful clumsy, but they *are* my parents, and I *would* like to see them again. Have you come looking for them too?' Luke asked wistfully.

'I *am* looking for someone, and who knows? Perhaps we shall find out something about your parents on the way?'

'You want my help,' he stated with certainty.

'Yes,' conceded Amanda, 'you see, I think someone is hiding in the house, and I would like you to show me where they are.'

'Why should I?' Luke asked, reasonably.

'Because,' — Amanda twisted herself on the stairs and leaned against the banisters to give herself time to think —, 'one of them may be a very bad person.'

This excited Luke. 'A pirate? A heretic?' he asked in awe.

'A murderer,' Amanda answered gravely.

He continued to examine her face. Luke came to a conclusion.

'I will make a bargain with you. An you find my parents, then shall I show you the ghost hiding place.'

Amanda protested at once, 'But I don't know where your

parents are!'

'That's the bargain,' Luke repeated stoically, brushing a speck of dust off one knee.

'But ... I'd need to go to the library!' Amanda objected. 'I can't ask anyone until tomorrow....' But Luke was fading. 'Wait!' Amanda entreated.

Boil ... fizz ... gone.

'Now what?' asked Amanda, in exasperation. Tempest walked towards the kitchen waving his tail like a plume.

'Food, yes I know ... wait ... YOU!' She ran after him. 'You can help me. Tempest, please.'

Tempest eyed her with the same what's-in-it-for-me expression she'd seen on Luke's face, minutes earlier. Amanda investigated the possibilities of the fridge. But it was at the back of a cupboard that she struck gold. The ultimate Tempest bribe.

'Look at thi-is,' she sang to him, showing him the small round tin.

''Caviaaaaar,' she uttered seductively. His eyes lowered to the prize in her hand. 'That's got your attention, hasn't it?'

Tempest climbed onto a kitchen chair, seating himself at the table expectantly.

'OK. Half now, half when the job is done.'

He rumbled a purr, and blinked slowly once, for 'yes'.

Chapter 34

❧

THE HIDEY-HOLE

Amanda opened the caviar, forked out half onto a plate in front of Tempest, then hurried to the bathroom and ran the taps into the tub. She unearthed her sponge bag and poured bubble bath into the stream of hot water. Next Amanda went around the house, switching off the lights, and making sure that every door was open.

When the bath was full, Amanda turned on her torch and extinguished the bathroom light. She disrobed and lowered herself into the fragrant, steaming water. Soon she was relaxing and luxuriating, releasing the tension of the shock of finding a body, the eerie half hour in the stacks, the encounter with the teasing Ryan Ford, the warning from Mr French, and the demands of Luke the Ghost.

Amanda began her meditative inner chant: *Wicc'hudol sihtlak, agertyn widstoz. Peath cathes Tempest fosiglow, me alymdisquez. Wicc'hudol sihtlak…*

And gradually the acute night vision of Tempest became one with her own. Through his eyes, Amanda was in the kitchen, looking at the handle of the fridge door. Tempest was aware she was present with him, and co-operatively began to tour the room. She saw under the appliances and inside the cabinets. He let her examine the tiles, then went out into the hall.

'Upstairs,' she urged him. He climbed the staircase elegantly, past Luke sitting astride the banister by one of the newel posts, watching him idly. Tempest toured Emerald; the bedroom Amanda had leaned out of to call down to Trelawney, then Peacock where she had found the body. He was methodical and thorough, … until Scarlet, the room on the other side of Peacock.

A red quilted four-poster with a nightstand either side stood against the wall on the right. The bed was hung with matching velvet curtains, like the ones at the window opposite the door. To the left, was a tall chest of drawers that stood between the window and the fireplace. The mantelpiece was of stone, adorned with an ornate pewter bowl between candlesticks. Over it hung a large portrait. During the daylight, she'd seen the plaque that identified the armoured hero on the rearing black horse as a Dunkley ancestor.

Tempest stood at the door looking in. Suddenly Amanda saw a tiny dark shape skitter across the floor at lightning speed. Tempest reacted in a flash of feline instinct and plunged after it. He dashed under the bed, but his quarry had frozen breathlessly. Tempest scanned and sniffed …. Mouse. Slowly, he moved in under the four-poster. The tiny creature made a break for it, fleeing towards the nightstand, scrambling up it in a second.

The cat shot out from under the bed, and reached up just too late to grab the mouse, who had gained the curtains and was racing towards the pelmet. Tempest pursued, catching his claws in the aged fabric as it ripped at their scything touch, and lowered him back towards the carpet. The mouse, having gained ground, scratched its way onto the chest of drawers. The cat tore himself free of the drapery and, seeing a corner to cut, leapt onto the dresser. In the split second before the cat made contact, the mouse sprang towards the mantelpiece, landing on a candlestick. It then dived for a barely visible opening, just below the picture frame, pushing a sensitive trigger as it squeezed through. Tempest hurled his much bulkier frame onto the candlestick. It treacherously tipped forwards but remained anchored to a small, square, hinged section of the mantel, leaving the cat hanging indecorously in midair with scrabbling legs. At that moment, a tall strip of the wall on the left of the fireplace grew darker as the panelling swung open just enough for Amanda to see that there was now an entrance.

Tempest lost his hold on the candlestick, dropped, twisting onto his feet and galloped into the newly revealed cavity, but the mouse was nowhere to be found.

'Tempest! Good kitty!'

Amanda rose to full consciousness, reared out of the bath, hastily dried and damply dressed. Dizzy from the hot water and the magic vision, she hurried up the stairs, putting on lights as she went. She had to pause twice on the way for breath, but made it to Scarlet. Amanda pulled the panel door wide open.

'Well done, Tempest,' she praised him fervently.

The space inside was the size of a box room. Judging by the side of the fireplace to the right, it had been at least partially cut into the wall. There was a sleeping bag on a foam mat on the floor, together with evidence of food and drink, jumbled up with crumbled trousers, tops and underwear. Amanda examined it. 'A man's clothing,' she informed her familiar. 'Maybe the man I found on the floor was hiding in here. He came out, and was struck. But how did he get into the house, and why was he here?'

Tempest was deep in the hidden room and poking at a tiny gap in the floor, in the corner by the chimney.

'What have you found there?'

There was a loose flagstone. Except it wasn't. It was plywood, painted and covered with a vinyl tile that mimicked the real deal.

'Hmm,' Amanda said with interest, 'what have we got under here?'

She prised up the pretend stone and exposed a deep hole with a ladder lining it.

'Aha! The way in. Or out.'

Amanda shone her torch inside. All she could see was the ladder running down inside the thickness of the wall and following the line of the chimney.

'OK. You'll have to wait here, Tempest. I'll be back soon.'

Amanda summoned her mask. It was likely dusty down there. She checked for good measure that she had her inhaler. Looking into the shaft, she estimated the distance between the rungs and eased her way onto the ladder. She held on tightly to the sides as she carefully let herself down, counting the stretchers to help her judge the distance she was about to travel.

By the time she reached the bottom, Amanda was sure she was well below the level of the ground floor of the house, even under the cellar. She shone her torch up to see Tempest's head at the top of the shaft, then directed the beam around. There was an opening to her right, the beginning of a tunnel. She followed it, able to smell, even through her mask, that it was musty and mossy. The earth underfoot was compacted, but man-size footprints were just visible going in both directions. The tunnel was shored up with planks of wood that had rotted in places, but other struts were new. Finally, it ended in makeshift stairs of wooden crates. There was a door in the ceiling above. It was latched. She opened it and climbed up and out into the night air. She was inside the copse she'd searched earlier. Just a few feet further in than where she'd stopped looking.

So … that's how the occupant of the hidey-hole had got in and out. But why had he been concealing himself there? How had he known about the tunnel? And where now was his assailant?

Elsewhere in the village, through binoculars and telescope, the lights going on and off at the Manor were being noted, with anxious frustration.

Chapter 35

༄

TEMPESTS

Amanda waited for a few moments, taking in lungfuls of the blessed fresh air. She retraced her steps back up to Tempest, sitting expectantly above in the box room behind the secret panel in Scarlet.

Using her mobile phone, she took photos of the cavity and its contents, the trapdoor and the ladder below. Next, Amanda closed the panel, testing the opening mechanism to see how it worked.

'Tea,' she said decisively. 'And more caviar for you.' She smiled down at her familiar. 'Clever Tempest!' He put up his head to have his chin scratched, and accepted due adoration.

Amanda and Tempest ate and drank at the table.

'Now,' she addressed him, 'maybe whoever killed the man we found came through that tunnel and up the ladder. But they didn't leave the same way because the trapdoor in the copse was locked on the inside.

'Maybe,' she continued, 'they left the house by the front door, or one of the side doors. Although they'd risk the all-seeing eyes of Gordon French. Plus, where did they hide the body? Hm … I wonder.' Amanda went to the stairs.

'Luke. Thank you for the offer, but I've found the ghost's hiding place,' she said breezily.

Luke promptly appeared looking seraphic. 'No, you haven't,' he sing-songed.

'I have,' affirmed Amanda.

'You found one. And not the important one either,' he smiled cheekily.

'So the bargain is still on. I find your parents and you tell me where the hiding place is?'

'Yes,' Luke said, and vanished.

Tempest was absent. Amanda found him curled up asleep on a claret-upholstered Georgian armchair in the library, manifestly exhausted by the night's escapades.

'There's nothing more we can do tonight,' she said to herself and her somnolent familiar. 'If anyone's here, then they know that we are too. Let's go home.'

Amanda picked him up and put him on her shoulder, still sound asleep, collected her bag, went out to the car and home.

Surprisingly, Amanda slept. She dreamt of Granny and Grandpa under a tree in Madley Wood. They welcomed her with hugs. Grandpa gave her an acorn.

She was awakened by the sound of thunder. It was getting light. Amanda got up, dressed, fed Tempest, who was bright-eyed and bushy-tailed, excitedly staring out at the hint of his namesake.

At 9.15 Amanda put on her jacket, pulled up the hood and dashed between the slanting raindrops out to the car. Tempest raced in, planted himself beside her, and off they went. She was waiting outside the library when the staff, first, Mrs Pagely then Jonathan, arrived to open up.

'My word, you're keen!' remarked Mrs Pagely, ushering Amanda in and closing out the wind.

'Good morning, Mrs Pagely. I just wanted to pop in before I start work.'

'Oh yes, you're doing the banister rail at the Manor, aren't you, dear.' Mrs Pagely's diminutive stature accentuated her comfortable frame, and made her appear rounder than she was. It suited her motherly demeanour.

'That's right,' replied Amanda, 'Well, I just wanted to know about the first family who lived there, who had the house built, or their children or grandchildren who lived there. Would there be anything in the archives? Perhaps Jonathan —?' Strangely enough, today, he seemed perfectly normal and harmless. So different from down in the basement the day before.

'Oh, he's busy setting up, dear,' said Mrs Pagely, shuffling off her purple quilted and hooded coat. 'But if it's local history you're interested in, I can help you there. What is it about the family that you want to know?'

'Well, was there a tragedy? Were the owners killed? Parents who left a son behind, perhaps?'

'Hm, now let me think … Yes … there was a story ….' Mrs Pagely hung up her coat and sailed to the history section. 'Under Hertfordshire gentry perhaps? …. Nope. Let's try the biography section.' She ran her finger along the book spines as she searched. 'Not here … what about … the pamphlet section…. It's here somewhere, but … I remember the story. It was a legend in these parts when I was a girl … Sir Henry Dunkley, the second owner, and his lady Mary had gone out to Hatfield in Hertfordshire for the day as guests of the Cecils. The Dunkley's groom was unwell, and Dunkley had driven the carriage there himself.' Suddenly Mrs Pagely spotted a reader and looked around the library. 'Oh, where's Jonathan? Just a moment, Amanda, I'll just issue young Graham his books.'

Amanda waited in suspense, while the librarian scanned and stamped. Finally, she returned from behind the counter.

'Dunkley had driven himself and his wife to Hertfordshire,' continued Mrs Pagely. 'They didn't stand so much on ceremony in those days, I expect, or he was a keen driver — carriages were primitive and the roads were appalling — or else he was involved with Cecil on some secret state business and didn't want any servants around. Who knows? Anyway, coming back at night, a wheel came off the carriage. A storm came on, one horse was lame and the other bolted, but the Dunkleys weren't far from home as the crow flies, so they took the track through the forest.'

The wind was rising outside, flinging the raindrops against the library windowpanes in a quick succession of thuds. The fifty-year-old cedar beside the building was sent into a slow sway from side to side.

'It was dark, and well — much like this! — Oh, Sandra! You out in this?' she called to Ms Cooper.

'I just need … it's all right, I know where to find it,' answered Sandra, making her way into one of the aisles. 'Oo, here it is!'

Mrs Pagely bustled off to serve the publican of the Snout and Trough.

Tempest had insinuated himself into the library, but the villagers were used to his perambulations. He sat a few feet behind Amanda, tucked behind the teen shelf.

'They were close to home …,?' prompted Amanda as the librarian came back to her side.

'Yes, but in the dark and rain and whatnot, they got lost — oh, Jonathan! Good, you're back. You know dear, I think I know where it might be.' She went to a section of the shelf opposite the DVD display stand. 'It's under the author's name, of course. Now, what was it? …. yes, I remember.'

She pulled out a yellowed pamphlet. 'Here it is.' She walked nearer to the window with it and into better light from the lamps above. Amanda followed her.

Mrs Pagely showed her the front cover. 'Do you see? The Legend of the Dunkley Oak by Dorothy Drake. Written in 1858, some 200 years after the event is supposed to have taken place.' She carefully opened it. 'This really should be in the archives where it's temperature controlled. It's probably the only one of its kind …,' she murmured reverently.

'So, … their carriage broke down and they lost their horses in the storm, so they set out on foot …?' Amanda prompted.

'Yes … here …,' Mrs Pagely read aloud from the pamphlet, '"And in the midst of the tempest, Dunkley and his lady strayed from the path through the Wood and there, some two miles from the Old Manor, in a grove of elm trees, stood a mighty oak from the time of the Ancient Forest and there, up in the branches of the tree, had footpads, fleeing from the arm of the law, built a dwelling …"'

'Footpads? Robbers? Living up in the tree? They murdered the Dunkleys?' pre-empted Amanda.

But she was not destined to hear what followed. For at that moment, an overwhelming gust of wind ripped a branch from the cedar next to the building and sent it, with a shocking crash, barrelling into the library window. It punctured the glass, and the resulting blast of air whipped the pamphlet from Mrs Pagely's hands, as the two women ducked. Amanda dared not expose herself by using magic, but threw herself around Mrs Pagely, pulling her back and trying to protect her from the battering ram and flying crystals.

Fortunately, the DVD shelves stopped the branch's progress, but the impact toppled them, in slow motion, onto the floor beside Amanda and the librarian, burying The Legend of the Dunkley Oak in a blanket of display stand, plastic cases and disks.

'Mrs Pagely! Amanda!' Jonathan called, rushing to their aid. They straightened up.

'We're fine, we're fine Jonathan,' Mrs Pagely assured her assistant, peering around. 'Oh, my saints, look at this mess! Right. Jonathan, call the tree surgeon. Never mind looking it up, I've got the number on my phone. You all right, dear?' she asked Amanda solicitously.

'I'm fine,' said Amanda, breathlessly.

'Now you go and sit down in the children's section. Jonathan, get Amanda a glass of water from the cooler.'

'No, no, I can do it,' offered Amanda.

'Sit down and have some of your inhaler,' the librarian insisted.

Mrs Pagely was on the phone in seconds to the tree surgeon, then the insurance company, then the local council.

Amanda sipped at the water, and her breathing returned to normal.

'You'd better go home, Amanda,' Mrs Pagely advised. 'We'll have to close the library until this is sorted out: health and safety. Jonathan, get something to pack around this break in the window, we have to keep the wind and rain out!'

Tempest rubbed against Amanda's legs.

'You knew, didn't you?' she said, stroking him. 'That's why you stayed back behind the teen shelf, isn't it?'

He stretched his neck, cocking his head as if to say, 'Maybe.'

'Well, now what? I have to bring Luke his parents' story, and I still don't know what happened to them.' Tempest stared into her eyes, blinked, then trotted towards the library door and looked back expectantly. To Amanda, it was the 'follow' command. She zipped up her jacket, pulled up her hood and went after him, calling over her shoulder, 'Good luck, Mrs Pagely!'

'You too, dear!'

Chapter 36

ᥱᥲ

INTO THE WOODS

They made a dash for the car and Amanda drove slowly and carefully, wipers a-blur, along the road to Madley Wood. She left the vehicle in the lee of the nearest house, checked her wand was still in her pocket, and resolutely walked to the edge of the trees.

Tempest padded forwards, then sat down to wait. Amanda knew where he was leading her. She stopped, lifted her wand, crossed her arms and bowed her head. Respectfully, she asked the Wood to reveal its secrets.

'*Eoda hydnessdal onhiddeskovra.*'

The air in front of her billowed, the trees appearing to bend around the sides of a distorting bubble. It pulsed three times. And stilled. Amanda felt it was the answer she wanted, and moved on.

The low, grey clouds were grumbling now, but the rain was easing off. Tempest struck out into the heart of the wood, and Amanda's trainers were soon clogged with mud. The thunder quickly built and seemed to be touring the air above the canopy, escorting a party of lightning bolts that fizzled down to the treetops. Amanda ducked instinctively at each crash and flare, but Tempest was in his element. Frisky as a kitten, he bounced ahead, waiting at intervals so as not to force her pace.

As they pushed their way deeper into the Wood, Amanda rubbed her eyes. What was near appeared distant, and what was distant, close. She was seeing as through a fisheye, and there was a mist around her. Amanda recognised these effects as signs of a time boundary; once she crossed the border, she would pass into the Wood of the 16th century and leave the 21st behind her.

She stood, her mouth dry and her breath short, rehearsing the words of the spell to open the portal between the two. This was difficult and dangerous magic. There was an ocean of difference between lines learned in the safety of the dining room, with Granny nearby, and bending time around the real world, in the midst of a hurricane.

But there was something else that made her hesitate: a strong premonition of a wider-reaching, personal risk. The feeling came upon her with searing intensity. Then it was gone. Amanda gave a little shake of her head, dispelling any lingering doubt that she must pronounce the spell.

Amanda planted her feet, held her wand to her heart with both hands, and, looking into space, addressed Lady Time,

'*Hiaedama Tidterm, Hiaedama Tidterm, Ime besidgi wou. Agertyn thaon portow, hond agiftia gonus fripsfar faeryn ento than aer deygas.*'

There was a jolt in Amanda's vision.

Her eyes cleared and showed her that, abruptly, the scene had changed. The modern fir trees were gone. In their place stood beeches and elms. The scent of pine in the air had changed. Tempest trotted on, then stopped near a tall and wide oak with low hanging branches. The rain had intensified again and was falling fatly thought the canopy. One drop splatted onto Amanda's hood and ran into her right eye. She put up her hand to wipe it off, and then, when she looked up … she saw people.

A young couple now stood under the tree. The man, with a small pointed beard and black hair, in doublet and breeches, was holding his cloak over the woman's head as well as his own. They were both dressed in a dark cloth trimmed with bronze brocaded silk, and each had a white ruff at the throat. The lady was pushing her brown hair back into some kind of order and trying to keep the hem of her floor-length skirt off the wet ground. They were laughing at the absurdity of their plight.

Unseen above them, was a makeshift treehouse, unoccupied and balancing perilously in the fracturing and wildly waving branches. The thunder rolled too loudly for them to hear it rip and tear. As Amanda watched helplessly, the supporting branch parted company with its trunk and toppled, house and all, down ....

They never knew what hit them.

'A house fell on them?' said Amanda to Tempest. 'Like the Wicked Witch of the West?' Suddenly the storm was over. Rumbling away into the east. The couple, now transparent, stood up in bewilderment, stepping out from the wreckage and their un-noticed, once-solid selves.

'Oh, my dear! You are all right!' cried the man with relief, taking his wife's hand.

'What a fright was that! We must get home to Luke,' she urged him. 'He will be worried.'

He put his arm about her shoulders. 'Luke adores storms, my love.'

'Yes, but he will be wondering where we could be so late.'

The couple began walking, but it was clear that they were lost and going round in a circle. They spotted Tempest.

'Oh, here is a cat!' exclaimed the woman, bending towards him with her hand held out. 'Can you not show us the way, pusskin?'

Amanda realised that, although they could see Tempest, she was as yet invisible to them. Looking towards the couple, she flicked her wand and pronounced. '*Onlideskovra meh.*'

'Sir! Madame!' she called after them.

They looked around and saw her, with surprise. 'Why

mistress, what make you here in this weather? Are you the woodcutter's daughter?' asked the lady, concerned.

'In a manner of speaking,' Amanda replied vaguely. 'You are Lord and Lady Dunkley, are you not? Will you allow me to lead you home? That is my cat.'

'You know us? Yet I know not your face.' Lady Dunkley peered at Amanda. 'Are you the new witch of the village and this your familiar?' she asked in hushed tones, cupping her hand to her mouth. 'You are full young for it.'

'I know that your son is waiting for you,' Amanda said elusively. 'Come, if it please you,' she added, beckoning them on. They looked at one another doubtfully, then followed.

Chapter 37

❧

Revealed, and the Way Home

Tempest led Amanda and the ghosts of the Dunkleys, by the shortest route, to the Manor. Amanda thought the car would just confuse them. It was something of a hike for her, but it would be worth it to get the information that Luke had promised.

The village of the 16th century was close to the Wood. Amanda had a glimpse of Sunken Madley as it was 400 years ago; thatched cottages, pigs and mud figured prominently, and she was not sorry to reach the Manor and open the unlocked door.

'Luke!' called his mother, hurrying into the hall. He instantly appeared.

'Mamaaa!' he cried, and sailed down the stairs into his parents' arms. Amanda saw that the dustsheets and her materials were gone; the banister, the stairs, panels and furniture glowed with polish.

Once the reunion was over, Amanda cleared her throat and got the attention of the trio.

'Luke has something to tell me, and then I have something to tell all three of you.'

'What have you done, Luke?' Dunkley asked his son, regarding him with suspicion.

'Nothing, Papa,' Luke replied innocently, 'but I struck a bargain with this lady that, if she found you, I would reveal a secret of the house.'

'Which secret?" enquired his father, sternly. Luke stood on tiptoe, and Dunkley bent down to allow his son to whisper in his ear. Dunkley's face cleared and he appeared satisfied. 'Ah, that one. Very well.'

Luke stood to attention and addressed himself to Amanda, 'Open the chest by the wall'.

Amanda looked around and saw the wooden seat she'd collapsed onto yesterday.

'This one?' she asked, pointing.

'Yes,' Luke confirmed.

She went to the chest saying, 'It's just full of old blankets', and pulled up the seat. Momentarily, Amanda had forgotten that she had gone back in time. But sure enough, the box was as packed with them as it would be 400 years on.

'Lift them out,' Luke instructed. She took them out in two armfuls. 'Reach inside. Feel in the middle of the sides of the chest. You'll find two catches. Release them, and you'll find everything that you are seeking,' said Luke mischievously. 'You have my word upon it.'

Amanda bent to look inside.

'And what did you want to tell us?' interrupted Lady Dunkley, curiously.

At once Amanda straightened up and took a deep breath.

'Ah, well … this may come a bit of surprise. But … you see ….' She told them the year from which she had come and the name of the current head of government. '… And the monarch now is Queen Elizabeth II.'

'But how …?' Lady Dunkley shook her head in bewilderment.

'You're dead, you see,' Amanda said gently, 'I'm not sure

how it was with Luke, but you and your husband … died in the forest.'

'Died?' uttered the shocked Lady Dunkley.

'Footpads!' exclaimed Sir Henry in disgust.

'No,' said Amanda.

'What then?'

She didn't see any other way to say it but baldy: 'A house fell on you.'

'A house in the forest?' marvelled Dunkley. 'Was the storm so terrible that it lifted a house?'

'It was a tree house,' Amanda explained, 'in the branches above the oak where you'd stopped and sheltered from the storm.'

Dunkley absorbed the startling news. He reasoned, 'But hold. Why have we remained bound to this earthly realm?'

'I think it is because you have been looking for Luke, but you couldn't leave the forest.'

'And I have been looking for you and Mama, but I could not leave the house!' added Luke.

'On the bright side of things,' said Amanda positively, 'now that you are all together again, you can join your friends and the rest of your family.'

'In paradise?' asked Lady Dunkley, anxiously.

Amanda smiled. 'I believe so. You are ready to go?'

'Indeed, we are,' Dunkley assured her, putting his arms around his wife and son.

'Before we leave,' said Lady Dunkley, who had something further on her mind, 'what of our Catholic friends, whom we concealed here?'

'They are most likely waiting for you,' Amanda said reassuringly 'But no one is persecuted in England now. We have Catholics in Parliament and universities and not just Catholics; Jews and er … Musulmen.'

'How is this?' asked Lady Dunkley, in wonderment.

'I'm sure that where you are going someone will explain it to you,' replied Amanda patiently.

'And witches?' asked her husband with interest.

'I don't know if there are any in Parliament, but witches have the protection of the law as much as anyone else now.'

'And what of …?' began Dunkley but his wife interrupted him affectionately,

'I think it is time we were on our way.'

Opening the portal was advanced magic, and Amanda wondered if she could pull it off with her first ever attempt. '*Agertyn* …,' she began, but there was no need. While she stood with wand raised, a tall, glowing, opaque glassy pane appeared a few inches off the ground and, with a decisive hum, slid open. Bright light shone out of it. The Dunkleys looked into it excitedly then back at Amanda.

'You *are* a witch!' exclaimed Lady Dunkley.

'A good one, I promise,' Amanda assured her.

'Indeed you are, mistress,' said Dunkley. 'For you have brought us back to our son, and now, I believe that you are sending us home,'

Luke stroked Tempest goodbye, then stood up straight.

'Thank you for your great service, mistress,' he said looking up at Amanda then bowing.

'And thank you for yours, Luke,' she returned, curtseying as best she could. Suddenly she remembered something that happened the day before, just after Trelawney had left, 'Oh and thank you for closing the front door that day when I left it open. I felt someone was keeping me safe.'

Luke look puzzled. 'T'was not I, mistress. It must be another of the ghosts,' he said cheerily. It must have been Granny or Grandpa, Amanda concluded, as Luke bade her, 'Farewell.'

'Until we meet again,' said his mother.

Dunkley nodded. 'Farewell.'

'Goodbye,' answered Amanda.

The three turned, stepped inside and the door closed behind them. Suddenly all was silent and ordinary daylight. The rain had stopped. The dustsheets were in place. A prosaic roll of masking tape lay on the bottom step, next to a spare packet of polythene. Amanda released an audible sigh, staring at the empty hall, trying to take in what had happened in the last hour and that she was back, and safe.

It dawned on her: the enormity of what she had accomplished. She had actually time-travelled. She had reunited spirit Luke, trapped in this house, with his parents, who had been caught in the forest. And she had sent them on their way. Jubilation replaced disorientation. She longed to tell Granny and Grandpa. If only they were here. Never mind. It was time to celebrate.

Amanda had forgotten the premonition she had had in the Wood. But when she had disturbed the boundary between her time and the past, somewhere far to the West, in a once ancient kingdom, something had stirred. Only the faintest ripple had passed through Amanda. Senara and Perran felt it, and heeded it anxiously. Their granddaughter, however, was too elated by her success to give it so much as a passing thought.

'Well, now, Tempest.' She rubbed the fur behind his ears. 'A good morning's work. Time for tea and then ... the chest!

Chapter 38

ↄ

THE EPERGNE

Amanda looked wistfully at the banister, waiting for its first coat of industrial stripper. Her life as a furniture restorer had been so simple that she felt a twinge of nostalgia. However, she had to admit that the last thirty-six hours had been among the liveliest and most stimulating of her life.

Amanda turned her attention to the wooden box by the wall. As a precaution, Amanda patted her pocket to make sure her wand was still there. She wasn't sure what she was going to find while following Luke's instructions.

With Tempest beside her, Amanda knelt and opened the chest. It was as full of old blankets as before, though of more recent date than the last ones she had moved. This time, however, she levitated them out to avoid the dust and exertion. Witch and familiar inspected the smooth wood interior.

'Aha, there they are!' said Amanda, as she spotted the catches in the cedar. She reached in and fiddled with them until she felt something give.

The floor of the chest sank slightly. She stood up, put one

leg in and pressed the base with her foot.

It swung down, and Tempest daintily hopped onto the deep top step. Followed by Amanda, flashlight in hand, he descended some wooden stairs until they were level with, what she estimated, was the cellar floor.

She flashed her torch around. Instantly she heard a shriek as the beam lit up two wide eyes and a hand wielding a large, ornate silver vase.

'Who are you?' simultaneously uttered Amanda and the armed woman standing before her.

'What are you doing here'? asked Amanda emphatically, 'more to the point!'

The woman retreated further into the passage behind her, over bedding, food, drink, and Louis Vuitton luggage.

'What are you doing with that vase? Have you stolen it?' demanded Amanda.

'It's not a vase; it's an epergne, and certainly not!' responded the woman, in well-bred tones of indignation.

'Then, what are you …,' began Amanda. But a faint light of recognition was dawning, of this tall, thin woman, with short blonde hair, aquiline nose, narrow lips and grey contemptuous eyes. She wasn't the sort Amanda would cross paths with often, but once or twice in the post office ….

'Mrs Dunkley-McVitty? Caroline Dunkley-McVitty?'

'No!' denied the woman, 'I'm … Victoria….'

'Victoria who?' Amanda pursued.

'Er … Beckham!' answered the woman, snatching at the first name that occurred to her.

'Mrs *Dunkley*,' Amanda said firmly but with concern, 'what on earth are you doing here? Are you all right?'

'I'm hiding from my husband — he's after me,' claimed Caroline Dunkley dramatically.

Amanda gently approached the agitated women. 'I see. Put that down; I'm not going to hurt you. I want to help,' she said.

Mrs Dunkley slackened her grasp on the epergne and placed

it in on the ground. But as Amanda's torch tracked its progress, she saw that a patch of the decorated silver surface was covered with a dark red pigment. Mrs Dunkley followed Amanda's glance and lunged for the vase. Amanda whipped it away, took a step back and looked at Caroline suspiciously. If the discolouration wasn't blood, why was the woman so anxious to get it back?

'That's my property!' Mrs Dunkley raised her voice.

'I think it might be evidence,' corrected Amanda.

Caroline changed her aggressive tack. 'No, you've got it all wrong. It was an accident.'

'OK, I'm listening,' said Amanda, cautiously, moving a hand to her pocket and undoing the top of the Ikea pencil that held her wand, just in case.

'You have to believe me,' said Caroline, plaintively.

'Try me,' Amanda encouraged her, reserving judgement.

'It was *him*,' Caroline began, her nostrils quivering with indignation, 'it was *all* him, he spent it all, gambled it away; I had to have the paintings copied so I could sell the originals. We couldn't keep up the house. It was mortgaged to the hilt. Our friends, our families avoided us because he kept asking them for money.'

She spread her hands helplessly. 'We had to sell up. It took a year to find a buyer. Gregory said he was going to live with his cousin in Iceland. I thought he'd gone. I knew the money from the sale of the Manor would barely cover the debts, and that once it was handed over, I'd have nowhere to go. So I had this little place built.' She gestured around the dim passage, as her attitude changed from beseeching to pride in what she regarded as her ingenuity. 'I got a carpenter who I used to know to come from Scotland,' she added.

'What did the carpenter think you wanted it for?' asked Amanda, curiously.

'I told him we'd fallen on hard times and were going to open the house to the public as a local museum, and I explained that a secret passage would add value,' she said smugly, pressing her thin lips into the semblance of a smile.

'I see,' said Amanda, noncommittally.

'So after it was sold I camped down here until I could work out what to do, where to go. I was expecting to inherit some money from Great Aunt Mildred, to make a new start somewhere, but she's inconsiderately hung on and hung on in the face of all the doctor's fatal predictions!'

Amanda wasn't feeling complimentary towards the selfish creature before her. 'So you're the infestation of mice that has been raiding the kitchen?'

'Well, I've only used what I needed,' Caroline returned defensively.

'It's *stealing*, Caroline! — Oh, but never mind that. Tell me what happened with the va — epergne'.

'It was a day or so after I thought the Poveys had left. I heard them talking about a trip to Provence, but then I heard noises. *You*, I expect,' she said, scornfully.

'Yes. Go on,' said Amanda.

'I heard the front door close when you left, so I knew you'd gone. And then, early yesterday morning, while it was still barely light, I heard sounds upstairs. It had to be a burglar. Who else could be here? He could be stealing the silver in Peacock. It's all that's left of the family fortune but it's locked in a valuable piece of furniture and we lost the key! I thought a thief was up there jimmying the lock. So I sneaked up, saw a silhouette of a man closing the curtains, and bashed him on the head!'

'And then you saw that it wa—'

'Yes. Gregory! I never meant to do it,' protested Caroline. 'I was protecting the house from, er … someone breaking and entering! I was defending the Manor. But when I realised … I was horrified. Much as I abhorred the despicable toad, I would never have —'

'Yes, yes, go on,' prompted Amanda, unsympathetically.

'I covered him up for decency's sake, but then I heard you, so I hid next door in Scarlet, and that's when I saw the open panel, and I knew! I knew he'd been hiding in the house too! Graceless rogue!'

Amanda interrupted, 'So then I found him … then the bell went … I went into Emerald and it was while I was in there —'

'Yes, fortunately, the hullabaloo outside of hoots and shouting covered me while I dragged his poor dead body back into Scarlet. And I hid it and myself behind the panel.'

'Good grief,' said Amanda. 'Well, the body isn't there now!'

'No, I brought it down here as soon as you left,' Caroline declared complacently.

Amanda shone the torch around. 'Well, *where* is the body?' she demanded.

'I thought it would start to smell, so I put it in the cellar,' Caroline replied matter-of-factly, with a toss of her blonde hair.

'What part of the house is this then?' asked Amanda, looking down the passage.

'This is a partitioned-off part of the cellar.'

'You got his body back upstairs through the wooden chest and then back down through the kitchen to the cellar?' Amanda marvelled at the woman's strength, manhandling a body all that way.

'No, through the sliding door in the wall I had built, in case I had to get into the main part of the cellar,' said Caroline confidently.

Amanda sighed. 'Of course, you did. So … what made you think the body would keep … er, fresher in that part of the cellar than this?'

'Oh, I put it in the freezer,' Caroline answered, as though stating the obvious. Amanda momentarily visualised the one in the kitchen with four small drawers. 'The freezer?'

'The chest freezer,' clarified Mrs Dunkley.

'When were you going to tell the police?' asked Amanda, severely.

'I needed time to thiiiink,' wailed Caroline. 'I was on private property, I do admit that. And besides, who was going to believe me?'

'The penalty for trespass is a lot less than the penalty for concealing what might be considered murder, Mrs Dunkley!'

'I didn't *mean* to murder him!' she insisted.

Amanda exhaled and gathered her patience. 'All right, if you want me to help you at all, we'll go to the cellar together now, and you can show me.'

Caroline nodded and beckoned. 'Over here!'

Chapter 39

༄

SPELLS

Caroline Dunkley moved further into the passage, the original stone wall of the cellar on her right and a new, wood sheeting barrier to her left. She put her finger into an indentation in the latter and lifted a latch. With a little effort, she pushed aside a three-foot width of wall, which comprised a sliding door. This created an entrance into the main space of the cellar.

Amanda followed her warily, stepping out between two piles of cardboard containers. Caroline switched on the light, and pointed to a stack of crates and cases of bottles on top of a white chest freezer. But the piles of containers, balancing on top of the large appliance, looked lopsided. As Amanda and Caroline approached, it became clear that the lid was propped open with the toe of a shoe.

'Oh, heavens!' cried Mrs Dunkley, and hastily pulled the cases off the appliance. Amanda aided with the discreet help of her wand. Instantly, the lid flew up, revealing the enraged countenance of what could only be Mr Gregory Dunkley-McVitty.

'What the …!' he uttered with a short invective at the sight of his less-than-beloved wife.

'You're alive!' she uttered, relief briefly overcoming loathing.

'No thanks to that burglar! What are you doing here?' he blustered, as the women helped him out of the freezer.

'Er … well … I … you see,' Caroline Dunkley began nervously.

'Mrs Dunkley-McVitty has been —' Amanda began, but Gregory cut her short and, ignoring her, addressed himself to his wife.

'Did you catch him? Damn burglar! Seven feet tall, attacked me upstairs in Scarlet. A rare old tussle we had, I can tell you, until he overcame me with an illegal move and laid me out cold! Woke up with a blasted headache, feeling like billy-oh, in some damn coalhole. Couldn't see a thing. Slept it orf, then heard a noise, sat up with a start and hit my head in the dark. Out cold again, then woke up incarcerated in that thing!' He looked at Amanda. 'Who the dickens are you?' he demanded rudely.

'Amanda,' she replied with composure. 'I'm working in the house. You're lucky you weren't frozen.'

'Switched it orf to save electricity ages ago. New occupants hadn't used it yet. Knew it was our freezer; recognised the brand of ice cream left inside. Bit in the bottom of the tub. I ate it. Tasted ghastly. Then I was running out of air. Couldn't get the lid up but managed to get it open a crack and wedge my shoe in there.'

'Why didn't you call for help?' asked Amanda.

Gregory Dunkley became vague. 'Thought whoever answered might get the wrong idea. Called Dennis on my phone. Left a message. Only person I could trust. Well, thank heavens you found me …' The narrative flow suddenly ebbed. 'Hang on … just *hang* on a minute … how did you know where to find me?' Dunkley was growing suspicious of his rescuers. 'And what are you doing in this house? You said you were going to stay with your Great Aunt Mildred.'

'First, you tell me what *you* were doing upstairs,' insisted his wife, regarding him narrowly.

'Please, don't tell us that you were checking on the house, Mr Dunkley,' interjected Amanda, 'because we found your er … digs upstairs.'

He waved his hand in annoyance, 'Oh, very well! It was all *her* fault. The money we had was nowhere near enough to support her champagne and caviar habit, and the flat in London and her pathetic horses that fell over in every race they ran —'

'Don't you *dare* say a word against Crumpet and Muffintop. With all you'd been spending on Grand Montecarlo!' responded Mrs Dunkley, furiously. 'That's his precious online casino,' she added hotly for Amanda's benefit.

'Never mind that now,' Amanda interrupted. 'Go on.'

Dunkley addressed himself to Amanda as to the more sympathetic of his magistrates. 'So I thought I'd just tuck myself away to get some breathing space. Work out the next move and so on. I thought she was moving to New Zealand on the strength of her Great Aunt's Mildred's bequest. That's what she told me. Not that I had any reason to believe a word that came out that perfidious —'

Amanda stemmed the flow with, 'Yes, Mr Dunkley. But it took you a year to sell the house. You had plenty —'

'I had nowhere to go,' he insisted, 'so I got a chum who owed me a favour, to loosen up that panel upstairs, and there I was all right and tight. Then the other night, I remembered we used to keep a couple of bits and bobs of silver in one of the cupboards in Peacock. Thought I might be able to fiddle the lock somehow. Thought I'd better close the curtains and then …'

He leaned towards his wife. 'It was *you*, wasn't it?' he said with acute distaste. 'You who bashed me over the head. Getting your revenge, at last. Trying to lay me out like a corpse!'

'It was a mistake,' intervened Amanda. 'She thought you were a burglar.' Over the sound of Dunkley spluttering with incredulity, she continued, 'Now. Let's get out of this cellar. After you, Mrs Dunkley, Mr Dunkley.' Amanda wanted them in front her, where she could see them.

She saw a brief glance flicker between the couple like static. Gregory laboured up the stairs with a hand to his head, groaning. Caroline followed slowly behind him. Near the top, quick as a flash, the Dunkleys hurled themselves through the door to the kitchen. They slammed it shut in Amanda's face, and locked it.

But Amanda was prepared. She already had her hand on her wand. She whipped it forth, whispered, '*Agertyn!*' and the door flew open. Amanda ran out and flicked her wand towards the couple fleeing for the front door.

'*Understeppith!*' she said quickly under her breath.

Immediately, they fell over their own feet and one another, and landed in an untidy pile of Dunkleys, cursing Amanda and one another. She hid her wand.

'Who *are* you? What did you just do to us?' Caroline asked, accusingly. The Dunkleys looked up furiously at her from the hall rug, united in their new-found dislike of Amanda.

'What have you got behind your back? A gun?' cried Gregory.

'Who am I? Someone who can stop you leaving, who can hand you over to the police, or let you go.'

The pair glanced towards the front door.

'Don't even think about it,' said Amanda levelly. She gestured toward the library. Bruised and unsteady, the pair got up and went reluctantly into the book-lined room.

Amanda had formulated a plan, but she needed a brief breathing space to execute part of it, and short of tying up the Dunkleys, which they would understandably resist, there was only one course of action that she could think of. First, she would need to distract them.

'Sit down,' she instructed them.

Mr Dunkley reared up to his full medium height and took a position by the fireplace.

'Both of you,' commanded Amanda.

'Oh, sit down, Greg, for heaven's sake, you idiot!' ordered his wife impatiently.

Dunkley plumped himself down, and Amanda stood before them. 'Now,' she said. 'Mr Dunkley, you said you left a message with your friend. Is he on his way?' Gregory checked his phone.

'Yes,' he replied.

'And about time,' Caroline added derisively, 'the useless, sponging pile of ...'

Amanda put up a hand to cork the tirade 'How long till he gets here?' she asked. Dunkley calculated.

'About ten minutes,' he replied, sullenly.

'Look again,' said Amanda. 'And you'd better check too, Mrs Dunkley.'

They were both looking at the phone when Amanda took out her wand again, this time cupped in her palm.

Chapter 40

୧ఎ

CONFESSIONS

'*Aestendivath!*' Amanda whispered and froze the Dunkleys immobile, side by side like naughty children '*Cusslaepeth.*'

They slumped back into a dreamless sleep.

Now was her chance. Amanda went down to Caroline's cellar. A few minutes later she was back in the library. She found two sheets of paper and, using a dictation spell, set two pens writing. When the documents were ready, Amanda directed her wand at Caroline and Gregory.

'*Awaecdenath.*'

The couple roused themselves into an upright position, Dunkley rubbing his eyes, as Amanda hid her wand.

'What happened there?' he demanded.

'If you both agree to my terms,' Amanda began sternly, ignoring his question, 'I will allow you to leave here. If you refuse, I will call the police. I will give them photographic evidence that I have just obtained, and emailed to myself and someone one else, proving your unlawful entry and trespass. As well as fraud in your case, Mr Dunkley — the valuable paintings you included in the sale that are actually copies — and assault in your case, Mrs Dunkley.' They bridled.

'What do you want us to do?' asked Mrs Dunkley, grudgingly.

'You will each sign a confession that I will keep on file with my solicitor,' replied Amanda. 'If you should ever be seen anywhere near this house, or anything untoward should befall me, it will find itself in the hands of the authorities.'

The pair were silent. Mrs Dunkley's chin was up, attempting to gather the shreds of her lost dignity. 'Very well,' she conceded.

Mr Dunkley was sitting with hunched shoulders and arms folded. 'Humph!' he uttered by way of assent.

'You will, furthermore,' Amanda continued, 'work together to find some way to reimburse the new owners of the Manor for what you have stolen, beginning with a hamper that you will send the Poveys to wish them well in their new home, in one month from now.'

'Work *together*!' exclaimed Caroline Dunkley, horrified, leaning away from her spouse. 'With him?'

'With *her*?' replied her husband, revolted.

'I'd rather work with a tarantula!' opined Caroline.

'I'd rather work with a scorpion,' he countered. 'Oh. Sorry. I *will* be!'

'Yes, you're used to that, aren't you?' returned his wife, 'Your blackmailing moron of a mafia cousin who went and stashed the goose that lays the golden egg and then got himself knocked down by a bu—'

'Have you no respect for the dead, you harpy?'

'Enough!' interrupted Amanda forcefully. 'Both of you. Have *you* no respect, Mr Dunkley for your father's esteemed name? My grandfather always spoke of him as a fine, good-hearted gentleman, as did everyone in the village. If you have any decency, you will sign this, get away from here and try to make amends before you compromise your family's reputation.'

Dunkley grunted emphatically, which Amanda took as

acquiescence. She offered each of them a pen. They went to the desk, signed the papers, and slammed or threw the offending writing implements down beside the documents.

'You'd better hurry and gather your belongings,' advised Amanda. 'I assume they are your belongings and not looted from the surrounding shops. Like the kebabs,' she added, pointedly.

Mr Dunkley muttered, 'I don't even like foreign food.'

Amanda handed out refuse sacks. She sent Gregory upstairs, dispatched Caroline to the cellar and locked the door behind her. Amanda was climbing the stairs to check on Dunkley's progress, when she heard yowling, screeching and yelling from Scarlet. She dashed in to find Dunkley, half out of the window and with Tempest pinned to his head. The cat's teeth were sunk into Dunkley's left ear, it's back feet competing for a grip on the right ear, and claws in his collar.

'My ears! My ears!' shrieked Dunkley, hopping on the one leg still inside the room.

'*Entednion*,' ordered Amanda quietly. The enchantment pulled the man's leg back out of the window. He landed on a sheet-covered commode with a yelp.

Amanda put a locking spell on the window with the word '*luxera*'. Tempest released his hold on Gregory, with the satisfaction of a job well done. She kept a strict watch on Dunkley, who eyed her resentfully at intervals while he packed his bedding, food and clothes into the plastic sacks she'd given him.

By the time she escorted him back downstairs, Mrs Dunkley was banging on the cellar door. Amanda released her, and she immediately recommenced railing at her husband:

'This is all your fault, you know! Draining the family fortune away year by year with your gambling! I should never have married you. Your mother —'

'Don't you *dare* say a word against Mumsy!' he shouted.

'I'll say whatever I like!' she riposted.

'Stop it!' ordered Amanda. 'Remember you have to work together if you want to get out and keep out of trouble. Isn't it worth it to stay out of prison?' she reasoned, but to no avail.

'I've been in prison! For the last twenty years married to —'
began Dunkley.

'Here's your friend!' Amanda interrupted him. Thankfully,
a battered red Alfa Romeo was drawing up outside.

'About time too, you —' started Mrs Dunkley

'Oh, get out of here, the pair of you,' said Amanda in
exasperation. The couple, bearing their stuffed bin bags, struggled
towards the front door.

Amanda had a sudden flash of inspiration. What if she
could make them be nice to each other? It would wear off all too
soon, but it might be enough to give them a start in formulating
a plan to repay their unwitting hosts.

Amanda tapped her wand towards each of them, whispering
'*Beoth deraweg toa agweilia.*' Dunkley, as though he couldn't
stop himself, opened the door and held it back for his wife. She
stared at Dunkley in astonishment but thanked him with helpless
politeness as she tottered through it and out to the waiting car.

Chapter 41

৽

THE APPOINTMENT

Amanda shook her head in disbelief as she made sure the Alfa Romeo removed the repulsive couple. Tempest felt it was lunchtime.

'I need lunch too,' said Amanda, 'and I'd have a drink if I didn't have an afternoon's work ahead of me. But I need to find some way to concentrate. Tea first, then I'm going to clean up the hidey-holes. And I'll make sure I leave enough DNA behind, in case I need it at a later date!'

Tempest sat in front of her, fixing her with his livid, yellow stare.

'Fine,' Amanda surrendered. 'I'll feed you first.'

Predictably, the Dunkley-Mcvittys had left behind their crisp packets, sweet wrappers, kebab boxes and empty bottles. Amanda dealt with it all, and then washed her hands thoroughly. She went to the corner shop to get a snack and ate it out in the fresh air of the Manor garden.

Finally, she could get back to work. In overalls, work boots, thick gloves and a mask, Amanda began the noisome process of applying stripper, letting it activate, boil and bubble, brushing off the old polish, and scraping it away where it clung obstinately. She took her time and did a thorough job, rinsing with methylated spirits and reapplying the stripper until one flight and two newel posts were innocent of all traces of old polish, paint splashes and dirt.

It was too late to start another section of banister. 'That's enough!' Amanda declared. 'Time for a blessed hot bath, sleep, dinner, a film and more sleep.'

Amanda cleared up for the day, checked her wand was still safely in her pocket and left the house. Tempest stepped slowly into the passenger seat of the car, exhausted too by the day's events. Within twenty minutes, Amanda was dozing in hot water under a comforting blanket of bubbles. Her last thought was that she had never cast a spell on a living thing before, and today, in the space of an afternoon, she had cast four ... and each time she had been conscious of the slightest vibration in the air ... it was probably nothing ... nothing ... at ... all....

At 5.15 Tempest pushed the bathroom door open and burbled.

'Ghhhrhhm,' muttered Amanda.

'Grrrrllllllrrrlllll,' said Tempest informatively.

'Hmm ... I'll fid you s'n,' she slurred sleepily. Tempest stood up, paws on the rim of the bath.

'Rrlllrlrlrlr,' he insisted. Amanda opened one eye.

'What?'

Tempest jumped onto the windowsill and pushed Amanda's watch onto the laundry basket.

'Don't do tha to my wa ... Time? ... The time? ...What? ....' She sat up and leaned forward to look at her watch. '5.20. So? ... I've got nothing on this eve — oh good grief! Trelawney! 6 o'clock. Nooooo! Tempest, you're a treasure.'

Amanda raised herself from the bath. 'What does he want? Hope he swallowed the story I gave him at the door of the Manor yesterday, about being busy and out of breath, and whatever other yarn I spun him.'

A few minutes later, Amanda stood in her bedroom, viewing the clothes in her wardrobe. Tempest was kneading the quilt ready for a protracted doze.

'I expect we'll have dinner … but it's business, so I don't want to look like I've made too much effort.' She chose jeans, boots, a blue silk shirt and a casual jacket. She added a woollen scarf. It was, after all, May in England; there was no point in taking chances and catching a chill. 'It's usually warm in the Sinner's Rue, so I won't need a coat.'

Amanda arrived punctually and walked in under the familiar inn sign depicting a red-robed, well-endowed young woman with flowing flaxen locks. She was soulfully casting her eyes upward and clutching a yellow-petalled herb. Amanda ducked beneath a low-pitched oak lintel and saw that Trelawney was already there. He was seated in a corner away from the bar and facing the door that she'd come in through. He saw her along the sight line from his table, past the spacious, double-fronted fireplace with its blazing logs. Trelawney rose politely as Amanda approached, greeted her and complimented her on the local hostelry.

'What can I get you?' he offered.

'Oh, no, that's all right,' replied Amanda, digging for her purse.

'No,' Trelawney insisted, 'it's the least I can do after interrupting your work yesterday, and calling without an appointment.'

Too right, thought Amanda. 'Then hot chocolate, please,' she said aloud.

'Don't feel you need to go teetotal because I must,' said Trelawney considerately.

'No, really, that's exactly what I would like.' She also felt the need to keep her wits about her. He went to the bar and ordered.

'They'll bring it,' he said, returning to the table, and thinking about how to break the ice. 'So … charming name.'

'Mine?'

'Yes, that too, but I mean the pub.'

'Oh, Sinner's Rue. It's a flower.'

'Really?'

'Yes. You see, in the old days, suicides weren't allowed to have a grave in the churchyard because it was consecrated ground, and they were regarded as personae non gratae. Instead, they were buried at a crossroads. Like where this pub stands. Anyway, it was said that a certain flower would grow there at the burial site. People believed that suicides were sinners, like the lady in the pub sign, who, in the afterlife, would regret — rue — what they'd done, and so they called the flower Sinner's Rue.'

He looked sympathetic, but she gestured around the homely tavern, with its rosy, 500-year-old bricks and mellowed wood beams. Even the empty tables and chairs basked in the warmth of firelight, amidst friendly chatter. Amanda continued:

'And now there's a pub here, where people can come and eat, drink and be merry, and hopefully put their troubles behind them, long enough to feel that life is worth living,' she ended with a grin.

'What a wonderful way to finish the story,' Trelawney said, cheered. 'Just one question about ye olde village inn, and not as a policeman,' he added with a smile.

'All right then,' she answered, warily.

'How does the pub afford to have a fire burning all hours, with the only logs it's legal to burn in these parts costing a fiver a bag? Whenever I've been in here, it's been crackling away, day or night.'

'Ah,' Amanda dimpled. 'Did you see the hopper outside? It looks like a wooden wheelie bin.'

'I did.'

'Well, that's for the villagers to contribute wood. Most people have gardens with waste branches and twigs, and the dog walkers pick up a stick or two in the woods, and there are other generous souls who contribute so ... you see?'

'Hmm. No regulations?'

'Well …,' she said slowly. 'Whenever there's any inspection, they get the lawful briquettes out. But you didn't hear that from me!' Amanda added, playfully.

'Quite. This conversation never took place,' he said solemnly. 'Now that that mystery is solved … have you had dinner?'

'No. Shall we?' They consulted the menu.

'Braughing Sausages?' Trelawney queried.

'Not "Braw-ing", "Braffing",' she corrected his pronunciation. 'We're on the Hertfordshire border here, and this pub celebrates the county food. The Braughings have made sausages since way, way back in —'

'The 12th century?' he guessed.

'1954!'

'Well, that's a good half-century. It just about qualifies as a tradition,' he said good-naturedly.

'There is a legend associated with the village of Braughing to make up for it though, if you'd like to hear it,' she offered, grinning.

'Oh, please do. I can hardly wait,' Thomas enjoined whole-heartedly.

'It was 1571,' Amanda commenced, 'and the village was mourning Matthew Wall as his coffin was carried to the graveyard. Suddenly, one of the bearers slipped on some autumn leaves, and the coffin fell to the ground with an almighty thud. All at once they heard a knocking noise from inside the coffin. They prised it open, and there was Matthew Wall alive and well, having been rudely, but fortunately, awakened from unconsciousness by the collision of his coffin with the earth.'

'Lucky Matthew!' commented Trelawney.

'Indeed. He went on to marry his sweetheart and live for another glorious twenty-four years. In his will, he left some money to pay for the bells to be rung on that day every year, and, perversely enough, for the children to sweep the lane where "the incident had occurred", as you'd say in police-speak.'

Trelawney applauded. 'You are an excellent storyteller,' he complimented her. Amanda wondered if that was a trait policemen particularly appreciated.

'I have to have the sausages now,' he said, 'with mashed potatoes.'

'I'll join you,' said Amanda.

Trelawney went to the bar. 'Bangers and Mash for two, please.'

'I'm paying for pudding,' Amanda insisted.

They continued to talk about food and local customs, while the courses arrived and they ate. The occasional person recognised Amanda, nodded, waved or said hello, and scrutinised Thomas. Joan the post-lady was paying him particular attention.

Trelawney leaned closer to Amanda and asked in low tones, 'Why is that lady looking me over like I'm a bull at the county fair.'

'Oh, that's Joan. She's considering your potential as a suitable match for the Cadabra estate owner,' she said, saucily.

'Ah,' he responded, doubtfully. 'Not sure she considers that I measure up.'

'Well, you're not Village, you see,' Amanda explained kindly.

'So that's my crime?' he asked, fatalistically shaking his head.

'Yes, and one has to serve long years as a village resident to atone!'

'I have been duly cautioned, madame.'

There was a pause.

Amanda had been enjoying his company, albeit somewhat guardedly. However, she was curious about why he'd come to see her, and wanted to find a way to make the transition from pleasure to business easy.

'Perhaps you'd like to share with me now, what it is that brought you here yesterday,' she tentatively invited him, with a smile.

'Hm. Not really. I've been having such a nice time this evening. But yes, I do have something I would like you to know. It may be nothing at all momentous.'

'About the incident, the family accident?'

'Yes.' Trelawney rotated his teacup in its saucer slightly, while he prepared himself. He looked up at Amanda. 'The day before yesterday,' he began,' there was an anonymous call made to the station. Detective Constable Nancarrow took it. She thinks it was a woman's voice. The caller said it had been troubling her for many years and she was putting her affairs in order. She was old and she wanted this off her mind. Thirty years ago, she was driving along a road in Cornwall near a cliff. She was behind a minibus full of people.'

'My family?'

'So it would seem. She saw it swerve off the road and, right in the path of her car, was a patch of black ice. It was a misty day, but not cold, not anywhere nearly cold enough for that. She managed to dodge around it but was so shaken up that she didn't see what became of the van. It was only later, much later, that she heard about the accident. She didn't want to get dragged into giving evidence or insurance business so she didn't report it.'

'Black ice in September?' asked Amanda, curiously.

'Yes,' Trelawney confirmed. Then he added casually, 'Can you think of any explanation?'

Chapter 42

༄

PUZZLE AND INNOCENCE

'Witchcraft,' pronounced Granny, 'is a private affair. Being a witch is like having a birthmark on your ... er ... leg, dear. It's not something you show to just anyone.'

Seven-year-old Amanda sat thoughtfully at the dining table, with her hands folded in her lap, and considered this new piece of information gravely.

'What if it's summer and I don't have socks on. Wouldn't they be able to see it?'

'Above the knee, Amanda, dear,' Granny said patiently.

'Oh.'

'Now, there may, in the course of your life,' Senara continued carefully, 'appear certain persons who may develop curiosity about you and your grandparents. You will now begin learning how to deflect their interest and to depress pretention.'

Amanda looked uncertain.

'You do not, thankfully, have much to do with the village children, so this kind of inappropriate enquiry is most likely to come from an adult, who may invite your confidence. They may, for example, say, "Is there something about your family that you would like to tell me?"'

'And I say "no"?' asked Amanda.

'First,' asserted Granny, 'and better still, you must master The Innocent Gaze.'

'But I am innocent. I haven't committed any criminal acts,' replied Amanda accurately.

'Indeed you are innocent, and your expression should reflect that, and your absolute conviction of it,' said Granny rousingly. 'Now… open your eyes … and look straight into mine. No, don't stretch them wide, just … yes, that's better, dear. Now add an air of confusion, bewilderment at their question ….'

* * * * *

'Can you think of any explanation?' asked Trelawney.

Amanda, snapping back into the present from the archives of her memory, assumed a guileless, perplexed demeanour as perfected under Granny's coaching. Of course, she could think of an explanation. Although her grandparents had, at all times, avoided discussing it, Amanda had long considered that the use of Darkside magic was a strong contender. However, she intended to keep Trelawney well away from that line of enquiry. She had to come up with some plausible ideas for an ordinary explanation.

'Freak weather conditions?' Amanda suggested. 'Could it have been a particularly sheltered hollow where the sun wasn't reaching? I don't know how hot or cold it was that day; I expect you could find out. Could there have been a chemical spillage from a lorry, shortly before it happened? Would the company responsible have been obliged to have recorded it for health and safety …. Erm … I don't really know much about police work, I'm afraid.' Amanda was implying, ever so subtly she hoped, that it wasn't her job to come up with a solution to his puzzle.

'I was just asking,' Trelawney said apologetically, 'in case your creative mind may be able to see something we more mundane Mr Plods could not.' Grandpa had introduced Amanda to the Noddy books by Enid Blyton. Toy Town's ponderous policeman was certainly no model for Trelawney.

'Well, it is an enigma,' admitted Amanda, 'and I will think about it. The woman's account of what she saw, raises more questions than it answers.'

'Yes. It explains why the vehicle containing your relations may have gone off the road, but … no more than that,' he said tactfully.

'Not what killed them, you mean?' asked Amanda, coming to the point.

'Yes,' Trelawney confirmed.

'Because they didn't die from the injuries they received as a result of the accident.'

'Precisely.'

'Well,' said Amanda becoming brisk. 'It's not something I like to dwell on, to be honest. I couldn't have had better parents than the truly grand ones I've had.' She shrugged. 'I didn't know or remember the others. The inheritance from any of them is immaterial. I'm so well provided for. How many people my age own a house and a little land and a workshop, a thriving business, have few outgoings and the means to earn a living in a way that is satisfying?' Amanda added firmly, 'I've put the incident behind me, if ever it was in front of me.'

Trelawney accepted this rebuttal, saying, 'Would you prefer it if I didn't come to see you unless I have something concrete to report?'

Oddly, Amanda knew at once, that she wouldn't prefer it at all. However annoyingly timed and sometimes challenging his visits were, for some reason, that she did not stop to fathom, she would miss them.

'Hm ... no ... I think, on consideration,' she responded more mildly, 'that if Chief Inspector Hogarth thought it important for you to keep an eye on me, then I respect his judgement, just as my grandparents did.'

Trelawney nodded.

'Very well then. I shall see you soon. And if any other explanation of any kind at all occurs to you, however outlandish it might seem to the average person, I hope you will share it with me. It can be off the record, if you're worried about being regarded as too bizarre,' he said, smiling kindly.

Bizarre! What was he implying? Supernatural? It was all too close for comfort. Amanda became formal.

'Inspector, I was three at the time. That day I was probably playing with Lego and learning Baa Baa Black Sheep. I really have no idea what happened.'

Trelawney nodded acceptance of her calling an end to the subject.

'Of course. Well, I must be on my way.' He stood up and put on his raincoat. 'Thank you for your delightful company. And I'm sorry about the temporary blight on the evening,' he said, warmly.

'Perhaps that's the explanation: temporary blight,' she suggested cheekily.

'Thank you, Miss Cadabra,' he replied with feigned solemnity, pulling out his notebook and pretending to write her remark down. 'Duly noted!'

Amanda chuckled. The air was cleared. She walked him companionably to his silver Ford Mondeo. There, Thomas turned to Amanda and said, 'You have my card. The offer still stands: if there's anything you need help with or want to talk over, then contact me. See you soon.'

They shook hands

'See you soon,' echoed Amanda.

Thomas got into the car and wound down the window.

'Safe journey,' she said, with a smile.

Waving, Trelawney drove down the road, the Manor in the background. And that's why she saw it. On the ground floor of the house, a light had flashed.

Chapter 43

❧

SURPRISE, SURPRISE

Could the Poveys be back? Amanda wondered. Had the Dunkley-McVittys been so audacious as to return? She almost called after Trelawney to stop. But the light she'd seen in the Manor had gone. And what if he started asking questions about the house? No, she would deal with this herself. Whoever was there was making a mockery of her caretakership of the Manor.

Amanda flicked up the top of the Ikea pencil wand-holder in her jacket. She made her way by the shadows through the graveyard to the house. No lights. The walls were so thick that it was impossible to detect any sound through them. She looked in at the front ground-floor windows. Softly, Amanda stole to the front entrance and put her ear to it ....

All quiet.

She put the key in the lock and turned it as silently as possible, eased open the door and stood listening ....

There was someone upstairs. She could sense, more than hear, it.

Was this foolhardy? What if she had to use magic to defend

herself? Should she risk exposure? There was more at stake here than the flying jam pot test from Aunt Amelia.

Her station cut off any intruder from exiting through the front of the house, or using the stairs unseen. Where could she hide to keep watch? She crept over to the chest, raised the lid, silently levitated the blankets and lowered them into the shadows under a console table.

Amanda reached inside and released the catches. But as she pushed the base, the chest creaked loudly, letting a shriek rip through the house, and the bottom clattered open. She got inside hurriedly, stood on the steps, pulled down the lid leaving just enough gap for her to see out of.

In the streetlight coming in through a small window at the front of the house, a figure appeared at the library door. It stealthed across to the drawing room. Whoever it was, knew better than to switch on the light again, and all Amanda could detect at first was a darker silhouette against the gloom. Then she made out the helmet of a bobbed hairstyle. Black leggings and top defined a lissom figure that she'd seen twice over the weekend.

Jessica either hadn't believed that Amanda would search for her bracelet, or finding it had become a matter of urgency. The model crossed the hall, heading towards the library. Amanda raised herself quietly out of the box.

'Jessica,' she said softly, so as not to alarm her. The model spun round. 'It's OK, it's me, Amanda!'

'Oh, thank goodness!' Jessica sighed.

'Why didn't you trust me?' asked Amanda, 'I was going to look for your bracelet.'

'I felt awful for involving you. And I can retrace my steps; I know where to look. But let's not draw attention, all right?'

'Yes, be careful how you use your torch,' Amanda urged her. 'I saw it from the road.'

'Really? I was lucky it was you who spotted it then, I guess.'

'Never mind. Now I'm here, we can search together. Wait,' said Amanda, pausing as an urgent question occurred to her, 'how did you get in?'

Jessica was reticent.

'Tell me! If you want me to help you,' Amanda insisted.

'All right. There's a pitched roof above the front side porch. If you climb onto it, you can swing a triangular section of the half-timbering inwards, and then crawl across to the — I'll show you later. Can we please not waste time?' Jessica begged.

'OK,' agreed Amanda. 'Let's be methodi… what's that?'

There was a hollow clanking in the kitchen. A click, a squeal and a thud. The women switched off their torches and got behind the open door. Amanda squinted through the jamb. The kitchen was spacious with units lining the right-hand wall, a scrubbed pine table in the middle, and on the left, cupboards either side of the chimney that housed a substantial set of ovens. Right now, Amanda could only see what was in the faint light coming through the glass in the door to the garden. Most of the room was in pitch darkness.

Amanda and Jessica strained their ears. Simultaneously their heads turned. Muted, hesitant footsteps were treading into the hall. A light flashed around and briefly reflected off the mirror there. Amanda caught a glimpse of blonde hair on the top of a man's form. Ryan. Of course. Amanda had guessed that the two village VIPs were an item. He'd obviously come to Jessica's aid and was looking for her bracelet too.

Amanda exhaled and came out from behind the kitchen-hall door.

'Ryan!' she whispered. 'It's OK. Jessica's already here. We can all look together,'

'Jessica?' he whispered. The model joined them.

'Ryan?' she said.

Amanda opened her mouth to demand an explanation of how he had entered the house. But before they could exchange any more conversation, the three fell silent. There was a sound coming from above and behind them: a shuffling that ended by the landing.

They looked up, eyes wide.

A creak and a muted tap later, insufficiently careful footsteps, set the lower flight of the staircase loudly proclaiming its warped treads. Amanda fired a beam of light at the stranger's head.

'Jonathan!'

'Amanda?'

'What are you doing here?' she demanded, aghast.

'Jonathan!' cried Jessica in accents of joy and relief, as she propelled herself forward into his arms.

'What?' uttered Amanda, staring in disbelief at the couple she was tactlessly spotlighting. 'Jonathan is the er…?'

Jessica turned a rapturous face towards her new friend.

'Yes. You will keep our secret, won't you, darling Amanda?' she pleaded.

''Well … of course, it's just that I assumed ….' She looked at Ryan.

'What?' he asked, puzzled.

'Well, that you and Jessica —'

'Oh no!' he said, in mildly horrified accents, then realising he may have sounded rude, hastily added, 'I mean, don't get me wrong, we've been pals since the year dot, and Jessica's the best, but honestly, no … we're really not —'

'Then why are you here?' she asked persistently. 'You're not a special constable, are you?

'No, I … what's that?'

'Nothing. Now tell me!' she insisted, her patience fraying. 'How did you get …' Amanda heard it too.

There was a suggestion of a scraping noise in the porch. Oh no, thought Amanda, not another intruder, surely? She hadn't had explanations from the two men yet.

The grating sound was followed by a mechanical sighing groan moving up the side of the Manor. Four pairs of eyes stared in the direction of the sound, and four torches clicked off. Jessica and Ryan looked at one another.

'The turret?' they said, simultaneously.

'The turret is solid, purely ornamental, isn't it?' queried Jonathan doubtfully.

'We thought so,' replied Jessica.

'How do you get to it?' Amanda asked urgently.

Ryan answered, 'No access on the ground floor. Only from upstairs.' He set his foot on the bottom tread. Jessica put out a hand to stop him.

'I'll go first; I know where the creaky loose boards are, or where they used to be.' Ryan followed, with Amanda and Jonathan in their footprints. As they approached the top of the stairs, Amanda thought she saw, in the light through the open curtains, a movement of the window seat in Emerald.

She clamped Jonathan's shoulder. He, in turn, stopped the other two dead in their tracks.

There came thuds against the wood as though something was stuck. They tiptoed in quickly and stood at a distance from the source of the sound. Whoever was in the window-seat, was having trouble getting out. They moved cautiously over to it. Ryan dropped to his knees and tried the various planks that made up the structure. Suddenly the front panel came free, and Ryan reached in and grabbed the arm of the intruder. It belonged to a short, slim figure, whom he slid along the floor of the room and into the beams from three torches. Amanda pulled off the stranger's balaclava.

Jessica gasped.

'Mum?' Irene James, her enduringly elegant figure, clothed in black, shook off the startled Ryan and stood up, brushing herself down.

'What are you doing here?' demanded her shocked daughter.

'Mrs James?' enquired Ryan.

'Irene?' asked Jonathan, her tenant.

'Good grief!' exclaimed Amanda, in relieved annoyance. 'This place is like Piccadilly Circus! Mrs James! What are you doing entering this house? Please explain yourself.'

Before Irene could answer, Jessica interrupted.

'Mum,' she said, her astonishment was rapidly turning into embarrassment. 'How did you find out about Jonathan and me and the Manor?

Amanda had no intention of letting a mother-daughter conference take precedence over Irene's answering her own pressing questions.

'First, Mrs James, I would like you to tell me — ' But again Amanda was forestalled by Jessica.

'You shouldn't be here, Mum I can handle this mysel...'

The noise from the turret was back, but now it was at the top of the structure. The five fell silent, Amanda in mounting frustration, and padded to the bedroom door and out into the gallery. Amanda flicked a beam along the passage, but it was clear. A sudden squeak from the door at the end drew her light to the handle, which was unmistakably turning.

Amanda switched off her torch, and withdrew with the others into the shadow of Scarlet. They heard the sigh of the door along the rug, shoes treading carefully with long pauses between the footfalls. The figure leaned on the banister, level with Scarlet. The five pounced, grabbing and pulling the tall stranger to the ground. They aimed their torches at his face as he struggled and spluttered.

'Gordon!' came Irene James' cry of concern.

'Mr French?' Amanda almost dropped her torch in disbelief. They released their flustered captive, who quickly straightened his clothing once they had helped him to his feet.

Amanda's strained patience broke.

'No! This is enough,' she declared, asserting her authority. 'I am in charge of this house. And if any of you want to get out of here without me calling the police, and reporting the lot of you for trespass, you will each explain, right now, what you are doing on Mr and Mrs Poveys' property!'

Chapter 44

ଏ୬

LOST LOVE

'Except you, of course, Jessica. I know why you're here,' Amanda said in a calmer tone. 'And er ... you, Jonathan. But you Mr French? And Irene?' She turned to each of them. 'And you, Ryan?' she asked, accusingly. But French had gone to Irene's side.

'Are you all right?' he asked her anxiously, 'You shouldn't be doing these things ... what if —'

'I'm perfectly fine, Gordon,' replied Irene firmly. 'I remembered it all very well, I promise you. As well as you do.'

'Mr French!' Amanda said inexorably.

He led Irene to the edge of the bed so they could sit down and recover, although Jessica's mother seemed to be full of life and thoroughly enjoying herself. Ryan spoke up.

'Let's go into the library; we can close the shutters and make it pretty light-tight and discuss this in comfort. What do you say?'

'Very well,' agreed Amanda. 'Shall we make tea?' she suggested, with a hint of uncharacteristic sarcasm.

They migrated to the ground floor, blacked out the windows and turned on the desk lamp. Amanda was pleased and not entirely surprised to find Tempest curled up in his current favourite chair, refusing to have anything to do with the unseemly brouhaha. Gordon and Irene sat together on the sofa.

'Mr French, now will you please explain what you are doing here?' Amanda asked as politely as she could. He looked at Irene, they smiled, and she nodded.

'Many, many years ago,' he began, 'I fell in love with a young lady in the village. She was just 16, and her family felt that she was too young for boys. Irene's mother ...'

Irene took over, '... was a maid here, and a very bright woman with an eye for detail. It was she who found the entrance to the turret that Gordon came up, and the way in that I used that comes out at the window seat in Emerald. And so this is where we used to meet,' said Irene, fondly glancing at her former swain, 'coming in from different directions and different entrances, during the occasional evening when the Dunkleys were out at a party.'

Her voice slowed and took on a regretful note. 'And then ...'

'... I was called up for national service. I went away for eighteen months,' Gordon said sadly. 'Of course, I came back when I could, but we were both very young, especially Irene —'

'I fell for someone else,' said Irene candidly. 'Harry and I got married and then later...'

'I met my Elsie,' said Gordon, 'and we put it all behind us. Almost.'

'You see,' continued Irene, 'while we were still dating, Gordon had saved up and bought me a present for my seventeenth birthday. I used to make a point of wearing it when ... we were together... and the last time before he had to report for training ... I lost it. It was a pendant ... his grandmother had left it to him to give one day to his bride.'

Irene shook her head and looked into her lap. 'I felt awful but what could I do? I couldn't tell my mother. I used any excuse I could to get into the house, offering to help her clean so I could search but … I never found it. But I never forgot either. I always knew that if anyone discovered it, they could use it to cause Gordon a lot of trouble, being a teacher at the school and then headmaster and a pillar of the community.

'Then the Poveys bought the place,' she said eagerly, 'and I heard they were away for a fortnight, and that you were working here during the day. So I thought, finally, here's my chance. To make things safe for Gordon once and for all.'

He turned to her. ' You did this for me?'

'Of course. I've never forgotten what we had. I know I was only a silly teenager, but you were always so good to me. I was such a fool. When Harry came with his charm and his car and his cash, and my parents thinking he was such a good prospect for me, well …. But you were happy with your Elsie, and I was always glad of that. I was sorry when she passedWhile Jessica, Jonathan and Ryan sat in respectful silence, Amanda's brain was busy. She was seeing some pieces of two mysteries falling into place. First of all, Miss De Havillande had told her about hauntings in the Manor long ago when she was young. Of course, Amanda realised now that it had been the teenage Gordon and Irene.

Furthermore, Luke had spoken of 'other ghosts'. To him, the living appeared as spirits. Why, the Manor had been full of them over time: The Dunkleys, The Poveys, Irene, Gordon, Jonathan and Jessica, none of whom, presumably, could see him and be of 'much use' to him in finding his parents.

Meanwhile, it was as though Gordon and Irene were telling their story to one another, with no one else in the room.

'Well,' Gordon sighed, 'that was two years ago, and after I started getting over losing Elsie, and making a sort of routine for myself, I started thinking about you again. I wanted to ask you to tea, or however they do things these days, but somehow … I couldn't get up the nerve, and then, as you say, the Poveys left the Manor empty, and I thought, if could get the pendant back and give it to you, it would be a gesture that might mean something.'

'That means a lot to me, Gordon; just that you wanted to.

And it's enough. Even if we don't find it, because I don't think it's to be found.'

'Yes … it is,' he stated quietly.

'It is?' asked Amanda.

'Yes,' Gordon said with certainty.

'You know where it is?' asked Irene in amazement.

'I do. You see … it wasn't in the house at all. The gardener hid it. He'd known my grandparents, knew what that pendant was and what it meant to us, and he intended to give it to me rather than to you, because he didn't want to cause you embarrassment. But I didn't come back in time. He was retiring to Norfolk, and he put a note through my parents' door while I was away on national service, telling me where he'd left it. But then I came back, and there was never a chance to retrieve it, and then I was away at college and came back to teach here. I couldn't risk being seen skulking around the Manor; what would people have thought? And then … well … I retired, and I had nothing to lose and everything to gain.' He put his hand over Irene's. She gave him a glowing smile.

'I hope you're going to put us all out of our misery,' she said impishly. Mr French looked at Amanda.

'May I lead the way?' he asked deferentially.

'Please do,' said Amanda. 'I expect we all want to go, do we?' The group murmured eager assent. 'Lights off, then. Let's not advertise this midnight party on Poveys property to the neighbourhood. Oh, and on the way, I want to see how you both got in, thank you very much,' she added firmly.

Gordon and Irene grinned conspiratorially like two teenagers. Irene went to the side door that led onto another part of the hall. She opened it and pointed downwards. The walls of the porch formed an arc. The floor was a complicated arrangement of tiles, and, by torchlight, Irene showed them where there was a large circle in the pattern. She pushed a brick at the bottom of the wall and the circle dipped slightly. She put pressure on one side of it and it tipped up into a recess just big enough for a slender person to fit in. Amanda shone her torch down to see aged wooden stairs. She'd attend to this later.

'OK. Thank you, Irene. Gordon, how did you get inside the Manor?'

He walked confidently to the back door. They paused while Amanda hastily carried out Mrs Povey's instructions on how to unlock it and applied the correct key. Checking that no one else was around, they crept out into the garden. Gordon halted at a spot close to the flowerbed, that lined the left-hand wall, and was mostly buried by laurels. He took a penknife from his pocket and bent over to wriggle a blade under a paving slab. Finally, his fingers could get a purchase and he heaved it up. Beneath the stone was a drop that led to a tunnel. Amanda leaned in. 'Good grief,' she said, disconcertedly, 'this house is more labyrinth than manor. It's so riddled with cavities, it's a miracle it stands up!'

'Yes, er … well, anyway, this particular way in leads to the bottom of the turret,' Gordon explained, 'and there's a dumbwaiter arrangement to get to the top.'

'All right. Thank you, Mr French,' she said, mollified.

'And now!' Jessica urged Gordon. 'Where is the pendant?'

He nodded. 'I'll need some water.'

'There's a watering can by the kitchen door,' said Amanda helpfully.

'I'll get it,' offered Jonathan, eager to have some part in the action, and vanished into the house.

'It wasn't the crown jewels,' said Gordon, 'just what my young grandfather could afford to give my grandmother on their anniversary. It probably cost a pretty penny in those days, and I daresay he had to save up for it'. While they waited for Jonathan, Gordon kept them in suspense about the hiding place of the trinket, like a magician about to disclose the secret of his star turn.

Jonathan returned a few minutes later with a brimming container. Gordon took it with thanks and walked to the fountain in the middle of the garden. He leaned over and shone his torch on the inside of the ornamental stone bowl. Then he slowly and carefully poured in the water, feeling inside the rim every few trickles.

'There's a mark,' he whispered. 'You have to get the water level dead on it …. There! Now! Look at the bottom of the fountain.'

They directed their torch beams downwards, to see that it was constructed of marble-faced bricks. 'The weight of precisely this amount of water frees a mechanism that allows this.' He grasped the bowl and turned it anti-clockwise. They heard it grinding protestingly, as a rectangle of stone was pushed out from the base. They knelt around it and there, in a hollow in the block, was a piece of disintegrating sacking, tied with gardener's twine. Gordon took it out and gave it to Irene.

'For you, my dear. Then, now and always.'

Irene unwrapped the packet in the beam of her daughter's flashlight, and there it was, tarnished but still glowing, a yellow gold heart, and, set in an etched starburst, a sapphire with a circle of diamond chips around it. She stood with it in her hand, looking first at the necklace and next, overcome with emotion, at her sweetheart.

Ryan moved the basin back, and the brick retreated into place. The young people discreetly walked into the house, leaving Irene and Gordon to their moment. Amanda looked back to see their two silhouettes becoming one.

Chapter 45

❧

THE FINDING SPELL

Amanda, Ryan, Jessica and Jonathan returned to the library, somewhat subdued after the intensity of the scene they had just witnessed between their elders. They plonked themselves down on the sofa and chairs, but Amanda immediately bounced back up.

'Right. I think some tea would help us all,' she said brightly. Jonathan followed into the kitchen.

'Anything I can do to help?' he offered.

'That's kind of you, Jonathan,' said Amanda, surprised.

'Well, I also wanted the chance to say sorry.'

'For what?' she asked.

'Mrs Pagely told me about your asthma. I would never have taken you down into the library archives if I'd known; I'd have brought the maps upstairs to you.' His remorse seemed sincere.

'That's all right,' she said, 'but yes I did feel … out of sorts in that … basement.'

'Oh, I don't blame you, Amanda. Quite apart from the dust and everything, it's a strange place. Got quite a history. I'll tell you about it some time.'

'Yes, do. But right now we have some more recent history to deal with.'

By the time the kettle was boiled, the tea had brewed, milk added and the mugs and sugar were on the library table, Gordon and Irene were back, and they were all again assembled.

'Mum?' asked Jessica, tentatively.

'Yes, darling?'

'Diamonds and sapphires?'

'Yes, where do you think I got the inspiration for your bracelet, my little Ice Princess?' Irene teased her daughter affectionately. They grinned at one another, showing a startling family likeness.

'I'm happy for you both. Truly,' said Jessica sincerely.

'I know, my honey, but it doesn't solve your problem, does it?' replied her mother sympathetically.

'Let's all search,' suggested Jessica. 'We can divide up the house into sections, and each of us can begin in a different place and move round systematically. That way, we each cover the whole of the Manor. That's six minds and six pairs of eyes. Agreed?'

They earnestly concurred.

'After the tea break then,' said Amanda.

'Any biscuits?' asked Gordon. As unintentional hostess, Amanda headed for the kitchen. She wondered at what point mass trespassing had turned into a tea party. He called after her, 'If you've got any Hobnobs ....'

They closed the curtains and shutters in each room before switching on any lights by which to search. Even with four experienced secret-passage-finders, pressing and pulling, twisting and prodding any surface likely to open a hatch, they drew a blank. It was 3 o'clock in the morning, and they were back, exhausted, in the library with another tea tray.

'What now?' asked Jessica listlessly.

'Yes,' said Jonathan anxiously.

'I have an idea,' said Amanda, who'd been turning a plan

over in her head, during the last half hour of the search. Five faces turned expectantly towards her. 'I have a technique. It might be worth trying.'

'You can try voodoo as far as I'm concerned,' said Jessica, 'if it helps get the thing back.'

'Not exactly voodoo. It's … well never mind, but I'll need something from you, Jessica. Do you have a ring or a necklace? Earrings?'

'I have a necklace. Mum made it. I usually only wear it at home.' She put her hands behind her neck, undoing the clasp of something hidden under her top.

There was nothing of the Ice Queen about the thick, warm rose gold string of small leaves, linked by a chain, and each set with an amber stone. The tip of the central and largest leaf pointed down. Jessica took it off and held it out to Amanda.

'Will this do?'

'Perfect.' Amanda smiled. 'Couldn't be better, in fact.' There was a great deal of love invested in this shining composition, from giver to wearer and back again. It was just what she needed.

Amanda went to Tempest and knelt by his chair. She stroked him, leaned close to kiss his cloudy head and whispered, 'Please, help me, Tempest. You know what's in it for you.'

Tempest growled, and his disgruntled gaze gave her to understand that she was a nuisance, and he didn't know why he put up with her and, yes, all right, but she'd owe him big time. He roused himself with exaggerated effort and jumped off the chair.

'Will you wait here, please,' Amanda said, addressing the men, 'Jessica and Irene? Come with me, please.'

Amanda remembered reading from Great-great-great-great-grandmother Jowantet Cardiubarn's primer: 'Finding spells be tricky if the thing be not your owne.' This enchantment was another first for Amanda. And the grimoire was specific: the owner of the lost item was supposed to be present when the witch cast the spell, and then be directed to the object. But this witch had no intention of revealing herself.

Amanda led them into Peacock and asked them to look towards Scarlet.

'Please face this wall.' She spoke with more confidence than she felt, but she needed Jessica and Irene to be as positive as possible. 'I'll be the other side of it. Hold hands and think only about the bracelet and imagine finding it. Don't stop until I tell you, and don't move, OK?'

'All right,' they agreed nervously.

Amanda closed Peacock's door behind her, and went next door into Scarlet. She shut herself and Tempest in. She went to the window to check the moon, just before the half-full. 'Waxing,' Amanda reported to Tempest. 'Good for attraction spells. Now, let's try facing the bed.'

Witch and familiar turned towards the four-poster. Amanda released her Pocket-wand from its disguising pencil. She twisted the necklace around her hand, letting the gold leaf rest in her palm with the point facing away from her. Amanda pointed her wand at it, and chanted,

'*Kibmielise presiusonesse en mina handoarn, almdiszquez meh ernpelle luronellez afundia.*'

The point of the pendant began to wobble. She put the wand away as she watched it. It shifted right, and Amanda turned. It slid right again, and Amanda moved with it. It acted like a compass. It took her to the window then back to the bed and then towards the fireplace wall and then to the panel behind which Dunkley had had his hiding place.

The pendant's leaf pointer became still.

'It's behind here,' Amanda whispered excitedly to Tempest.

Clutching the necklace, she pushed her finger into the recess beneath the painting and pulled the candlestick, so that the panel released and she could shove it aside. Amanda opened her hand and stilled herself. The leaf rotated until it was facing the left inner wall of the hidey-hole. She moved up to it and shone her torch. She pushed and pulled at the bricks. Nothing happened.

Amanda was half-crouching, as she inspected the wall. Tempest unexpectedly bumped against her legs, and she gave a little cry, stumbling off balance. Her fist closed on the necklace but not before the leaf had slid out of her hand and was now dangling freely. Amanda straightened up and frowned.

'That was no accident. Where is the leaf pointing now? Towards the floor. That must mean the lowest bricks.' Amanda got on her knees and started trying to wriggle them. Not a single one budged.

She sat back on her heels. 'Lets be logical,' she said quietly to her familiar. 'If whoever made the mechanism for opening the panel, also made the hiding place behind these bricks, then maybe they used a similar system. To open the panel, we have to pull the candlestick and push the pin under the painting. So maybe we also have to do two things at once here, in order to open the hiding place.' Having got that far, she paused for further thought.

'The spell and the necklace can show me only one thing at a time,' Amanda said looking down pensively at Tempest. He returned her gaze with intensity. 'So let's see if it shows you something different to what it shows me.' She put the pendant around his neck. He sat down, paws neatly together and it rested against his chest. Inert.

'OK. That doesn't work. Let's try something else.' Amanda took it off him and laid it on his paws. The pendant rotated and tilted up, pointing directly at a single brick, three courses above floor level and three from the corner furthest from the fireplace.

'Yes!' whispered Amanda, triumphantly. 'That's your brick then. Now, my turn.' She put the necklace, leaf dangling, on her hand and holding it close to the same wall, lowered it slowly. Reaching the bottom course, it began to swing. Amanda moved it from left to right, and when it was held opposite the second brick along, suddenly it agitated wildly.

'Bingo. Right, this is mine. Let me try manipulating the two at the same time.'

Amanda took a breath and pushed both bricks. Everything

stayed firmly in place. She tried pulling them. Nothing. Then she pushed Tempest's brick and tugged at her own. She felt hers loosen. Using her nails, she got it sufficiently free of the wall to use her fingers. After some wriggling it came out a little way, she was able to see that only the façade of the block was brick. The facing was attached to a wooden box with a lid. She had to pull it clear of the wall to open it. Inside, within a clear ziplock bag, was the unmistakable treasure they sought.

'Good work, Tempest!' Amanda rubbed his head. She ran next door to the ladies in waiting.

'You've got it!' came Jessica's ecstatic whisper. Amanda held out the bag and Jessica opened it saying, 'Oh, my goodness! Where was it?'

'In a box in the wall,' replied Amanda, leading the way back into Scarlet and pointing to where the bracelet had been concealed. The women were astonished. 'I didn't know this hiding place was here!' said Jessica.

'Neither did I!' agreed Irene. 'In all the years my mother cleaned here she never found this, and I'll bet she knew about this secret room behind the panelling.

'Well. You have your bracelet, Jessica,' Amanda said with relief. Jessica hugged her.

'Thank you soooo much! I owe you.'

'That's OK. Come on, let's tell the others.'

They hurried downstairs to share the news. The vocal volume was starting to rise as the gentlemen congratulated Jessica.

'Shhh!' Amanda cautioned. 'Remember, you're not supposed to be here. Now before we leave, Jonathan, how did you get in?'

'Through the porch roof and out through the cupboard on the landing,' he answered helpfully.

'Ah, that's how Jessica got in then. Thank you, Jonathan. OK, let me make it clear to every one of you that any future visits will be made by coming to the front door! Now, let's all go home as discreetly as possible. One at a time.'

A keen observer would have spotted a stately figure with a walking stick creeping out of the Manor garden by a side gate. Then a tall woman, then a shorter one, and then a man of medium height, could be seen leaving from different parts of the house.

Two of the company remained in the building for a few minutes.

'Before you go, Ryan,' said Amanda, 'why did you come here tonight? For Jessica?'

'No. You,' he said simply. 'I saw activity here, lights flickering, a couple of people hanging around the house. I thought you might be in danger.' Amanda was touched.

'Thank you, Ryan. That was very neighbourly of you.'

'Not exactly ...' he replied vaguely.

'But how did you get in?'

'Oh, through the back of the chimney at the side of the house and out through the upper oven in the kitchen.'

'Good grief!' Amanda was appalled at her clients' unwitting total lack of security. 'Doesn't anyone use doors anymore!'

'I didn't want to alert the intruders. What if you were being held hostage?'

'That's very gallant, Ryan,' Amanda marvelled appreciatively. 'Perhaps you can tell me exactly where the chimney access is another time.'

'Why don't I draw you a diagram?' he offered.

'All right.'

'Over dinner as soon as I get back. We can try The Snout and Trough. My treat.'

'But I haven't done anything for you,' she objected.

'You helped my friend and you kept yourself safe. That's more than enough,' Ryan said warmly.

Amanda blushed in the darkness. This was all very gratifying. But by now she was flagging and needed to get home.

'Yes. OK. Thank you. When you get back? You're leaving in the morning?' she asked, conscious of a twinge of regret.

'Back in ten days, though,' he said enthusiastically. 'Friday week. 7 o'clock, yes? The Snout and Trough?'

She laughed 'Yes, yes!'

Soon a watcher could have seen a tall man detaching from the black shape of the Manor, and finally a medium sized female with a cat. But it was 3.45am, and the village was asleep.

Chapter 46

❧

TEMPEST THE HERO, AND CLAIRE RETURNS

Amanda slept two cycles of the sleep of the just, knowing that the mysteries of the Manor were solved and that the house would soon be secure. In between, however, she tossed and turned in the wakefulness of Trelawney's troubling tidings of an anonymous witness of the incident all those years ago, and black ice.

However, the next morning was full of May sunshine and hope. By 11 o'clock, later than usual after the long night before, Amanda was back at the Manor. Fortunately, this time she had only Tempest for company, and he was soon purring loudly in a patch of sunlight coming through the hall window.

Amanda's first self-imposed task as chatelaine was to check the secret routes into the house. She found a cupboard on the landing that swung out from the wall when a catch was flicked. Amanda put on her mask, collected some tools, crawled to the inside of the porch roof and screwed the cunning door shut on the inside. Up in the turret, there was a seat that rotated to reveal a shaft with the dumbwaiter that Mr French had ridden up. Tempest peered down it and then wandered off while she fastened it down.

When Amanda came to examine Emerald's window seat, he seemed more interested. The day before yesterday, when she had been searching for secret entrances, she had tried to get it open by lifting the top. Now, however, Amanda knew better, after having watched Irene emerge the night before. Amanda opened the front panel by wiggling a screwdriver into a join and prising it open.

'Aha,' she said to Tempest. 'Now we can lift up the seat'. They looked inside. There were wooden stairs descending in the thickness of the wall. Tempest suddenly pre-empted her and jumped down onto the top step. She waited while he gave consideration to the next one. He moved onto it, and Amanda followed behind him. It was on the third step that he planted himself and barred her way.

'Come on, furry prince, next step,' she urged him.

But Tempest settled himself firmly and directed a piercing gaze at her. Amanda looked back at him thoughtfully.

'Hm. Tempest. You know something that I don't.' Amanda went off to her tools and got a roll of polythene that was stiffened with an inner core of cardboard. 'Come out, Tempest.' She leaned into the hole and bashed the end of the roll against the fourth step. Abruptly, without warning, the staircase collapsed, the treads falling deep into the shaft and crashing and smashing on the stones far below.

Amanda put her hand over her mouth in horror. It was unlikely she would have survived the perilous drop if her familiar had not stopped her progress down the steps.

'Oh my goodness! It's like a dungeon. I wonder if there are bones down there! Thank you, Tempest. My guardian angel, my hero.' She cuddled him, drawing comfort from her warm furry companion, after the narrow escape from the ghastly fate from which he had saved her. Amanda took a puff from her inhaler.

'Phew … Right. Let's look for the other end of this passage.'

Amanda took some tools and materials and went onto the

side porch. She made a show of looking at the timbers in the frame, just in case anyone was watching. She cast a surreptitious glance around to check that the coast was clear. Satisfied that she was unobserved, Amanda squatted and opened the circular lid of bricks, just as Irene had demonstrated several hours earlier, and lowered herself in.

She took the stairs down into the thickness of the wall until the shaft became a level tunnel leading around the angles of the house. Amanda followed it until she found the broken rectangles of wood that had once been the treacherous stairs and looked up at the light coming down through the window seat.

'No bones,' she reported, calling up to Tempest. 'I'll bet there was more than one booby-trapped stair. Well, at least no one else is getting in this way.'

Amanda regained the surface and went in search of Ryan's entrance, to make all safe there too.

All of this would have to be reported to the Poveys somehow. Bit by bit. She'd likely be working in the house on and off for a while to come, and would break the news of the hidey-holes and secret tunnels one at a time, as though she herself was just discovering them. There was no need to make known the private histories of the two couples. Amanda planned to start with the tale of a game of cat and mouse in Scarlet. That would be the most innocent of circumstances in which to discover a hidden entrance.

It was a profound relief to get back to the ordinary tasks for which she was engaged. Amanda arrayed herself in mask, gloves, boots and boiler suit, and began applying noxious liquid to another section of unoffending banister rail until it yielded its remaining polish to bubbling, brushing and scraping.

That evening, Claire was home after a long stretch of overtime in London, and hailed Amanda from an upstairs window as she got out of the car.

'Hello, sweetie! Just out of the bath. Let yourself in and we'll have a catchup!'

They had one another's keys, so Amanda locked up the car and soon made herself comfortable on Claire's teal velvet sofa.

'Well!' declared her friend, coming into the room wearing pyjamas, and towelling her hair. 'Whoooo is he?' she asked suggestively. They hugged, and Claire continued, 'While you reveal all, let's have a bracer.'

'Who is who?' asked Amanda, bewildered, as her friend clinked about with glasses and bottles.

'You, my darling, came home in the wee small hours of the morning, so ....?'

'Ah, I see,' smiled Amanda. 'I was sleuthing.'

'Oooo, do tell.'

'I thought I saw a light on at the Manor. It took me ages to make sure that the place was secure. The house is huge, and has more nooks and crannies than the Roman Catacombs.'

'I heard that there have always been tales of strange lights and sounds at the Manor,' remarked Claire. 'It's obligatory. What little tourist trade we have in Sunken Madley would collapse without it. Oh, and the tale of the ghost at the house too, naturally. Remember your former neighbour, Mr Jackson?'

'Yes?'

'Well, he had any number of stories. 'Them ghoolies, they get aba-oot in tha-at houn.'' said Claire, giving a convincing impersonation of the Cadabra's former neighbour. 'Have you, by any chance, met the legendary poltergeist of Sunken Madley Manor, in the course of your professional duties?' she teased.

Amanda laughed. 'As if. '

'While I was in the process of buying the house, Mr Jackson and I had some rare old chats, and he filled me in about the Manor and village,' recalled Claire, handing Amanda her G&T and curling up beside her on the sofa. 'He had a lot of respect for Mr Dunkley-McVitty senior, said he was a fine gentleman of the old school, but he hadn't much to say for the son or the nephew.'

'Thank you, Claire,' said Amanda, taking her glass, 'Really? He didn't think much of Gregory, then, or… Vernon, I think his name was?'

'No. According to Mr Jackson, both went off to boarding school then university but came to no good; all but sunk the family in scandal.'

'What kind of scandal?'

'Cheers,' said Claire, raising her wine glass to clink Amanda's highball. She drank and then continued, 'Blackmail, it was rumoured. Something about something hidden in the house and … oh, I don't know — Why? Do you think someone was searching the property?'

'Possibly, but it was all quiet when I left it,' Amanda said truthfully.

'"Possibly",' Claire seized on the word excitedly. 'Right! I'll get my nunchucks, you grab a mallet, and let's go over there!'

'Let's not,' soothed Amanda.' You're in your jimjams, and we don't want to get involved in any violent altercations.'

Claire's ardour for battle subsided. 'What about the Poveys? Could they have brought something with them to the house and someone wants it? Secret treasure from the East?' she asked dramatically, and took a sip of her white wine.

Amanda shook her head. 'Hugh and Sita really don't seem the kind to have secret treasure. Or even secrets.'

'Oh, everyone has secrets, darling. Even you.' Claire looked at her quizzically.

'Me! From you?' said Amanda, giving a fair rendition of surprise.

'Things you don't tell me.'

'Only boring things about the commode I restored or the ball and claw foot that I cleanly spliced back onto its leg,' Amanda replied prosaically, having some of her gin and tonic.

Claire was regarding her keenly but affectionately. 'Whatever your secrets are, they are safe with me.'

Amanda remained outwardly relaxed, saying, 'You're the best of friends.'

However, her mind was racing. Did Claire know that

Amanda was a witch? Even just suspect? Amanda remembered the black ice and how it had sounded like a deliberate supernatural intervention to cause the minivan to go off the road, and what Granny had said about enemies. Would the time come when Amanda would be in danger and need Claire's help and so need her to know what Amanda was?

Claire changed the subject.

'It must have been late when you saw the light. Working all hours, were you?'

'I'd had dinner out,' Amanda admitted.

'Alo-ooone?'

She knew an impulse to tell Claire about Trelawney's visit. She recalled Granny's words about impulses, and thought it through. The black ice was just a piece of evidence. If Claire knew about Amanda's magical heritage, then she might think it significant. If Claire didn't know ... then Amanda had nothing to lose by telling her about the Inspector's call. After all, Claire already knew about the open case of the incident.

'I had a visit from Trelawney,' she said.

'Checking in or ...?' asked Claire.

'It could be nothing,' murmured Amanda.

'Tell,' coaxed her friend.

'Someone came forward and said she remembered that, years ago, she was driving behind the minibus with my relations in it just before it went over the cliff. She said she saw black ice on the road, saw the minibus in front of her skid and only just swerved to avoid the patch herself.'

Claire was sceptical.

'After thirty years, she remembers this all of a sudden. Who was she?'

'Anonymous call.'

'Why now?' pondered Claire.

'She said she was getting old and sorting out her affairs and didn't want this on her mind or something,' Amanda explained.

'Why anonymous?' Claire asked suspiciously.

'Didn't want to get involved in making statements and reports and giving evidence.'

'Gosh.' Claire's excite-ometer was rising again. 'I bet she could tell us more. Under hypnosis. I'll bet she could remember the registration number and something about the people in the minibus. We have to find her!'

'Oh, come on, Claire. If the police can't find her, then how can we?' Amanda asked reasonably.

'I bet you might have some ideas if you put your mind to the problem. It's the only lead for thirty years. You do want the money, surely?' asked Claire, curiously.

'I'd rather let sleeping dogs lie,' Amanda replied soberly.

'Are they dogs, Ammy?' asked Claire intently. 'Or something else? Something Granny told you that you should be wary of?'

Amanda didn't know how to reply.

'The reason why you keep a low profile?' Claire suggested.

'I don't,' objected Amanda, 'I go out with you, I work in the village and all over the place, Hertfordshire, London …'

Claire seemed to give up.

'It's probably nothing,' she said, resignedly.

'Yes,' Amanda agreed, 'maybe just an oil slick, a leak from another car, anything ….'

'Sure,' said Claire. She had a thought and brightened up. 'How's Trelawney?'

'Fine, I think,' said Amanda.

'Still with the girlfriend?'

'I didn't ask,' replied Amanda in reproving accents.

'Pity.' Claire winked.

'We had a nice meal, and it's kind of him to be protective and informative,' Amanda stated.

'Of course, it is,' Claire said, gently mocking. 'So did you meet Ryan over the weekend?'

'Yes,' said Amanda noncommitally. 'Actually,' she said, changing gear, 'I have something to ask you.'

'Judging by that smile,' Claire remarked judiciously, 'I'd say it involves a — Ha! Can it be? Ryan …?'

'It's nothing! He's invited … I mean, he's giving me two tickets to see him play at his next match, and I thought you might like to come, that's all.'

'Absolutely, darling. And afterwards, I'll make myself scarce at the crucial moment,' she offered, naughtily. Suddenly, Claire became unusually grave.

'Or perhaps I won't,' she added slowly.

'I hope you won't,' agreed Amanda. 'We just chatted at the cricket match,' she said accurately. Amanda looked at her friend's face, trying to decipher her expression. 'Why? Do you know him?' She laughed. 'Of course, you do. You know everyone.'

'Slightly,' said Claire. 'He seems nice. But I'd reserve judgement on Ryan Ford, if I were you.'

'That's what Gordon French said,' Amanda responded, reflecting. And not just about Ford, she thought. There was a silence.

'Oh, we're probably being parochial!' Claire dismissed the sombre mood with a wave of her glass. 'They b'aint local, mo-ee dearie! '

Amanda chuckled.

Chapter 47

ᥱᢙ

GOLDEN RULES, AND UNEXPECTED FLOWERS

Three days later, Amanda was polishing the wall handrail at the Manor when she became conscious of an unsettling sensation. It was a feeling that took her back to when she was 15 years old, and railing against the limitations of her asthma. And then Granny and Grandpa had given her Tempest.

Where was the contentment she'd enjoyed before the antics at the Manor? It had been eroded by time-travel and trespassers. And now Amanda felt restless. Maybe even a little bored with her life. Oh, not with her work exactly, but she'd had a taste of excitement, even danger, and there was no going back.

Amanda took her luncheon in the garden, sitting next to Tempest on a sun-warmed stone bench, not far from the fountain. That was not currently in working order, as she knew from thta busy night, but surely, if the Povey's had their way, it soon would be. A statue of Aphrodite, with bluebells around its base, looked down on her beneficently from one side. A marble angel on the other was contentedly absorbed in its book, undisturbed by the burble of a skylark, and the chatter of a rook.

Amanda had just finished her Angus beef, English mustard and watercress sandwich, and was offering a shred of meat to her familiar, when Granny and Grandpa appeared either side of her.

They were in good humour. Amanda was torn between pleasure, at being reunited with her grandparents, and indignation at their absence in her hour of need.

'Hello darling,' said Granny, brightly,

'Hello, love,' Grandpa greeted her sunnily.

'Well, hello. So you've decided to return? The prodigal grandparents,' Amanda commented drily.

'We've never been far, you know,' Granny told her.

'So you know what's been going on?' queried Amanda.

'We do,' affirmed Granny. 'The Dunkley-McVittys, Luke and his parents, time-travelling in the Wood, the commotion at the Manor. You've done very well indeed, Amanda, dear.'

'We're *pur* proud of you, *chiel*,' Grandpa added, with a touch of Cornish.

'Ha!' expostulated their granddaughter. 'Was that all an exam? Have I passed Ghostbuster 101 and Sleuthing Primary?' responded Amanda, aghast.

Yes,' answered Granny, unabashed. 'As a matter of fact, you have. With flying colours for a beginner. And you enjoyed it. Admit it.'

'Enjoyed!' huffed Amanda. 'Dealing with two bickering trespassers, a body, blood, intrigues, dark, dusty holes playing havoc with my asthma!'

'Perhaps not "enjoyed" then,' conceded Granny, 'but wasn't it stimulating? And look how well you dealt with it. You used your resources.'

'Now you've had a few days off, aren't you feeling just a little ... bored?' asked Grandpa, affectionately ribbing her. Amanda's honesty overcame her.

'Well, all right, I suppose I do miss the challenge.'

'So,' said Granny, 'there may be more coming your way. And you can embrace them. Provided you follow these golden rules. You can write them down later, but for now:

'One: keep your Pocket-wand on you at all times. In fact, write to Dr Bergstrom for a spare.

'Two: always use the least powerful spell you know.

'Three: look for potential allies and expect the best from people, but allow them to earn your trust rather than giving it away, however strong the impulse.

'Four: be sensitive to any strange feelings you may experience when casting a spell, and remember them.

'And five: always carry a tin of caviar, in case a certain person needs more persuasion to help you than out of the goodness of his heart,' she said pointedly, directing her gaze at Tempest. He began cleaning his paws disdainfully.

Once they had reappeared, the grandparents were as much in evidence as they had been before the 'test'. Amanda finished the banister rail and repaired the scratches and gouges in the furniture. It was superficial work, and she could see that a great deal more restoration needed to be done around the Manor.

Amanda removed the polythene, the dust sheets, and the masking tape. The Hoover was summoned from its place under the stairs, and set to work sucking up the wood shavings, bits of crumbled old polish, dirt and dust. She took photos of the 'after' of the banister and furniture by way of a record. Changed out of her overalls, Amanda locked the back door, had a last look round, closed up and headed home with Tempest.

The Poveys returned that evening, and Amanda visited the next lunchtime, after they'd had time to settle back in. They were full of praise for her work and of tales of their two glorious weeks in Provence: the light, the wine, the food, and the kindness of the owner of the villa where they had stayed. They settled the bill, promised to be in touch soon with more commissions, and Amanda gave herself the rest of the day off.

* * * * *

The same week, Thomas got a call from Hogarth inviting him to dinner, that is, asking him to pick up fish and chips on the way.

Thomas watched with awe as Mike made a neat incision in the batter of his cod, peeled it back, saturated the white fish with vinegar and topped it with a generous sprinkling of salt.

'Don't you worry about sodium?' he asked Hogarth.

'This is pink Himalayan salt, Thomas. Does your detective's eye not tell you that?' his senior teased him.

'Ah. That's all right then,' said his junior doubtfully.

'How did Amanda take the news?' Hogarth asked.

'Like she wished I hadn't told her,' answered Thomas with a hint of regret. 'I think it disturbed her in some way. She got a bit defensive, but we mended the fence and parted friends of sorts.'

'Hm. Well,' said Hogarth, 'I want you to make real friends with Amanda Cadabra. Not just "of sorts".'

'Are you matchmaking, Mike?' Thomas asked in surprise, and then added ruefully, 'If my overtures are too friendly, she may think it rather odd in the … er circumstances.'

'Oh?' enquired Hogarth

'I told her I had a girlfriend,' Thomas confessed.

'Did you now? Well, I don't think Tamsyn in The Smuggler's Chest chatting you up while she pulls your pint really counts as a girlfriend. She's barely of legal drinking age,' joked Mike. 'What did you go and tell her that for? Trying to maintain a professional distance? Never tell me Amanda made advances to you?' Mike was enjoying himself.

Thomas had the grace to blush. 'No, of course not,' he insisted.

'Never mind, son. The Cababras are a family that gets under your skin. But no, to answer your question, I'm not matchmaking.' Mike became serious. 'No. But I do think she may need a friend one day. Something in the air is shifting. We've stirred the coals, and now smoke is rising. We've only made the embers glow, and they may come to nothing at all, may die down and be extinguished. But it's better to be safe than sorry. If I'm right, and every Cornish instinct I possess tells me I am, Amanda Cadabra is on the side of the angels even if she is at the heart of this case. And she deserves your trust, and your help too if it comes to it.'

After the plates were empty and, knowing Thomas was staying alcohol-free for his drive home, Mike kept him company with a mug of tea. They cupped their drinks as they leaned back comfortably, stretching their feet out towards the fire.

'I'm going to be taking a holiday,' said Mike, cheerfully.

'Good for you. I'm sure you've earned it,' Thomas responded sincerely if drowsily.

'Could be protracted. Actually, I'm going to stay with my sister in Spain.'

Thomas's policeman's radar was picking up something unusual about this.

'Oh? I rather thought you were interested in seeing if this old case was reviving,' he said, looking into his tea.

'That's just it, Thomas. I rather think it is reviving. And I also rather think that the trail of revival is going to lead to me. And if that trail is followed t'were better I were not found where I am expected to be.'

'Sir?' In his concern, Thomas reverted to the familiar professional form of address. 'Are you in danger? What has all this got to do with you?'

'Old families, Thomas. Old families. Remember what we talked about? The St Piran?'

'The symbol of the fight by good to overcome evil?'

Mike chose his words carefully. 'Not all of Cornwall's ancient clans are gathered to the standard, my boy.'

'Is this about witches and magic?' asked Thomas sceptically.

'Remember Shakespeare's words: "There are more things in heaven and earth —"'

'"— than are dreamt of in our philosophy."' Thomas

finished impatiently. 'I don't understand where all this is going.'

'And right now, you don't need to. Fear not, Thomas, I'll leave you with contact details and you can get hold of me anytime. And I'll be back; you may be sure of that. Meanwhile …. Amanda. Yes?' Trelawney felt he had to be content with what Hogarth was willing to tell him. He would like to have been trusted with more. Thomas could at least assure Mike that he was up to the assigned task.

'Yes, sir. I will regard her as my sacred trust.'

The following weekend began with an unexpected event. It was Saturday morning, and Amanda had planned a picnic for herself and Tempest in a choice spot, after a quick visit to the workshop. She was just checking some glueing had dried as it should, with Perran chatting to her, when Granny appeared with explosive suddenness.

'Amanda! You have to see this!' she announced portentously.

'What?' asked her granddaughter suspiciously.

'Guess who's putting flowers on our graves?'

'Er …?'

'Go! Go and see — get your gloves off, girl — hurry! But don't run!'

Amanda took the car, drove up to the speed limit and fairly skidded to a halt in the church hall car park.

There was Trelawney in the graveyard, standing, flowers in hand, before the engraved granite markers of Senara and Perran. Amanda had hastily grabbed two early blooms, from the Princess Margaret rose bush in the front garden, as an excuse to visit them herself.

'Hello', she hailed Trelawney in a friendly voice.

'Hello, Miss Cadabra. I was just up for the weekend and …'

'It's very thoughtful of you,' she said with an appreciative smile.

He saw her two roses and suspected a rush job. News certainly travelled fast in Sunken Madley. Or else ….

'It was actually Hogarth's kind thought,' Trelawney explained. 'But I'm happy to be carrying it out. Honoured, in fact,' he added graciously.

'Well, thank you.'

'I also wanted to check that all is well with you,' Trelawney admitted.

She rapidly cast her mind back over all the commotion during the last twenty-four hours, following his previous visit. She assured him honestly,

'All is well. I'm fine.'

'Manor assignment going well?'

'Yes,' confirmed Amanda, 'happy customers and will very likely commission more work, so, yes, indeed …. Would you like to try The Big Tease?'

He laughed. 'Very much. But my family's expecting me, so this is just a flying visit but … next time I'm up here, in a few weeks, if you're free — one Saturday? — I'd like to get to know this corner of the world a little better, learn the history of the village, for example, where the name comes from.'

'I'd be happy to show you.' Amanda added as an afterthought, 'As long as your girlfriend wouldn't mind.'

'My what?'

'Your girlfriend? The one you'd been neglecting and were taking to dinner …?'

'Ah. I see … well … that didn't work out. I don't think she was really cut out to be a police detective's wife.'

'Oh, I'm sorry,' said Amanda automatically and then wondered if what she'd just said was strictly true.

'So …?' he asked.

Amanda nodded. 'Then, of course, I'll look forward to showing you the delights of our hamlet and surrounding countryside,' she said, happily.

Thomas grinned. 'Great.'

'Well, I won't hold you up,' said Amanda. 'Thank you for coming.'

'Oh, there is just one more thing before I go,' said Trelawney, 'Your name.'

'Amanda?'

'Cadabra.'

She smiled. 'Grandpa's family were French. His great-great-however-many-greats-grandfather, Aristide, was an undertaker. And during either the Revolution or under Napoleonic rule, he found it prudent to cross the channel for a new and safer life in Cornwall. When the customs or immigration official came to record Aristide's name and profession, he couldn't understand what our ancestor was telling him about being an undertaker. So Aristide used the French word "cadavre" to explain that he worked with the deceased. The official finally recognised a word that sounded similar to an English one, and recorded Aristide's surname as "Cadabra". Goodness knows what the official thought Aristide's profession was!'

'Aha. Well, thank you. Great story,' he complimented her, cheerily. 'OK, see you soon.'

'See you soon.' She waved him off, feeling gratified and not a little excited that she now appeared to have two suitors, even if one wasn't entirely to be trusted and the other was a policeman investigating her history.

Amanda drove with Tempest to their favourite place: the priory ruins, where she could climb up and look down on her little village kingdom, lying snug in the embracing trees. She could see one or two of her neighbours going about their business. Amanda shook her head ruefully as she considered what the inhabitants were capable of getting up to.

A cloud covered the sun.

There was a lot to think about. Her first ghost-busting. The time zones in the forest, her first time using magic against humans and … still lurking unexplained … the black ice … the woman who had called the police … the strange still-unsolved deaths of those of her blood. Her narrow escape on the secret stair. Her inexplicable panic in the library basement. And then there were the new labs, of course. Maybe a chance for a cure for her asthma. But where they were going to be built! On the lost village with its dark past. And then there was Granny's dark past, her enemies ... these were matters to be pondered and seriously.

The cloud passed.

Amanda breathed in the pine-fragrant air and turned to look north toward the rolling hills of Hertfordshire, bright with spring green and studded with apple blossom. Tempest settled warmly on her feet. 'Matters to be pondered ...,' she repeated to him. The playful breeze stirred her hair. She smiled up at the blue vault of the sky. '... But not today,' said Amanda Cadabra.

THE END

Author's Note

Thank you for reading Amanda Cadabra and The Hidey-Hole Truth. I hope you enjoyed your visit to Sunken Madley.

I would love you to tell me your thoughts about the book and would be thrilled if you wrote a review. You can post in on the e-store where you bought the book or on Facebook, Twitter or your social platform of choice. It would mean a lot to me.

Best of all, drop me a line at: HollyBell@amandacadabra. com so we can connect in person. If there is a character you especially liked or anything you would like more of, please let me know. Amanda Cadabra Book 2 is in the making and I am writing it for you, dear reader.

For titbits on the world of Sunken Madley and to keep up with news of the continuing adventures of our heroes Amanda, Tempest, Granny and Grandpa visit www. amandacadabra.com, where you can also request to enter the VIP Readers Group. This is a limited numbers group. Members can be invited to receive and review an advance copy of the next book.

If Tempest has endeared himself to you and reminds you of your cat or one you know, in any way, you are invited to enter a photograph in The Tempest Competition.
Details are at:
http://amandacadabra.com/the-tempest-competition/
You can also find me on Facebook at:

https://www.facebook.com/Holly-Bell-923956481108549/
Twitter at: https://twitter.com/holly_b_author
Pinterest: https://www.pinterest.co.uk/hollybell2760/
and Instagram:
https://www.instagram.com/hollybellac
See you soon.

About the Author

Cat adorer and chocolate lover, Holly Bell is a photographer and video maker when not writing. Holly lives in the UK and is a mixture of English, Cornish, Welsh and other ingredients. Her favourite cat is called Bobby.

Acknowledgements

Thanks to TJ Brown, my writing mentor, who gave me the lint and the kindling for my creative spark. Thank you to Philippa for encouraging and reassuring me throughout the writing process, to my brother for editing the book with a fine-tooth comb, to Flora Gatestone, my first beta reader, for a wealth of valuable feedback, and to my first teen beta reader who said, 'I love it!'

Thanks are also due to the rector of 'Sunken Madley' whose fund of information helped me to shape the village, and to the brother who taught me my way around a workshop.

Thanks to Tim for helping me conceive the layout of Sunken Madley, sketching it out before my eyes and for adding the key and title that gave it the finishing touch. Thanks to Methmeth who skilfully turned the sketch into the drawing in the book.

Thank you, in fact, to all those without whose support

this book would not have been possible.

Finally, in whatever dimension they are currently inhabiting, thanks go out to my cat who inspired Tempest, and to my grandfather and brother for Perran and Trelawney.

QUESTIONS FOR READING CLUBS

1. What did you like best about the book?

2. Which character did you like best? Is there one with whom you especially identified?

3. If you made a movie of the book, whom would you cast and in what parts?

4. Did the book remind you of any others you have read, either in the same or another genre?

5. Did you think the cover fitted the story? If not, how would you redesign it?

6. How unique is this story?

7. Which characters grew and changed over the course of the story, and which remained the same?

8. What feelings did the book evoke?

9. Which was your favourite group characters, and why?

10. What place in the book would you most like to visit, and why?

11. Was the setting one that felt familiar or relatable to you? Why or why not?

12. Is there a character you would like to know more about? If so, who and why?

13. Was the book the right length? If too long, what would you leave out? If too short, what would you add?

14. How well do you think the title conveyed what the book is about?

15. If you could ask Holly Bell just one question, what would it be?

16. How well do you think the author created the world of the story?

17. Which quotes or scenes did you like the best, and why?

18. Was the author just telling an entertaining story or trying as well to communicate any other ideas? If so, what do you think they were?

19. Did the book change how you think or feel about any thing, person or place? Did it help you to understand someone or yourself better?

20. What do you think the characters will do after the end of the book? Would you want to read the sequel?

GLOSSARY

As the story is set in an English village, and written by a British author, some spellings or words may be unfamiliar to some readers living in other parts of the English-speaking world. Please find here a list of terms used in the book. If you notice any that are missing, please let me know on hollybell@amandacadabra.com so the can be included in a future edition.

British English	American English
Spelling conventions	
—ise for words like surprise, realise	—ize for words like surprize, realize
—or for words like colour, honour	—our for words like color, honor
—tre for words like centre, theatre	—ter for words like center, theater
A4 (paper size)	8.26" by 11.69"
An (Early Modern English)	If
Balaclava	Ski-mask
Beep (a car horn)	Honk
Biscuit	Cookie
Boiler suit	Coveralls
Chips (food)	French fries

Close of play	End of the game, end of play for the day, end of the day
Corner shop	Small grocery store
Cornish pasty	Disk of puff pastry filled with meat and vegetables then folded and sealed at the edges.
Curtains	Drapes
Deep Square Leg	Batsman's left near the boundary
Different from	Different than
Dressing-gown	Robe/bathrobe
Dust sheet	Drop cloth
Forsooth (Early Modern English)	Truly
Fridge	Refrigerator
Gastropub	Pub that serves high-quality food
GCSE General Certification of Secondary Education	Exam taken at 16 years of age after two years study.
Hairgrip	Bobby pin
Hold	Stay, wait
Holland covers	Large white cotton sheets for covering furniture
Hoover	Vacuum cleaner
Jewellery	Jewelry
Jumper	Sweater
Kebab	Gyro
Lorry	Large truck for carrying goods

Minibus	Van, minicoach seating 8 - 30 people
Mobile phone	Cell phone
Momentarily	For a moment
Motorway - M	Expressway, Highway
Musulmen (Early Modern English)	Muslims
Neighbourhood Watch	Neighborhood watch
Nightdress	Nightdress
Ought (Early Modern English)	Something
Passing (Early Modern English)	Very, surpassingly
Pavement	Sidewalk
Penknife	Small folding knife
Photocopy	Copy
Piccalilli	Pickle made of cauliflower, onions, gherkins, mustard and turmeric.
Pimm's	Gin herbs and citrus fruit
Pub	Quiet, family friendly, coffee-shop style bar
Publican	Owner of a pub
Scotch Egg	Hardboiled egg in a case of sausage meat coated in breadcrumbs
Solicitor	Lawyer
Sponge bag	Toiletries bag
Sweet wrapper	Candy wrapper
Takeaway	Takeout

Tap	Faucet
Tea towel	Dish towel
Tin	Can
Torch	Flashlight
Trainers	Tennis shoes
Victoria Sandwich	Sponge cake with jam and cream filling
Wellington boots	Rubber boots
Zebra crossing	Cross walk

A NOTE ABOUT ACCENTS AND WICC'YETH

The story includes a Swedish character and, to add flavour to his character, his accent has been approximated. In Swedish there are no 'th', 'j' or 'w' sounds. Therefore, for example, 'this' become 'sis', 'project' becomes 'proyect' and 'warm' becomes 'varm'.

One or two of the villagers have a Cockney accent, indicated by the missing 'h' at the beginning of words such as 'hello' becoming ''ello'.

Wicc'yeth, is a magical language peculiar to the world of Amanda Cadabra. If you are curious about the meaning of individual spell words, you will find a glossary at http://amandacadabra.com/wiccyeth/ and Amelia's Glossary with Pronunciation.

Printed in Great Britain
by Amazon